Murder
at
Corner Rise

A. K. Summer

DEDICATION

To Mum and Dad

ACKNOWLEDGMENTS

I would like to thank Roger for his patient beta reading and many cups of tea, and Louise from Refine Fiction for copyediting.

CHAPTER 1

Cyan Butler stopped to look at the new signpost that had been erected outside the Gatehouse. Finally there was something to direct the public to the correct path for the two cinemas on campus, and it had arrived just in time for the path to be closed due to building work. Cyan walked up to the Gatehouse and showed her staff ID card to the security guards. Beyond the Gatehouse, the dark stone King Building stood as a square guardian to Corner Rise University's Crown Campus. Cyan had just finished a brief chat with the new security guard, Jennifer, when there was a shout followed by a crash. Cyan jumped.

"I thought the demolition was over?" she said.

Jennifer laughed. "Would you believe they've nearly finished the building?"

"Not by that sound," said Cyan. "I bet you'll be glad when it's done."

"What? No. It's given me some good overtime. I really don't understand what all the moaning was about."

Cyan looked at Jennifer. "The noise for a start. And all those people without staff cards in the King Building? Just think. All those computers."

"All those people," said Jennifer. "Most people just want to see their film. They might look at some of the displays on the way to the cinema, but that's it. We let visitors into the main corridor and the only place they can get to is the back door."

Cyan nodded. "But has anyone 'accidentally' wandered off into the hidden rooms of the King Building yet?"

"Not unless they've got a pass." The desk phone rang. "Excuse me," Jennifer said as she reached for it. "Good morning, Crown Campus security." Jennifer waved as she answered the telephone. Cyan nodded a goodbye and walked up the short driveway to the King Building.

The Crown Campus got its name from its location on Corner Rise, which split naturally into three islands: Crown, Main and East. Crown Island got its name from the three capes at the north of the island, which made for impressive aerial photographs. Not for the first time Cyan reflected that the whole of Corner Rise was a geologist's dream with a low, narrow isthmus and several live volcanos that boiled under the surface of the sea to the south, one of which had almost become a new island. Cyan went through the glass doors at the front of the building, turned left and walked along the west corridor. Along the corridor were posters, some with information for students and others about various events. She walked past another set of glass doors to her right that led to the courtyard around which the King Building was built, and through the back door into the early morning sunshine.

The sky was clear and if the rain stayed away Cyan planned to sit under the canopy of one of the large cedar trees in the grounds at lunch. The Students' Union had insisted that Tuesday afternoons be left clear for society activities, which meant that the campus would be almost empty by mid-afternoon. Cyan was sure there were no appointments scheduled, so she hoped to attend a tea tasting at the School of Agricultural Science. She smiled at the School's name, which was shortened to SAS when they answered the telephone. In Cyan's mind she saw a group of agriculturalists swooping down on crop-filled fields clad in black with balaclavas, sharp farm tools in their hands.

Cyan was pulled back to the present by a voice from the university's latest building site. The new building, currently called the 'Student Centre', was a response to the Students' Union call for more study space. As a workman gave instructions within the site Cyan wondered if the path directly from her office to the Gatehouse would reopen once the construction work was over. Well it had to, her building also housed the cinemas.

She felt that the Crown Campus had become a perpetual building site. Only last summer the Portmore Building, unofficially known as the Hub, was finished. The idea was to move all of Corner Rise University's administration to the Crown Campus, which would free up space within the Main Campus for teaching.

And that worked really well, thought Cyan as she remembered the arguments between the Academic Departments and Senior Management. The Academic Departments had wanted their administrative support to stay with them.

As a result the Portmore Building was populated by Finance, Human Resources and Estates and each campus kept a branch of Student Services. Cyan had hated the move; up until a month ago her office had still smelt like a paint factory.

Cyan looked down from the glass and steel building to the path and saw Professor Cyrus Pepper well ahead of her. She looked at her watch: it was eight forty. Cyan looked up again and wondered why Cyrus was so early. His head was down as he fiddled with his mobile phone. Cyan quickened her pace. Cyrus had come to the islands with a slight limp, which made him walk slowly, and Cyan knew that she could catch him up. She was sure Cyrus could hear her shoes on the paved path, but he didn't look back. The building didn't open before nine o'clock, so when Cyrus reached the double doors he paused to touch the electronic lock with his staff card and Cyan was close enough to hear the bleep. He raised his left hand to push the door.

"Cyrus! The sign."

Cyrus paused. "Hello," he said as he turned, smiled and failed to notice that the door didn't move. He walked into it with a muffled thump.

"I'm sorry," Cyan said as the professor stood back. "That door's been out of use for three days now."

There was a small notice taped to the left door and a tiny arrow pointed to the door that worked. Cyan made a mental note to contact Estates Management about the door, or at least a larger sign, the last thing she wanted was for the university to be sued. Fortunately the door was left open during the day, which she didn't think was ideal. Cyrus stood back and rolled his shoulders, then gave the right door an experimental push. The door moved and he pushed it almost open. Almost, because it jammed at an angle of forty-five degrees. He was halfway through the gap when Beethoven's Ninth Symphony sounded from his mobile phone. He stopped to answer it. The door

3

came to life and tried to slam shut. Cyan blocked a laugh with her hands as Cyrus was caught mid-Hello.

It took Cyan a few seconds to compose herself before she went to the professor's aid.

"Electronic doors hate me," said Cyrus. "Last week the King Building's doors stayed resolutely shut as I approached them."

"Hello?" said a voice from the phone.

"Can I call you back?" said Cyrus.

Cyan waited until he rang off and then gave the door a hard push. It offered no resistance and she nearly ended up on the floor. *That door really hates you*, thought Cyan.

Cyrus's expression managed to combine surprise and embarrassment. "Hello," he said.

"Hi," said Cyan. "Why are you in so early?"

"Research breakfast," said Cyrus as they walked past the box office. "Getting up before the local ghosts have finished their night patrol is supposed to make me a focused and successful man."

"Who says you're not successful?"

Cyrus didn't answer, instead his mouth formed a straight line as they walked into the Cinema Cafe. "And there he is."

Cyan scanned the cafe and saw Dr Dayton King, eyes fixed on his laptop.

"Oh," she said. "Well I'd better—"

"Leave before he sees you," said Cyrus as if he had read her thoughts.

Cyan nodded. She would never have said that aloud but she was grateful as she headed towards the stairs.

Cyan's office was on the first floor with the rest of Student Services. The ground floor was occupied by Corner Rise University's showcases, the King Collection, a museum made up of items gathered when William King, who had once lived in the main building, had gone on his 'Grand Tour' in the eighteenth century, and the two cinemas, C1 and C2. The last two had been welcomed. As the then Vice Chancellor Ian Portmore had noted, "The inhabitants of Crown Island now have their own cinema and no longer have to travel to the mainland."

The shutters for the counter that separated the office from the main reception area were raised and the head of Crown Campus Student Services, Zoe Mandeville, stood by the counter with the morning's post. They exchanged greetings as Cyan sat down and switched on her computer. Zoe distributed the post and went into her office. Dylan Bligh, one of the other student support administrators, walked into the office just as Cyan opened her first email of the day.

"Hello," he said. "How's it going?"

"All good so far."

Dylan nodded towards the empty desk next to Cyan.

"Katherine's not in today."

"She wasn't in yesterday," said Dylan.

"She has some holiday to take before the end of the year."

Dylan raised an eyebrow.

"Yes I know," said Cyan.

Katherine Welman, the third student support administrator, was known for her absence. Cyan was surprised that Katherine had any leave left and knew that Dylan felt the same from the look on his face.

Dylan sat down and Cyan heard his computer come to life.

The rest of the morning followed the usual pattern – Cyan went through the rest of her inbox. There was a circular from the SAS that asked for tasters for a new range of blended teas. Cyan smiled. Maybe there would be iced tea on offer as well, and she made a mental note to head there at lunch. When she read the next email, Cyan sat back in her chair and puffed out her cheeks.

"How did that get through?" she asked herself. "This student has way too many resits to progress." She marked the email and dealt with other, less complicated issues.

She returned to the student and their multiple reassessments after lunch. Fortunately their personal tutor was Cyrus. Cyan hoped that a quick email exchange would sort this out.

"Cyan?" said a gentle English West Country accent.

"Hmm?" Cyan said, her attention on the student's records displayed on her screen.

"Not getting ready for the presentation?"

Cyan looked over the top of her screen at Dylan. Then her eyes flicked back to the bottom left of her screen. There were no messages, but behind her computer screen, pinned to the blue fabric-covered partition, was a printed programme for the 'All staff introduction to Safe Tracker', the new student records system.

Dylan got up and closed the counter's shutters. Zoe had left earlier for another meeting.

While he walked back to his desk Cyan checked the agenda – the presentation was due to take place in one of the computer rooms in the Mann Building. She looked at the student record on her screen and decided that this had to be dealt with that afternoon. As she locked her desktop Cyan hoped that the presentation would not run over time.

"Save me a seat!" she called to Dylan as he collected his jacket from a row of coat hooks next to the office door and walked out of the registry. He waved acknowledgement and closed the main door to the registry behind him.

Cyan grabbed her bag, travel mug and got up. She pulled some paperwork from her drawer and followed Dylan out of the office.

Cyan left the Hub and walked quickly along the path to the Mann Building, where she pressed her staff card to the lock, opened the door and walked in. The Mann Building had once been a set of barracks for navy personnel during the eighteenth century. The then landowner, William King, had given land to the navy in exchange for protection should enemy naval forces ever show up. There was nothing to indicate that they ever had, but when his one remaining descendent had left the land to Corner Rise University it became the Crown Campus, and the Mann Building was easy to convert into teaching space. Except for the top floor, which was a confusion of short passages and steps to single rooms. Cyan was pleased to only get lost once before she reached a small flight of stairs that she hoped led to the large computer room. The steps ended at a small landing and a fire door. Cyan paused outside the door to make sure that she had the details of the dummy students her team had created to test the new student records system – 'Zippy Zappy Zog-Zog' with the student number 26262626 was her favourite. She smiled to herself. For once data protection had been fun. She could hear voices from behind the door, but as she knew that the staff from the whole of Student Services plus those from the Department of Mathematics and Statistical Studies had been invited, she dismissed them. People always complained when a new system was introduced, so the tone of the voices didn't worry her.

Cyan was still with her thoughts when she opened the door

slightly. She froze. Through the gap she saw Professor Daniella Waldergrave standing, fists by her sides and feet apart. Opposite her, Dr Dayton King leant against the wall, one ankle crossed over the other, his arms resting across his chest while he looked at the ceiling.

"You seem to be forgetting that I did the lion's share of the research for this paper," Daniella said as she crossed her arms. "That's why my name should be first."

"And you seem to be forgetting that you're at Corner Rise University, on a set of islands in the middle of the Atlantic," Dayton looked at Daniella, "rather than somewhere more red-brick in England. There has to be a reason for that." His gaze returned to the ceiling. "I'm guessing plagiarism?"

"What?"

Cyan put her hand over her mouth to lock in a gasp.

"I'd better double-check that research of yours." He smiled. "Or was there something else?"

Cyan watched as Daniella shrunk back from Dayton as if he had pulled out a weapon. Guessing that this was not a conversation to walk in on Cyan retreated, allowing the door to close silently in front of her. She listened, but there was silence on the other side of the door. Cyan had no idea what to do. It felt like an age before she heard the click of heels. Cyan pushed the door open and rushed in before the heels reached the door, she didn't want to collide with the person on the other side.

"Oh sorry," Cyan said. "Am I late for—?"

Cyan's voice stopped dead when she saw the rage on Daniella's face. Cyan moved to her left and Daniella mirrored her. Cyan felt the temperature rise as Daniella glared at her. They repeated the two steps to the opposite side and this time Daniella growled. Cyan stepped back and out through the door. Daniella walked past her without a word. Cyan watched as the professor stomped down the stairs. Behind her a door opened and she guessed that Dayton had just walked into the computer room. She sighed and followed him in.

Cyan found Dylan and the rest of the Student Services staff near the front of the room. Dylan smiled up at her, but his expression changed when he saw her face.

"What's wrong?" he said.

Cyan told him what had just happened as she settled into her seat and logged on to the computer in front of her.

"Wow," said Dylan. "He really said that?"

"I know. Which university would risk hiring someone who plagiarised?"

Dylan shook his head. "I have told people over and over again," he said, "Dayton is not that smart. He just puts on a show."

Before Cyan could respond two large screens at the front of the computer room sprang to life.

"Oh no!" said Dylan. "I forgot my list of dummy students."

"Share mine," said Cyan. "But I get to be 'Zog-Zog'."

Fortunately for Cyan the presentation finished a few minutes after four o'clock.

"I really can't see the difference," she said as she walked down to the ground floor with Dylan. "It's just the same student records stuff with a new front end."

Dylan shook his head. "Nope. The new keyboard shortcuts will save your wrists. Believe me."

"That's true," said Cyan.

They continued to talk as they walked downstairs and through the corridors to the main entrance.

"Good afternoon. Did you enjoy the presentation?"

Cyan looked over her shoulder at Cyrus. "Good afternoon," she said to the professor. "At least it was short."

"Two hours for a system I barely touch?" Cyrus replied. "At least they could have provided some refreshments."

"I bought a tea on the way here," said Dylan as he pressed the green button to open the door.

"I wish I had," said Cyrus as they walked down the main path towards the King Building.

"Well—" said Cyrus as the path divided.

"Cyrus, have you got a few minutes?" asked Cyan before he could say more.

The professor nodded.

"See you back at the registry," said Dylan and walked away.

"I noticed that Daniella wasn't around," said Cyrus. "That will cause trouble when the new system starts."

"I'm not surprised," said Cyan as they moved out of the way of a group of students. "She looked ready to kill after her argument with Dayton."

"Oh, not again. They have argued non-stop since that paper was finished."

"Really?"

Cyrus nodded.

"For goodness' sake," said Cyan. "About what?"

"Who did the most research."

"Why is that important?"

"Authorship. The person who did the most work comes first in the list of names at the top of the paper."

"Huh," said Cyan. "I can see why Dayton would fight over that."

"Anyway. You wanted to talk to me?"

"Ah. Yes." Cyan looked around at the empty path. "It's about a student in your tutor group." She told Cyrus about the reassessment and progression problem.

"I'd better have a look. I'll also be able to get a tea, I'm parched." Cyrus stepped back to let Cyan lead the way to her office.

Half an hour later, Cyrus stared at Cyan's computer screen.

"Well," he said, "at least we have time to sort this out before the spring term. Send me a meeting invite." Cyrus got up to leave. "But for now I wish you a good evening."

"Thank you. You too."

Cyan followed him to the office door and closed the registry's main door behind him. She went back to her desk and sent Cyrus the meeting email, she then glanced at her watch. She had missed her bus, but would make the next one if she hurried. Cyan closed down her workstation and picked up her stuff and lowered the shutter. She closed the registry door behind her as she left.

Cyan was in good spirits when she got into work the next morning. For once she wasn't held up by roadworks and the sky was so clear that she felt she could see the whole Atlantic on her bus ride to work. Both Zoe and Dylan arrived shortly after Cyan and they started the day with a conversation about the latest celebrity mishap. When Cyan checked her email she was pleased to see that Cyrus had replied to her request sent the previous afternoon. Plus Cyan was on counter duty to answer student queries, the part of the job she really enjoyed. There was nothing better than offering solutions to problems, even if all she did was listen while the student sorted it all out themselves. Katherine Welman, the other student support administrator, arrived after both Zoe and Dylan had gone to different appointments. Katherine managed her usual sullen Hello before she picked up her mug and walked back out of the office. She returned after a few minutes, set her tea down and logged in to her machine. Cyan continued with her work. Most things were looking good that morning.

Cyan had just worked out which students required extra time for the end-of-term assessments when she heard the office door open and looked up in time to see a flash of blue hair as Katherine sped out of the office. Cyan was about to wonder why her colleague had moved so fast when she saw the reason on the other side of the registry counter. She felt her stomach contract as Dr Dayton King slipped through the partially closed door and approached her desk.

"Good morning," said Cyan, bracing herself. She knew from experience some form of confrontation would follow her next question, but she had to know why Dayton was now on the office side of the counter. "How can I help?"

"All I want are some old exam papers," said Dayton. "Is that too much to ask for?"

Cyan looked up at him. The exams would take place before the holidays, surely he should have written them by now. Cyan kept that thought to herself and carefully chose her words. "Examinations will be able to supply them. Just send a—"

"I don't have time to send a request. I want to publish a research paper before the end of term."

"The exam papers will arrive before the end of term."

"You do not seem to understand," Dayton said slowly. "I was asked to cover this module, adding to my workload, and now I have to write the exam for it."

Cyan glanced beyond the counter at the empty registry. Then back to Dayton who now stood over her.

"I have important work to do," said Dayton, "so I don't want to waste time on this exam."

He leant so close to Cyan that she could the see the green flecks in his hazel eyes. She wheeled her chair away from her desk to put some distance between them.

"You could call them?"

"Why should I?" Dayton replied as he took a deep breath.

Cyan tried not to sigh.

"Honestly, this is pathetic. None of you are focused enough. Your job is to support me, not stare at a screen all day."

Cyan sat back as Dayton continued to tell her exactly what he thought her job should be. Inside she silently cursed Katherine, knowing that Dayton would not dare to act like this if there was a witness. Cyan brought her attention back to Dayton and wondered if he would ever pause for breath.

"Good morning, Dr King. Is there anything I can do to help?"

The use of Dayton's title and last name, along with a voice that could freeze an ocean, made him spring upright and jump back at the same time.

Zoe stood in the doorway, her stance was passive, but her stare had the force of a prize fighter's right hook.

"I want some past exam papers for the basic statistics module," Dayton said.

"You should ask your department admin for that. Or have you tried asking your head of department?" said Zoe as she stepped away from the door. "I could help with that if you'd like."

"No, no need." Dayton refused Zoe's help quickly as he zipped through the door and across the reception area.

"Are you okay?" Zoe said to Cyan once Dayton had left.

"No," said Cyan. "And, I think he's getting worse."

"What do you want to do?"

"I'll avoid another complaint for now," said Cyan.

She was sure that the last one hadn't helped. In fact, it had probably added to Dayton's aggression.

"If you need to talk just knock," said Zoe.

Cyan nodded in reply as Zoe unlocked her office door and walked in. Katherine appeared with a half-empty cup and sat down without a word. Cyan knew better than to argue with a defensive Katherine, but neither was she prepared to sit there as if nothing had happened, so she got up and went to make a cup of tea.

The rest of the morning passed with few student queries. The sky was still clear at midday, so Cyan found an empty bench and enjoyed a quiet lunch. Dylan walked into the office shortly after Cyan sat at her desk.

"I saw Dayton with a new member of staff," he said as he hung up his jacket and walked towards his desk.

Cyan looked at the back of the monitor next to Dylan's. The

fourth position in the registry office had been vacant since she arrived.

"Does that mean we'll get a new member of staff?"

"You wish. Zoe's been asking since before you arrived and all she gets are blank stares."

"So," said Cyan, "who is this new member of staff?"

"He didn't introduce me, but whoever she is, she looks like she should be famous."

Cyan looked up at Dylan. "What makes you say that?"

"The way she was dressed," said Dylan.

"Really?" said Cyan, who had never known Dylan to comment on clothes. "So? How was she dressed?"

"Expensively. A long grey cardigan and an orange top—"

"Oh please," said Katherine. "Orange top."

Cyan looked at Katherine in time to see an exaggerated eye roll.

"Oh and I suppose you saw her?" said Dylan.

"I know her," said Katherine, "and so should you. She's a student on one of your courses. Something in textiles."

"Dayton was talking to a student?" Dylan stood, a look of surprise on his face.

"I bet that didn't last long," said Cyan. She chuckled. The way that Dayton usually talked to students was to point to the sky, say, "What's that?" and walk away while the student looked up. He could move pretty fast when he wanted to.

"No. This student talked and he listened." Dylan pulled out his chair.

"Dr Dayton King?" said Cyan, looking over the top of her computer as Dylan sat.

"Yes," he said. "I know. I couldn't believe it either."

"Did this student have magic powers?" said Cyan.

"Actually I had lunch with her." Katherine brushed a twist of blue hair over her shoulder. "The cardigan is antique silver, one hundred per cent silk, as is her top. Which is coral, not orange. If you need to look her up, her name is Orlanda Henry."

Katherine's tone reminded Cyan of those teen-queen films she would stumble across on television. She struggled to suppress a smile as Katherine rose from her chair and flounced out of the registry.

"Because I had lunch with her," mimicked Dylan, which caused Cyan to laugh. "Hey, Cyan," he said when Cyan stopped, "are you going to look this student up?"

"No," said Cyan. "First, she's not on a course I support so I really don't need to, and second, why give Katherine the satisfaction. If she asks if I looked up the student I can say I didn't. Will you look her up?"

"I've already seen her."

Cyan sat back in front of her screen and looked at the student records icon. She started to reach for the mouse, but the registry door opened and as she rose from her desk she decided not to. If it was one of the courses Dylan supported she had little business there, plus she had enough to do with her own courses. She approached the counter with a "Good afternoon."

There were no more student queries after that and an hour later Cyan decided to give her eyes a rest from the screen. She left the registry and walked to the nearest toilets, only to stand outside with her arms crossed; they were closed for maintenance again. The toilets in the Hub broke down so often that Cyan believed they were added as an afterthought. Probably by the world's worst builders. She walked towards the stairs and was halfway down when the argument started. She was tempted to reverse back up the steps to the first floor to avoid it, but then she recognised Dr Dayton King's voice behind the security door.

Cyan could tell from the volume of his voice that he hadn't got what he wanted. His voice got louder and she guessed that Dayton considered the person he was angry with to be beneath him. Cyan had to see who held out against him. She hit the green button and pushed the door open. On her left she watched as Dayton shouted at a porter. *Okay*, she thought, *Dayton has finally lost his mind*. It was an unwritten rule at Corner not to shout at porters. They moved the furniture, delivered the post and always knew which rooms were empty when you needed one for an emergency meeting – although nobody knew how. Cyan had met Trevor several times since he joined the Estates Department as a porter. He wasn't a small man, and even though he was half a head taller than Dayton, it was Dayton's pointed finger that jabbed the air inches away from Trevor's chest. As Cyan approached them she could tell from the look on the porter's face that if Dayton's finger ever made contact it would be broken.

"Hey," she said, hoping to stop the argument with her presence.

Trevor stepped back. "Afternoon," he replied, his eyes locked onto Dayton's finger.

Dayton ignored Cyan completely. "I keep telling you, you're not focused enough," he said, his finger stabbing the air in front of the porter's chest.

Huh-oh, thought Cyan. She knew Dayton's favourite phrase was always followed by an insult. "Maybe this is not the place," she added aloud.

It was five minutes past four on Wednesday afternoon and although Wednesdays were not the busiest days during term time, there were still students about and Cyan didn't want any of them to walk in on an argument between two members of staff. The staff in question appeared to read Cyan's mind. Trevor took another step back and Dayton, whose eyes had flicked briefly in her direction, slowly lowered his finger.

"This is not over, Trevor Furley," said Dayton and he pushed past the porter through another set of doors into the Cinema Cafe. "Pathetic! Completely pathetic!" he added as the doors closed behind him.

Cyan watched as rage sprang in Trevor's eyes and his jaw tightened, but he stayed still. A second later, he released a slow breath.

"What happened?" she asked.

"Missing package," Trevor answered quickly. "You'd think it was gold the way that man carried on." He focused on Cyan. "Thanks for coming when you did. I'd better get back to the post room."

Cyan nodded. "See you tomorrow?"

Trevor nodded. "Of course. Good afternoon."

Cyan echoed Trevor's words and watched him push open the double doors to the cafe. That had to be the first time she had ever seen Trevor without a smile. Cyan could not understand why Dayton's attitude didn't get him sacked. He had no respect for anyone in a black university uniform, be they caterers, porters or cleaners. *That man needs to learn some manners.* Cyan walked through the same doors, past the coffee bar and towards the toilets.

CHAPTER 2

Cyan walked through the King Building while she tried to work out if there would be enough time to get to the mini market in her lunch break. The idea of carting a bag of cat food on the bus did not appeal, but she had forgotten to go to the shops the previous night and really could not be bothered to go out again once she had sat down with a hot drink. This meant that Cyan's cat, Loki, got a rare treat of tinned tuna for breakfast, which wasn't a habit that Cyan wanted her cat to develop. She reached the back door at the same time as another figure.

"Sorry. Oh. Hello, Cyan." Cyrus smiled and pushed the door open for her.

Cyan smiled in return, it was the right door this time. "Hello," she said. "Another early morning meeting?"

"Not today. I'm off to the King Collection, I've got a bet to win."

"The Collection's closed. How are you going to get in?"

Cyrus glanced at his watch as he walked along the path. To their left a flatbed truck passed along the main path and turned into the building site.

"Looks like they're about to take the scaffolding down," said Cyrus.

"It does. But that doesn't explain how you'll get into the King Collection."

Cyrus smiled. "I promised not to say."

Cyrus pressed his staff card to the lock and pushed the door open after the bleep.

"After you," he said as he held the door open.

"Thank you."

"Have a good day," Cyrus said as he headed towards the museum. Cyan shook her head, she didn't want to watch Cyrus run into another locked door and turned towards the stairs. She would find out about the bet later.

Cyan walked up to the registry's main door and placed her card against the lock. It opened with a quick bleep and she was pleased to see the yellow shutters down on the counter, which meant that she was alone for a while. She always liked this time of the morning, it gave her enough time to prepare herself for the day. Cyan walked to the door at the left of counter and punched in the code to get into the office.

There was some post on the counter behind the shutters and Cyan hung up her coat before she picked it up. The parcel was for a different department and Cyan put it in the out tray for collection later, but after she had locked away her bags she decided to take it back to the post room. She couldn't open the registry while she was by herself, plus it was too early, and it would be fun to have a morning chat.

Cyan carried the parcel down to the post room in the basement and was surprised to see the counter closed. She was about to knock on the double doors when one opened, and she jumped back to avoid a collision.

"Sorry," said Trevor as he raised his eyes from the package he had tried to push into his post bag. "Hi, Cyan." Trevor's smile shone like a star.

"Good morning, Trevor." Cyan looked at the post bag, it appeared ready to burst.

"No one else is in right now." He rearranged the thick shoulder strap. "Greg's just called in sick. He was a bit peaky yesterday. Is that for us?" He nodded to the package Cyan was holding.

"This? No. It's for SAS, we got it by mistake."

"Sorry about that. Look. Come in, leave it behind the counter for now."

Trevor reversed back into the post room and Cyan followed. She leant over and added the parcel to the last bits of post on the table just behind the counter, took a look at the empty post room and gave up any thought of a conversation. She was about to leave, but Trevor rested the bag on the counter and stared at her.

"What?" said Cyan.

"Is that your hair?"

Cyan's hand rose automatically to her head. She gently pulled at one of the twists. "My cousin had an 'all natural' party. No straighteners, no extensions, no nothing. I didn't fancy an Afro so here they are."

"I have never seen you without a wig before." Trevor nodded rhythmically and slowly. "Why cover your hair? It looks good."

"I like wigs. Quick and easy. Actually, I nearly cheated and bought an Afro wig. Good thing I didn't."

"Why?"

"There were so many Afros the party looked like a 1970s dance show."

"Right on!" Trevor's head bobbed rhythmically as if to music.

"Stop that!" Cyan tried to keep the laughter out of her voice.

Trevor didn't try and laughed as he slid the post bag off the counter. They heard a scream. Cyan froze. Trevor slipped the post bag from his shoulder to the floor.

"Who else is here?" Trevor's eyes were round and the smile was gone.

"Cyrus!"

They looked at each other for a second then sprang to the open door. They reached it at the same time and for a moment they were both stuck in the doorway.

"Sorry," said Trevor and popped free.

Cyan rubbed her arm as she raced after him. Being tall, Trevor took the stairs two at a time and was on the ground floor before her.

Cyan pushed open the solid double doors of the King Collection to see Cyrus leaning heavily on a chest of display drawers. Trevor was standing by him, looking as if he wanted to help but wasn't sure what to do. He looked up at Cyan.

"What happened?" She nodded towards Cyrus.

Trevor shook his head. Cyrus's knees buckled slightly, the professor's eyes almost filling the wire frames of his round glasses.

"Whoa!" Trevor held Cyrus's arm. "Quick, get him something to sit on."

Cyan doubted that Cyrus's legs would support him much longer.

As she hunted for a kick stool she asked herself if one of the statues in the collection had come to life and spoken to him. It was the only way to describe his expression. She found a stool and kicked it slowly towards the professor, who had pushed Trevor's hand away.

"You're all right now," said Trevor as he tried to calm Cyrus. Cyrus didn't agree, he shook his head and his hand twitched as he pointed to the left of the porter. Cyan's eyes flicked in the direction of his hand. She froze for a moment. Then leant to her left. There was something on the floor between two of the tall display cabinets. She took a cautious step forward and saw shoes with blue leather soles lying on the floor, one in front of the other. Cyan took another step. The shoes were brown and shiny and they went perfectly with the red socks and the grey trousers. Her first thought was that someone was asleep on the floor. She remembered an incident after last year's Christmas party. Fayval had arrived at work the next day to see a junior lecturer snoring loudly beside one of the display cases.

The man Cyan stared at now looked asleep – he was on his side with both arms in front of him. Or at least Cyan thought he was until she saw the back of his head. The sight made her jump back, letting out a half-strangled yelp.

"What's up?" Trevor was by her side.

From behind her she heard Cyrus say, "Day-Day-Day."

Cyan and Trevor looked at each other and then at the feet. Cyan put three fingers on the corner of the first display cabinet and leant forward again.

There was something wrong with the shape of the head. Then she saw small shiny red droplets on the hard floor next to it.

"Oh no."

Cyan closed her eyes and took in a deep breath to try and calm her stomach. Instead she inhaled a light smell of smokey mint, which made her stomach churn even more.

"Blood," she said aloud.

"What? Where? Uh-oh." Trevor grabbed her shoulders as she heaved.

Then the shiny shoes no longer shone. Cyan looked at her breakfast and heaved again. She slumped against the cabinet and slowly slid to the floor, glad of Trevor's support on the way down. She closed her eyes, felt Trevor move and opened her eyes again. Trevor walked past the cabinet to the front of the body.

"No. Please don't—" Cyan didn't have time to warn him.

"My days! It's Dayton King!" said Trevor. His eyes were as big as Cyrus's had been, then they rolled to white. Trevor groaned, rocked back on his heels, balanced for a moment then collapsed like a flattened cardboard box. Cyan winced as he hit the ground. *At least he hasn't taken any exhibits with him*, she thought. She closed her eyes and hoped that her stomach would settle. How many times had she had to explain that her response to blood was the reason that she had not followed the women of her family into nursing?

"What ... what's going on?" The voice caused Cyan to open her eyes. She looked over her right shoulder and spotted a pair of brown shoes.

What is it with brown shoes today? she thought. This pair had slim heels and square toes. Cyan looked up into the round face of Fayval, the museum's curator.

"You okay?" Fayval asked as she got down on her knees.

"Call the police," said Cyan, leaning her back against the cabinet. Fayval hesitated. Then she started to reach for Cyan. "No. Really. Call the police."

"Why?" replied Fayval.

"Because Dayton King is dead." Cyan was surprised at how calm she sounded. Maybe she should get up, but when she raised her arm to indicate where the body was, it shook so badly and felt so weak that she decided against any further movement. Fayval looked beyond Cyan and gasped as she saw a pair of shoes. Cyan realised what would happen next. The last thing she needed was another person on the floor.

"No! Police. Call!" For a moment Fayval looked at Cyan, then leant to one side and spotted Trevor. Fayval's eyes grew bigger and she raised a hand to her open mouth, then she got up and stepped back.

Cyan intervened again. "I-I think Trevor's okay." Cyan paused for a second. "Call the police and an ambulance."

Finally Fayval's gaze moved to Cyrus, whose stance fought against gravity. Until he slumped a bit more. Fayval looked about, grabbed the kick stool and slid it under the professor. Gravity won and Cyrus dropped onto it and pressed his hands onto his thighs in what looked to Cyan as an effort to stay upright. He partially succeeded.

Cyan's gaze moved from the slumped professor to the King

Collection's curator. "Fayval?" The curator nodded. Cyan tried to look straight ahead. She failed and once again saw the soles of the doctor's brown shoes. The sight caused another wave of nausea. She closed her eyes. The next sound she heard was Fayval's shoes as they clicked along the parquet floor and then the sound of a handset lifted from its rest. She caught snatches of Fayval's call.

"Hello. Security? I need the police … dead body … King Collection, yes, the museum on the ground floor … yes, a dead body at Corner Rise University."

The end of the call broke Cyan's trance. Her eyes flew open at the last phrase. How could anybody be dead in a university? Especially Corner Rise University.

CHAPTER 3

Shortly after Fayval had put down the phone Cyan heard feet and voices behind her. Then Fayval touched her upper arm.

"Can you stand? The police have been called and they'll want the museum."

Cyan looked into Fayval's amber eyes and then over Fayval's shoulder to see three members of Corner's security staff, she recognised Jennifer, who nodded quickly in greeting. Cyan smiled back weakly. Another one of the three had his back to her and Cyan could hear the bleep of a radio.

"They're not the police?" Cyan said.

"No, security. They're here to help us to another room," said Fayval. "We can't sit here with a dead body."

Cyan glanced at Dayton's shoes and instantly wished that she hadn't, the sight made her shudder and she turned her head away. She looked at Fayval and nodded. "What about Trevor?"

"We can't move him, but an ambulance is on its way," said Jennifer. Cyan watched as she reached into the pocket of her black jacket and pulled out a small silver plastic packet.

"Cyan!" Fayval waved her fingers in front of Cyan's face. "Can you stand?"

Cyan slowly got to her feet, assisted by Jennifer and Fayval. Jennifer wrapped a silver sheet around Cyan's shoulders.

"She's not cold," said Fayval.

"It's to help with the shock," replied Jennifer.

Cyan smiled weakly at Jennifer and clutched at the sheet for comfort. All three followed Cyrus, who was supported by the other security staff, out of the Collection and into Cinema One where they were seated.

"I'll get back, make sure no one gets into the Collection," said the tallest security guard.

"Okay," said Jennifer, "we'll go back to the Gatehouse." She looked at Cyan and Fayval, unsure of what to say next.

"We'll just wait here," said Fayval.

Jennifer nodded and looked relieved as she followed the other member of security staff out of the cinema.

Cyan wasn't sure how long the police took to arrive. She felt as if she was surrounded by thick fog – everything felt distant. Fayval moved between her and Cyrus and tried to get them to talk, asking them about their plans for the weekend and what they had seen on television recently. Fayval had asked if they would like some tea, but the thought made Cyan's stomach churn again and when she dry-heaved Fayval rapidly changed the subject. Cyan tried to focus on Fayval but the security staff had left half of the cinema's double doors open. It was the sound of voices that stopped Fayval. Cyan saw two police officers walk past, one in a stab-proof vest. They were followed by paramedics in dark green uniforms. Fayval walked towards the door and briefly blocked Cyan's view. Before Cyan could say anything, Fayval slipped through the door and some people in funny white disposable overalls with face masks stood outside the doorway for a brief moment. Then another police officer looked into the cinema and pulled the door shut as he backed out. Cyan sank back in her chair.

She looked down at the shiny silver blanket she was wrapped in. It reminded her of natural disasters where she had watched earthquake survivors, staring shell-shocked into space while television crews panned out to show crumpled buildings or a lone child's toy. Cyan ran her palm across the shiny surface. This felt all wrong. She was in a university.

Right now I should be in the registry's office … Her thoughts tailed off as she remembered why she wasn't.

Fayval walked up the aisle to Cyan with two mugs of tea. Cyan's stomach gave a quick flip, then rumbled and she accepted the offered mug gratefully and used it to warm her hands while Fayval stood and took a sip from her own.

"It's just like TV." The excitement in Fayval's voice caused Cyan to stare hard into her mug while the muscles in her jaw worked silently. "All those SOCOs—"

"What?" Cyan's hands trembled as she tried not to shout. She slowly looked up at Fayval.

"SOCOs. Just—"

"Fayval. I just saw a dead body. I couldn't care less about soccer people."

"Not soccer. SOCO. Scenes of Crime Officers."

"Oh. Sorry. Thanks for the tea," said Cyan. She smiled at her friend and then looked around the cinema.

"Why would someone bash Dayton in the head?" said Fayval.

Cyan's eyes switched back to Fayval. "You. You looked?"

"Why whisper. Of course I did. It was definitely Dayton and he was definitely dead. His eyes were wide open." Fayval sipped her tea.

"Huh?" Cyan wondered how Fayval could be so calm.

"Well. When did you ever see him with wide-open eyes?"

Cyan was about to argue. No one should be that calm after they had seen a dead body. Then she stopped. She realised that she had never seen Dayton with his eyes wide open. "They were always half closed," she added aloud.

"That's because he was always looking down his nose at us."

"Fayval!"

"No, really. Even with those taller than him. He lifted his chin to do it."

"The man is dead," Cyan reminded her.

"And I would be a hypocrite to change my views now. Especially with the police walking about."

Cyan could only stare at her friend.

"Why look surprised? Those officers out there, they will want the truth."

Cyan looked beyond Fayval's shoulder. "I think one of those officers wants to talk to you now."

Fayval looked over her shoulder and then back to Cyan and nodded. Cyan smiled back and Fayval gave a wink in return.

"Good morning. I've been given your names by the guard outside of the …" the police officer looked down at her notes, "King Collection." She looked around the auditorium and then at Fayval. "Can I take your name please?"

"Fayval King."

"Ah. Hello, Mrs King?" Fayval nodded. "Please follow me."

"Of course," said Fayval. "Can I bring my tea?"

"Of course."

Fayval went through the door after the police officer, mug in hand and not spilling a drop. Cyan watched in admiration. She knew that Fayval was right about the police, they would be after the truth and once they had it all this would be sorted.

Cyan rested her head on the high-backed seat. The deep wine-coloured upholstery slowly relaxed her; it made her think of wine and she wished she were sitting on her balcony looking out over the sea on a Sunday afternoon. In her mind's eye Cyan could see the turquoise sky, with a hint of gold from the sun reflected in the waters. She took another sip of sweet tea and tried to work out if wine would be good for shock. One person who wasn't shocked was Fayval. Cyan smiled to herself at the thought of the investigators stuck in silence while Fayval was in full flow with full descriptions and a fuller vocabulary.

"Oh." Cyan remembered that she hadn't discovered the body alone. She heard Cyrus move in front of her. She pulled the crinkly blanket tighter around herself, rose and walked slowly towards him. The professor had looked better. He was as white as paper – even his veins had retreated. He turned round eyes up at her. "Is he … Dayton … really?"

"Yes. I think he is." Cyan reached for the seat to pull it down. She slipped, almost fell back into the newly upholstered auditorium seat. She heard the chair next to her creak lightly along with the movement of clothes. She didn't need to look at Cyrus to know that his head was in his hands. She was startled when he sat up as if spring-loaded.

"Wait," Cyrus looked at her, "where's Trevor?"

"In an ambulance."

"What?"

"Or probably in the hospital by now," said Cyan, looking back into the almost cold cup of tea. "I saw some paramedics a moment ago, so they must have taken him out of the Collection. But it felt like I was miles away."

"Or in fog," said Cyrus. They sat quietly for a moment. Cyrus pulled his arms over his stomach. "When I saw his face."

"Trevor's?"

Cyrus shook his head. "Dayton's. He just looked so. Surprised."

Cyan frowned. "Dayton was surprised?"

"Well. He was murdered. I'd be surprised by that."

"Cyan Butler." The officer made both Cyrus and Cyan jump. They hadn't heard her come in. Cyan looked at Cyrus, but his head was back in his hands.

Cyan stood up and pulled the silver blanket from her shoulders, folded it neatly and slid it between the chair seat and the back rest. Cyrus looked up as she left with the officer and tried to smile encouragement. Cyan smiled back. She then followed the officer through the double doors and along the short corridor. The Cinema Cafe was empty, even the bar staff were gone and Cyan kept her eyes on the officer's utility belt to avoid the scene that surrounded her. She had seen enough that morning. As they passed the main entrance Cyan automatically looked out. There was a small crowd behind the blue-and-white police tape outside and she knew that most of them would be students. Cyan easily spotted Katherine in the crowd – she could hardly miss her. Katherine was taller than most of the people around her and had swapped her blue extensions for deep cerise ones. Katherine caught Cyan's eye, waved and mouthed a few words, which caused Cyan to stand still and stare until she had lip-read the question, 'What happened?'

"Are you all right, ma'am?" said the police officer.

"Hmm? Sorry," she said. She pulled her eyes away from Katherine. "I saw someone I work with. Outside."

The officer looked quickly outside. Cyan thought about the counter in the registry and was thankful for it. At least Portmore hadn't been around long enough to implement all his ideas about 'removing all barriers' and 'better staff-student interaction', which translated as 'remove all the counters and let everyone roam freely'. Without the counter she could imagine herself surrounded by staff, and students, all over her desk to find out what had happened that morning. And how would she do her job with everyone around her?

There was a buzz from the crowd as the doors opened and Cyan watched paramedics wheel an empty stretcher through the main doors. She turned her head away and fixed her eyes on the officer's utility belt again. The officer led her to a blue-upholstered sofa just beside the main doors. Opposite the sofa was a single chair that had been taken from one of the tables in the cafe.

"Would you like a glass of water? Or some tea?" said the officer.

"No. Thanks." Cyan watched the officer leave and realised that she had left her half-empty mug on the cinema floor – she hoped that someone would pick it up.

"Hello."

Cyan looked up into the kind face of woman with a black reporter's notebook. The woman was wearing a long black dress populated with large, long-stemmed red flowers and a formal short-sleeved black jacket. Cyan noticed the ID badge attached to the jacket's lapel.

"Sorry you've had to wait so long." The woman pulled out the chair opposite Cyan and sat down. She looked briefly at her notes. "Cyan Butler?"

"Er. Yes?"

"I'm Detective Sergeant Phyllida Brookes."

In the end the interview wasn't that bad. Cyan remembered Fayval's words about truth and recounted the events of the morning, with any times and details as requested by DS Brookes. Cyan only stumbled when asked about Dayton.

"So he's really dead?"

"I'm afraid so," said the detective sergeant. "He was pronounced dead just before you were sent for."

Cyan glanced briefly towards the museum. "Will you catch—" The word 'killer' stuck in her throat.

"It's early yet, but in a place like this there are a lot of people who could become witnesses. Somebody must have the information we need." DS Brookes smiled and Cyan felt reassured.

"Well," Brookes continued, "thank you for your time. Sorry that we kept you waiting so long."

"Th-that's fine. I understand." Cyan rose to leave. She reached for her shoulder bag.

"Anything wrong?"

"No," said Cyan. "I thought I had my bag. I usually sit here for lunch."

Cyan got up and walked towards the lift, glancing around the large open cafe just as a stretcher was wheeled past. The body on top was completely covered by a sheet and Cyan knew it was Dayton. She stood still and watched. Not long ago Dayton stood over her and told her how to do her job. At some point she had stopped listening to him and began to imagine ways in which he could get lost. Cyan sighed. This was not what she had in mind at the time.

"Inspector?"

Cyan's head whipped around at the sound of the detective sergeant's voice. To Cyan the title 'Inspector' only belonged on TV or radio, solely for crime dramas or news broadcasts from elsewhere. She had never seen one in the flesh before. The inspector passed her as he walked towards the table she had just left. He wore blue chinos and a red polo shirt. His skin was the colour of almonds and his hair was almost black. But it was his eyes that startled her. They didn't threaten or probe, they were just the clearest deep green she had seen that wasn't jewellery or glass.

Cyan hurried to the lift. This morning had been too much for her.

CHAPTER 4

When Cyan got to the registry the counter's shutters were still closed. She hoped that the police would soon open the building, after all, the murder had taken place in the King Collection, so they wouldn't need to check any other rooms? Cyan wanted some noise, even Katherine's voice would do. In the quiet, her mind went back to the museum, which forced her to try and shake the image of Dayton's body from her head. Maybe the rest of the registry staff were still outside. The police would have to let them in soon, they couldn't keep the building shut all day? Where would the post go? She closed the registry's main door behind her, walked through the door at the side of the counter and pressed the button to raise the shutters. She watched them until they clicked open and then went to her desk.

As Cyan opened her email there was a tap at the main door. She hoped that it wasn't a student, she wasn't allowed to have any students in the registry when alone. Cyan looked through the long, thin window in the door. To her relief the woman on the other side of the door held up a staff card. Cyan smiled and let her in.

"Good morning," said Cyan, even though that morning had been far from good.

"Good morning." The young woman shifted her weight from one foot to the other.

"How can I help you?" Cyan asked after a few moments had passed.

"What? Sorry." The young woman looked up. She had almond-shaped eyes the colour of dark chocolate. "I should have caught you after the police ... I'm Miranda, from Human Resources. The Portmore Building is closed. Due to ... events."

Ah yes, thought Cyan, *the reason why the registry is empty. Events. Dayton's lifeless body in the university's museum.* "Of course," she replied out loud.

"We've booked you a taxi," said Miranda. "We'll call you this afternoon. At your home?"

"I'll just log out."

Cyan didn't remember the journey home, but one thing she did remember was that by the time she had got there, Dayton's death had made the midday news. Her phone rang and she switched off the radio. Cyan got to her mobile in three rings.

"Hello?"

"How are you?" Her mother's voice was full of concern.

"Not good." Cyan described the morning's events.

Then there was a pause. "Would you like me to come over?"

Cyan thought about it for a while. Earlier on she had wanted to be with people, but after she listened to the news, Cyan wasn't so sure. Everyone would have questions to ask. "No. I'm fine."

"I don't think so," said her mother. "In over thirty years of work I never saw one murdered body."

"I hope not," said Cyan. "How would you explain that to their families? I can see the headlines now, awful puns about angels and demonic nurses."

"No joking!" Cyan could hear her mother fighting to keep the smile out of her voice. "You could always come and stay with me."

"Yes, Mum, you're right. I'm not fine. But I've got Loki for company." Cyan looked around her. "Although I haven't seen her today."

"Probably in a bin somewhere."

"Loki doesn't do bins. I'd better go look for her."

"Call if you need to. Or just come over."

Cyan put her phone back on the table after her mother had hung up. She called for her cat, but there was no meow in reply. Cyan got up.

She began with the balcony. Loki wasn't on either of the two grey metal chairs, or behind the painted wooden box used as a table. Cyan stood by the rail and looked out over the bay. Although she was familiar with the view, she loved how calm it made her feel, especially today when it was almost still. There were no boats to be seen, the trans-Atlantic sailors having long left for Europe to avoid the storms that rolled in from the USA. She missed the sight of them and would sometimes travel to other more sheltered bays around Corner Rise to get her floating fix. Her dream was to sail. Not away from Corner, she had already left once, but to potter around the bays in a small sailing boat and in the evenings look up at the stars. Once again Cyan snapped her mind back to the present and started to look for her cat. It wasn't a long search, Loki wasn't in the apartment, so Cyan returned to the balcony and looked into the flame tree, the branches of which almost touched the balcony rail. Loki often climbed down through the thick branches and walked around her territory. There was no sight of a white cat with tabby ears at the foot of the tree, so she left her second-floor apartment. Cyan walked down the stairs to the ground floor. She had just reached the foot of the stairs when a voice made her jump. Cyan looked up to see Gustavo. He was wearing what Cyan called his working-from-home uniform: grey lightweight jogging pants, an emerald-green T-shirt and flip-flops.

"Oh sorry," he said. "I didn't mean to make you jump. This morning must have been tough, especially if they've sent you home."

"Er, yes. Actually I'm looking for Loki?"

"Oh, he's okay—"

"She," corrected Cyan.

"She? Loki is a boy's name? Why would Loki be a she?"

"I thought Loki was a he until the first visit to the vet. Have you seen her?"

"Oh yes. He. She's, in here," Gustavo indicated his apartment, "been here all morning." He opened the door and Loki strolled out. The cat crossed the floor and brushed her body against Cyan's ankles. Cyan pushed away a wicked thought, that Loki had wandered in and Gustavo gave her a treat when the news of Dayton's death came on the radio. Well, Gustavo was a journalist, mainly celebrity stuff, but the murder would have got him interested enough to try and keep Loki with him.

"Sorry about that. I'm sure if you stop feeding her she'll stop bothering you," Cyan said.

"Oh it's no bother," said Gustavo.

Cyan wondered why he didn't get his own cat, but only nodded in reply. She stooped down to rub Loki's ears. Loki's loud purr was just what she needed.

"How are you feeling?"

Cyan looked up into her neighbour's face. She could tell he wanted to ask what had happened at the university but she wasn't ready to answer any questions. Loki bounded up the stairs and mewed from the landing.

"Shaky. I had better go after Loki, she probably wants a treat or something."

"Aw come on, Cyan. Don't shut me out of this. You must have heard something about the murder?"

She had more than heard. "It's a police matter now," she said, echoing the police's statement to the media.

"But there's always gossip."

"Look. It's not fun going to work and—" She stopped herself just in time.

Gustavo nodded. "Yeah. I guess you knew him."

"Sort of."

"Well. If you need to talk things over," said Gustavo, who looked more like a concerned neighbour than a man after a story.

"Thanks. I just need some quiet right now."

Cyan walked up to her apartment, heard Gustavo close his door as she opened hers. Loki slipped in and Cyan followed.

The rest of the afternoon was too quiet. Every time Cyan switched on the television or the radio there was another update on the 'events at Corner Rise University'.

"There have been other murders on these islands!" Her shout at the TV had made Loki's ears twitch.

In the end she sat in front of her laptop and looked up wigs, then recipes and finally listened to music. Loki kept her company and sat either on her lap or on the keyboard. By the time Cyan forced herself to bed she had been contacted by Victim Support and HR. Initially she was sceptical about the call from Victim Support, surely Dayton had been the victim here. But by the end of the call the woman had gained a lot of respect from Cyan – it had been good to speak to someone with a calm voice, even though she was a stranger. Cyan wasn't sure if she would call Victim Support again, but she was glad they were there.

Later that day Cyan walked towards the kitchen area of her studio apartment to get a glass of water. The telephone rang. Cyan hesitated, shrugged and answered it.

"Hello?"

"Hello. This is Miranda Barry. We met this morning after the … er."

"Oh yes," said Cyan.

There was a long pause.

"Hello?"

"Oh sorry," said Miranda. "This is about the SSC."

"Who?" said Cyan. She wished Miranda had been given a script.

"The Student and Staff Counselling service."

Miranda gave Cyan the full details of the SSC in a voice that sounded as if she wanted to run away.

"Have you been contacted by Victim Support?" asked Miranda.

"Yes." Once again Cyan was tempted to point out that Dayton was the victim, but this time to see what would happen. She reasoned that the mention of the late lecturer's name would probably reduce Miranda to a gibbering mess and decided not to.

"Good."

After that Miranda seemed a bit eager to hang up, but she did manage to tell Cyan to take the rest of the week off and be back Monday. It was to be a late start – Cyan had to call into HR first thing.

"Well," Miranda said. "That's …"

Cyan waited for Miranda to finish her sentence.

"Thanks for calling," Cyan said when she could wait no longer.

"Yes. Well. Goodbye."

Miranda hung up swiftly. Cyan gently put the handset down. She smiled to herself. If Miranda drank she would be in a bar this evening with a large cocktail or the poison of her choice. Cyan picked up her glass of water. She drank it back, went over to the kitchen and pulled out a recently opened bottle of white wine from the fridge. She normally allowed herself one glass every now and then, but today was a two-glass day.

Cyan struggled to stay awake after her evening meal and headed to bed. She remembered Miranda's words and didn't set her alarm, the idea of a late Friday morning appealed to her.

Unfortunately cats don't have late mornings and she was woken up by Loki's purr as the cat rubbed her cheek against the bedside cabinet. Cyan swung her legs out of the bed, surprised that she had slept at all. A quick self-scan of her mind didn't expose any bad dreams. After a long stretch Cyan bent to scratch Loki's ears. Once the cat was fed Cyan thought about her colleagues in the registry. She didn't think that they would enjoy a day with police tape and various members of the police force in the building, they would feel strange, but it would give them something to talk about along with the news. There was no way that they could avoid Dayton's death. In a strange way, Cyan wished that she was with her colleagues. Not because of work, although she did enjoy her job, but for a sense of normality and some office banter. *Ah*, she had thought, office gossip. Then she thought of Katherine, who hardly spoke to anyone else in the office, but would want to know what happened. Katherine would bombard Cyan with questions until she believed she had received the whole story, regardless of how Cyan felt. She cheered herself up with the fact that by Monday the news coverage might have died down. Cyan reached for the radio, but it wasn't long before she switched it off. Every other item was news from the university.

Cyan got up and went to the bathroom for a comb. She decided to watch a film and removed the twists from her hair. She returned to the living room and sat down when the telephone rang. It was the police – she was to go to the police station to make a statement. She sighed as she went to shower and get dressed.

Cyan felt exhausted when she left Three Trees Police Station. She had sat opposite DS Brookes and Inspector Torrington who asked more questions about that morning. They wanted to know everything that happened, from when she arrived to when she first saw the body. Then there were questions about who she regularly saw on Crown Campus. She was surprised that she couldn't remember much about the people she saw every day. It went on for ages. As Cyan walked back towards her apartment she pulled out her mobile phone. She moved to the side of the street and called her mother. The call was answered on the fourth ring.

"Good afternoon?" said Vee.

"Good afternoon, Mum."

"Cyan," Vee said in a tone not to be argued with. "Are you

coming to stay with me?"

Cyan knew that it wasn't a question. "If I can?"

"What is this, 'If I can?'" said Vee. "Of course you can. I'll get your room ready."

Cyan smiled. "Thanks, Mum. I'll be there soon."

They said their goodbyes and Cyan hung up.

Once back at home she put out and filled Loki's automatic cat feeder, made sure that everything that should be switched off was off, and locked the doors.

Cyan caught the bus from her apartment in Three Trees to her mother's house on Trelissick Top. Vee was in her favourite chair on the veranda and after Cyan walked up the steps her mother wrapped her in a huge hug.

Cyan spent the rest of Friday sat in a white plastic chair in the small room at the back of the house with a good view of the sea through the French windows. She reflected that one of the joys of living on the coast was the sight of water, it calmed her, but didn't completely wash away the reason why she wasn't at work. Cyan was relieved that her mother was more concerned about how Cyan felt than the murder. Once she had convinced Vee that she wasn't about to hide away from the world forever she was left in peace. She selected a book from her mother's bookcase and read as the afternoon faded into evening, then she walked through the dining room into the living room and stretched out on an overstuffed terracotta-coloured sofa.

"I wonder if that place will be safe?" Vee said.

Cyan looked up from her book. "What, Corner Uni? Of course. There's no proof that the murderer came from there."

"Then how did they get in? Remember when you first started working there? You were surprised by the number of locks and guards."

"Yes, I remember. But …"

Cyan got up and looked at Vee, who took two place mats from the pine sideboard opposite the dining table. Her mother had made a good point. Only students and staff could come and go with the correct ID. Visitors and contractors could get into the Crown Campus when they were signed in by a member of staff, and that had to be done every time they came to the campus. They also had to sign out when they left. Cyan eyed the two place mats on her mother's dining table, the idea that the person who murdered Dayton had, and could still have, access to the campus worried her. She refused to believe it was true.

"Visitors are signed in every day," she said.

Vee walked back into the dining room, a bowl in her hands. She placed the bowl, filled with rice cooked with tomatoes and thyme, on the table and looked up at Cyan.

"You said?"

"What?" said Cyan. "Nothing really. It's just that visitors are signed in to Corner Uni every day."

"So," said Vee as she walked back towards the kitchen, "someone had to get in to kill that poor man. They didn't stand outside and magic him dead."

Cyan walked towards the table and looked at the bowl. It was white Pyrex and bunches of carrots, purple grapes and red tomatoes ran round its middle. Cyan loved this bowl, and could remember it at the centre of her grandmother's dining table. She smiled to herself, it had been filled with rice then.

"Need a hand?" she called as she walked towards the kitchen.

"Come and carry out the salad," Vee shouted over the sound of pots being moved.

After dinner they sat and watched *The Nation*, Corner Rise's evening news, and Cyan winced every time the Crown Campus was mentioned, which was a lot. The newsroom went back to the reporter at the campus several times, with the words 'Crown Campus Killer' appearing at the bottom of the screen.

"You'd think this island was all murder now," Vee said as she rose from her chair after the programme.

"I know," said Cyan. "I can do the washing up."

"I've done most of it, I'll just finish the plates. You sit." Vee pointed at the chair.

Cyan sat obediently.

Vee made two mugs of grated hot chocolate with vanilla and cinnamon. Cyan pushed back the thin layer of oil on the top to allow the steam out then sipped hers slowly. On the TV was one of her favourite detective series, a comedy where all the characters were surprised when arrests were made. Both Cyan and Vee laughed and made comments as the characters bumbled through their investigation and Cyan allowed herself to become lost in the story.

Once they had finished Cyan got up to wash the mugs, but Vee shooed her away again.

"Good night, Mum," said Cyan.

Vee looked up from the kitchen sink and smiled at her daughter. "Sleep well."

Cyan lay in bed for a while thinking about that evening's detective series *Find it How?* In sixty minutes a priceless vase was stolen, the crime was solved and the perpetrator was behind bars. Cyan wondered how long it would take the police to find the 'Crown Campus Killer'.

CHAPTER 5

By the time Cyan hugged Vee and caught the bus to Three Trees on Sunday afternoon, the TV networks had lost interest in Dayton's death. They could only repeat the same details so many times and, with no new information on the murder, other events had begun to take prime position in the news.

The next morning Cyan combed her hair, pulled on a wig cap and a new spiral twist wig. She pulled on a blue-flowered tunic and blue trousers. Loki looked up and meowed from Cyan's bed. Cyan looked in the mirror. A blue lady, in both colour and mood, looked back at her. Cyan sighed, she both wanted and didn't want to go back to work. It was Schroedinger's Monday.

"You're right," she said to Loki. "I should wear something brighter today."

Cyan changed into a sunset orange tunic. Loki purred. Cyan added a blue and orange headband and left her bedroom. She rolled back her shoulders and went to catch the bus.

Cyan looked at her watch – she was fifteen minutes early for her HR appointment and didn't want to sit in the Cinema Cafe. She got off the bus just as a delivery truck pulled up outside Vincent's Sweet Orchid Spice Shack. For a while she watched as white boxes were loaded onto a sack barrow and wheeled into the restaurant. Cyan remembered when Vincent used to open for breakfast and lunch only. She would treat herself to a sit-down breakfast every week, but since the cinemas had opened Vincent had changed his opening times to fit around the film crowd. It made sense, he had moved from Jamaica to Corner Rise to run a business and he wanted it to be successful. Cyan walked on towards the university.

Jennifer was on duty at the Gatehouse and they exchanged greetings while Cyan presented her staff card.

"How are you?" asked Jennifer.

"I thought I'd be better," said Cyan. "No, let's be honest. I never thought I would see ..." She trailed off.

Jennifer nodded. They swiftly moved the conversation on to different topics before Cyan left.

She went to sit in the King Building's canteen before her appointment and double-checked the location on her mobile phone. The meeting was awkward to begin with, for some reason the person who booked the room didn't check how big it was and Cyan had stood in the door for what felt like an age as she tried to pick one of the nineteen vacant seats. Miranda didn't help, she just watched Cyan as if she were on TV. Cyan eventually chose a seat near enough to Miranda to hear what she said, but with a two-chair gap between them. After that Miranda was more relaxed and Cyan's appointment didn't take long. Miranda spoke about the Student and Staff Counselling service and all that was on offer by means of support within the university.

"Of course," Miranda said, "if you have any issues please contact us first."

Cyan nodded. She translated that as, 'Please speak to us first instead of the press or a lawyer.'

"Well." Miranda closed her laptop. "If there is anything I can help with now?"

"No. You've been. Informative."

Miranda looked at Cyan expectantly.

"Of course, I'll make an appointment to see the SSC as soon as I get back to my office."

After awkward goodbyes Cyan left. She guessed that Miranda would be off Crown Campus before Cyan got to her desk in the registry.

Cyan delayed her return to the office, another cup of tea was what she needed. As she stood by the bar Cyan hoped that Katherine would have followed the news and also lost interest in Dayton's death. But when she opened the door Cyan knew that she had hoped in vain. Katherine rose the minute Cyan walked into the registry and approached the counter like a lioness. Cyan instantly felt empathy for antelopes. Katherine opened the door to the office just as Cyan reached it. She braced herself.

"Hello, Cyan," said Katherine.

"Hello."

"So. How are you?"

"Fine," Cyan replied.

Katherine followed Cyan to her desk. "Of course you're not. How's about I make you some tea?"

As Cyan sat down she raised her purple paisley travel mug. "I'm fine."

"Biscuits?"

"Aren't you on counter duty this morning?"

Cyan sprang up at the sound of the voice to see Dylan. "Good morning. Sorry. I didn't see you," she said.

Dylan smiled. "Hi. No worries." He glanced sideways at Katherine.

"Do you see a student waiting?" asked Katherine.

The registry doors opened.

"Yep," said Dylan, "I do."

Cyan sat down and kept her smile to herself as Katherine rose slowly and headed towards the counter. Cyan logged on in peace.

"How are you?" said Dylan.

Cyan looked over her screen at him. "Not good. You?"

"My parents called from Cornwall. They think it's all murder over here in Corner Rise. And as for my sister." He rolled his eyes. "If you need anything let me know."

Cyan smiled in reply. She knew that Dylan had more questions, she also knew that Dylan wouldn't ask too many questions. One day, if he was still interested, she would tell Dylan what happened, after the murderer had been caught, but for now the police had to do their work and she was glad to leave it at that.

"Oh," said Dylan, "before I forget, could you let Zoe know you're in?"

"Of course. Thanks." Cyan nodded and rose from her desk.

Zoe's office door was open and Cyan tapped on the frame. Zoe looked up from her screen.

"Hello, Cyan." Zoe tilted her head towards the door.

"Hi," said Cyan and closed it behind her.

Unlike Miranda, Zoe gestured to the chair closest to her desk. Cyan sat down and Zoe's computer bleeped. Zoe glanced at the screen then plugged her headphones into her computer.

"Right, no interruptions," she said. "You've probably heard this enough already. But how are you?"

"Yes, I've heard that from nearly everyone this morning," said Cyan. "Except HR."

"But you've had your appointment with them?"

"They were all business," said Cyan.

"Wow," said Zoe. If she had any other comments she kept them to herself. "Anyway. How are you?"

Cyan sighed. "Not good."

Zoe sat patiently as Cyan described her weekend.

"Thank goodness for support," said Zoe. "Speaking of which, if you need any time off or to leave early, please let me know."

"Thanks," said Cyan. "But I'd rather work. It keeps my mind occupied."

"I understand that. Oh. And I probably don't have to tell you this, but you don't have to answer any questions about that morning from anyone. If anyone starts to hassle you, please tell me."

Cyan tried not to smile. She knew that 'anyone' meant Katherine. "Thanks," she said.

Cyan nearly collided with Katherine in the short distance from Zoe's office to her desk.

"Your tea must be cold by now," said Katherine. "Why—"

"Nope," said Cyan. "Mum bought me a well-insulated travel mug. It will be nice and hot."

"Katherine?" Zoe's voice called from her office.

Katherine rolled her eyes and walked into Zoe's office.

"Please close the door," said Zoe.

Katherine closed it harder than was necessary.

"Thank goodness," said Dylan. "Katherine has been hovering over my desk ever since Zoe called you in."

"I'm surprised she didn't listen at the door."

"Even Katherine wouldn't do that in front of a witness."

Cyan smiled as she sat at her desk. She opened her top drawer, reached for a long-handled spoon and took the lid off her travel mug. A second later she sat back in her chair with a yelp. She had knocked tea all over her desk.

As the morning wore on Katherine's attempts to find out what happened grew ever more persistent. She began with, "I'm sure you want to talk about …"

Cyan raised her eyes from fee payment reports. "What?" she said.

"About Dayton. It must have been so traumatic." Katherine smiled.

"Yes, Katherine it was. But I had better go up to the Fees Office about these reports." Cyan got up.

"There is a thing called a phone," Katherine said and sucked her teeth as she went back to her screen.

Cyan ignored her and left the office. She was glad to get away. She walked slowly to Fees, which was only a few doors away. The query was quickly answered and she walked slowly back.

Cyan had barely sat down before Katherine tried again. "Did you really find Dayton's body?" To which Cyan could only stare back with large eyes.

Zoe stepped in at that point and called Katherine into her office.

Dylan peered over the top of his screen. "I don't think Katherine will be asking any more questions today."

"Good," said Cyan.

Katherine came out of the office and Cyan noted the determined look on her colleague's face. In the past Cyan had described Katherine as tenacious, or used less complimentary terms. She knew that Katherine would want to know what happened last week, regardless of what Zoe said.

Cyan stood and Katherine sat. "Katherine, Dylan?" They both looked up. Katherine had a hint of expectation on her face. "Just to let you know that I'll be leaving early today."

"What?" said Katherine. "Why?"

"I've got a planning meeting for the ECC, with Cyrus, at five o'clock."

Katherine looked puzzled.

"The Ealing Comedy Club?" said Cyan.

"Oh. That thing," said Katherine and went back to her mobile phone.

"What's wrong with a film club?" said Dylan. "I've been. Drinks, nibbles, watch a very good black-and-white English film and discuss it afterwards."

"I don't have time for old movies." Katherine looked up at Cyan.

"Anyway. Who says Cyrus will be there?"

"What?" said Cyan.

"I think the word you want is why?" Katherine looked back at her mobile phone.

"Katherine?"

Katherine put her mobile phone down and swivelled on her chair to face Cyan. "Well," she said. "The last I heard, he was helping," she added speech marks with her fingers, "the police with their enquiries."

"How do you know that?" said Dylan.

"I have my secret source." Katherine gave a smug smile. "Plus I didn't see Cyrus on Friday."

"You didn't see me either," said Cyan, hands on hips. "HR told us to stay home."

"I'm sure I saw Fayval." Katherine twisted a cerise hair extension around her finger.

Cyan didn't believe her. Fayval had seen Dayton, so why would HR allow her to work?

"And," Katherine threw the extension back over her shoulder, "Cyrus has been called to the station twice."

"So have I," said Cyan.

"But you didn't find the body." Katherine swung back to her keyboard. "And we all know that makes him a suspect."

"Cyrus!"

"Yes. Cyrus." Katherine smirked.

"For what reason?"

"Because he was jealous of Dayton."

Cyan shut her mouth firmly before the words 'Are you quite mad?' could escape.

"Is that so?" said Dylan.

Cyan looked over her computer at him. He appeared to be reading something on his screen.

"Yes," said Katherine as she sat upright and raised her chin.

Cyan tried to suppress a smile. Katherine didn't like her shock announcements treated with such flippancy.

"Hmm," said Dylan. "I remember when you tried to get close to Dayton. He was rather rude about it. Loudly. In a meeting." Dylan looked up from his screen at Katherine. "So wouldn't you have a motive too?"

Katherine ducked back down behind her screen as a thunderstorm made its way across her face.

"I wasn't in the museum before it opened," Katherine said as she tilted her face towards Cyan. "Tell me, Cyan. Why was Cyrus in the museum so early? And how did he get in? It was supposed to be locked."

"I don't know how he got in," said Cyan.

Katherine raised an eyebrow and smiled, then faced her screen while Cyan sat down slowly. Katherine had a point. How did Cyrus get into the King Collection? Cyan opened an email, typed Cyrus's address and got stuck on the title. 'How did you get into the King Collection' sounded a bit blunt. She closed the email and hovered the mouse over an icon of a telephone. Then switched back to the student records system. She would have to wait until she met Cyrus after work to ask him. He would be there.

Most of the morning passed before Katherine crept up on Cyan in the kitchen. Before she could open her mouth Zoe slid between them. Cyan had to admire the move. Katherine had been so close at the time their noses almost touched. After Zoe slipped between them, all Katherine could do was look angrily over the top of Zoe's head. Cyan had never noticed the difference in height between Zoe, five feet if her Afro was included, and Katherine nearing six feet, hair not included. After that, Zoe was there to interrupt Katherine nearly every time she tried to speak to Cyan, and if Zoe couldn't get there in time, Dylan did. By lunchtime his actions had convinced Cyan that he had developed the power of teleportation. That was the only explanation she could give for him suddenly appearing in the doorway of the walk-in stationery cupboard when Katherine had blocked Cyan's exit and suggested a 'nice chat'. Cyan would have gladly paid money for a photograph of the look on Katherine's face when Dylan asked for plastic punched wallets, A4. Katherine's expression was best described as a combination of furious disappointment and the look of a local flasher who had opened their coat only to find that their audience was a pack of savage, snarling dogs. How Cyan had managed to return to her desk with a straight face after that was a mystery. Not much work was done.

Cyan locked her desktop and glanced at Katherine. Katherine tapped at her keyboard. In one movement Cyan grabbed her backpack and got up. Katherine barely twitched, so Cyan was really surprised when they reached the office door at the same time.

"Mind if I join you for lunch?" Katherine smiled at Cyan.

Cyan blinked at her colleague. Katherine was shameless. The only time she ever joined any of the registry staff for lunch was when she was forced to at the Christmas party. Cyan looked into Katherine's eyes. "Erm."

"Oh, Katherine. Glad I caught you," said Zoe.

Cyan jumped at first and then relaxed. To her, Zoe's deep voice was like a cool breeze on a hot day. From the look on Katherine's face that was not the case for her. Her eyes closed slowly and then her shoulders sagged.

"See you later, Cyan," Zoe said.

Cyan could only nod her thanks as she tried not to skip through the door. Normally being overprotected would have annoyed her, but today she was grateful.

Cyan trotted down the stairs and walked out of the Hub's main entrance without a glance towards the museum and instantly felt guilty. Fayval had welcomed her to Corner Rise University two years ago and had become one of Cyan's closest friends. Cyan had not even called on Fayval that morning. She gave herself a shake and walked back into the building and into the King Collection. Fayval looked up from behind the computer monitor as Cyan pushed the door open. Her wary look changed into a smile. Cyan smiled back.

"They did a good job," said Fayval after they exchanged greetings.

"Hmm?"

"The company called to clean up."

Cyan realised that the only thing she had looked at since she walked through the door had been Fayval's desk. Her eyes moved towards the display cabinets, but her head refused to follow with them.

"It's okay. You can look. You missed the mess on Friday."

Cyan stared wide-eyed at Fayval. "You were here on Friday?"

Fayval shrugged. "I was told to stay home, but I couldn't. I said I needed to come in, just in case the police had to take something away. You know, I'd have to log it and nobody knows this place like I do. Anyway, I had to see this place without Dayton lying there. I could never come back otherwise."

Cyan turned to Fayval. At first she thought Fayval was mad. Why come back so soon? But then Cyan thought of the way she couldn't even sit in the Cinema Cafe and realised that Fayval was probably right.

"You should have seen it. White powder everywhere and they scraped something off one of the cabinets."

"Who's they?" asked Cyan, keeping her imagination away from the something that would have been on the cabinet.

"The police. Well, the forensic ones."

Cyan wobbled slightly.

"Oh dear." Fayval rushed from behind her desk and steered Cyan towards a chair.

"Oh this is just ridiculous—"

"No it's not!" Fayval said. "It just is. I can't eat pineapples. Can you imagine? Nearly every dish on Corner Rise has a pineapple in it. And that's before we get to the desserts."

Cyan took a few deep breaths. "Thanks. So. They cleaned up yesterday." Cyan risked a look around. The museum looked the way it always did. Spotless floors, polished glass cabinets. "At least they didn't take anything."

"Oh they did," said Fayval. "One statuette."

"Which one?" said Cyan after a while.

"Grand tour statuette. Colossus of Rhodes." Fayval pointed her chin to the second cabinet in from where Cyan sat. "You know. The guy standing across the entrance of the harbour."

"With hands on hips." Cyan finished Fayval's description as she got up and walked towards the cabinet, looking up to the top shelf. The display label was still there. "Why that one?"

"Dayton often looked at the statuettes. He even asked if he could hold them. The answer was no of course. I mean, he was mathematics, not art or history."

Cyan looked confused. "So how did he get to the statue?"

"I never used to lock my desk drawers. I don't keep anything personal in them and I kind of thought that no one would search them." Fayval crossed her arms. To Cyan it looked like a defensive movement. "As I told that Brookes woman, the doors to the Collection are locked and I have one set of keys, the library has a set to cover when I'm away and a spare set is locked in the key safe behind my desk. The keys to the display cabinets are also in the key safe and the combination is usually in my head. Well, that will have to stop now."

"Why change? It all sounds secure. Dayton didn't take the keys from your desk and he couldn't stand close enough to read the combination."

"He stood as close as he could when I said I had to open the key safe."

"So that's—"

"He was where you are now and the combination had recently been changed for security," Fayval continued. "I thought he was interested in the display, he had just asked about it. So I checked the number."

Cyan knew that Fayval would never open the safe while someone watched so she looked at the cabinet behind her. It contained a very ornate tea set with blue flowers and a gold trim. Cyan noticed that the cups didn't have handles. They were all displayed against a dark background to bring out the white porcelain. "Oh," Cyan said and looked at the glass instead of through it. A perfect reflection of Fayval nodded back at her.

"Yeah. I worked that out too. He saw me check the notebook and as I put it back in my desk. I had it disguised as a telephone number." Fayval took in then released a deep breath. "When the forensic guys took the key out of that cabinet's lock I checked my desk. All my stationery was out of order. He didn't even try to hide what he had done." Fayval looked as if she could have murdered Dayton herself.

"But how?"

"He asked for a cup of tea. He said he felt as if he was about to choke. I should have let him."

"But you locked the safe behind you."

Fayval nodded towards the fire door that opened into the kitchenette. Like all fire doors it had a damper, which meant it would have shut while Fayval made the tea.

"Oh," said Cyan.

"Like you said. I locked the safe behind me, so there was no reason to open it and check if any of the keys were gone. He must have thought he was so clever."

There was silence for a while.

"I'm sorry he was murdered," said Fayval, "but I doubt anyone disliked him as much as I did."

"You say that," said Cyan. "But so did a lot of Corner staff."

"No, really. Especially after he brought that group of students in."

Cyan looked at Fayval. "Dayton brought students here?"

"Something to do with what he taught at the Tech."

Cyan remembered Dayton's complaints about the college students. Dayton didn't understand why he had to teach at the Tech, the short name for the William King College of Technology, and let Dylan know on a regular basis, usually at full volume.

"They're foundation students. Not degree level," he had said to Dylan.

Dylan had informed Dayton's head of department.

Not long after that Dayton was reminded that as the Tech was part of the Crown Campus, and as he had signed a contract to teach at all of Corner Rise University's campuses, he had better get on with it.

"So he brought a group of students into the Collection," said Fayval, "which I am more than happy with, but he didn't book a slot or ask for a tour or anything. Anyway, he walks up to an inkwell, ignores the label and told his group it was a salt pot."

"You had to correct Dayton?" Cyan said. "Wouldn't it have been easier to argue with thunder?"

"Yes it would. But to be fair it is a pretty fancy inkwell. We only have the one." Fayval pointed to a cabinet to the left of Cyan. "Middle shelf."

Cyan looked into the cabinet – there were three silver stylised fishes arranged in a pyramid with their tails in the air, holding up a black ball.

"Easy mistake to make," said Fayval. "We eat fish. Anyway, he asks me why such a thing would be made, so I talk about displays of wealth and move him over to a silver sauce boat. You'd think he'd be grateful. On the shelf below the inkwell is a salt pot and I carefully avoided that."

"I can see why," said Cyan as she looked at a silver cylinder with a relief of classically dressed figures around it. It couldn't have been more clearly labelled. As was the salt pot. She could imagine the row that would have followed.

"Well at least that was over quickly," she said.

"No, it wasn't. He wrote to Karen, the ex-head of library, to ask why the curator of such an important museum didn't know the difference between a salt pot and an inkwell."

"Really?" said Cyan, her voice rising a few octaves.

"Oh yes." Fayval smiled. "She wrote back and told him that I did."

"Wow," said Cyan after a pause. "You can only be amazed at his sense of self-importance."

"I think you mean arrogance. Well it didn't do him any good this time."

"How comes?" said Cyan.

"Dayton chose his own murder weapon."

"He chose his own murder weapon?" Cyan echoed. "You mean, the Colossus statuette?"

Fayval nodded at Cyan, who looked at the space where the statuette should have been. They spent a few more moments in silence.

"How about we go outside?" said Fayval. Cyan nodded at the curator's suggestion.

They settled themselves on a bench between two trees and opened their bags.

"I've usually eaten a muffin and a piece of fruit by now." Fayval pulled a pink lunch box out of her blue canvas backpack, opened it and took a white plastic fork out of the lid. "All I did today was stare at the cabinets."

"I can still eat," Cyan said as she pulled a clear plastic box from her bag. "It's the cafe that bugs me. Every time I look at the museum's door I shudder." She rooted around a bit more and pulled out a fork with a look of triumph.

"You should try working there," said Fayval.

"Sorry."

"Don't be. The professional cleaners did a great job. They shined the glass in the cabinets and made the floors so you could eat off them. But still."

Cyan watched a brown pigeon land on a branch that looked too small to support the bird's weight. The branch dropped slightly and the bird flapped its wings briefly to stay balanced. Cyan watched until the branch stopped moving and the pigeon began to settle. Then there was a roar of a large engine from the building site that startled them both and the pigeon flew away.

"When are they going to finish that building?" she said.

"What? The new Student Centre? Soon I hope," said Fayval. "I've missed my bus more than once since they fenced off the path."

"Me too."

Cyan clicked open the box and they ate to the sound of heavy machinery. After a few mouthfuls each, the noise stopped.

Fayval leant close to Cyan. "Did you hear about Daniella?"

Cyan shook her head, her mind had wandered back to the pigeon.

"She's already been questioned. Apparently she was the last to see him alive."

Cyan turned to Fayval. "Who? Dayton?"

"Who else?"

"How do they know?" said Cyan. "I saw Dayton jabbing his finger into Trevor's chest on Wednesday afternoon."

"But Daniella was seen near the Hub late on Wednesday evening. And we now know that's no rumour. Then the next morning." Fayval shrugged.

"No." Cyan looked at the empty branch. "That's not possible. I mean, why would Daniella?"

"You must remember the arguments they had over that academic article thing?"

"Heard, I saw." Cyan told Fayval about the argument before the 'Safe Tracker' presentation.

"See," said Fayval. "I heard that they fought over everything. Even where to publish it."

"That's just daft. A journal is a journal."

"Depends on who reads it," Fayval said as she mixed the remains of her lunch.

Cyan glanced at the pumpkin chunks in a tomato sauce, she could smell the smoked paprika.

Fayval raised the loaded fork from her lunch box. "As Daniella did most of the work she wanted it published where her peers would read it."

Cyan went back to her own lunch. "That's really no reason to … You know … Dayton," she said.

"I know," said Fayval.

They ate in silence for a few minutes, each with their own thoughts. Then Cyan leant close to Fayval. "Do you think Dayton found out about Daniella? You know. Back in the UK?" she asked.

"You mean the affair?" Fayval looked around quickly, then lowered her voice. "With the research student?"

"Yes," said Cyan.

"I don't know," said Fayval. "I just wish I didn't. Why talk about such stuff in the registry?"

"To be fair it was a Tuesday afternoon and the shutters were down."

"But still. Vincent's would have been better."

"What? The Spice Shack? Do you know how many staff go there?"

"True," said Fayval. "But on campus?"

They both sat back on the bench and Cyan remembered that afternoon. All the staff had been called to a 'Crown Campus Briefing', where they were informed about the plans to build the Student Centre. There had been a heated discussion about the disruption that would be caused by the building works and the briefing had dragged on for over two hours. Zoe had looked at her watch and suggested that everyone head home and the other heads of department had done the same, so Cyan and Fayval had gone into the registry to retrieve Cyan's backpack.

"So every man and his pet rabbit have to go through the King Building now?" said Fayval.

"How's that gonna happen with all the card access?"

Fayval nodded.

When they walked into the registry and through the door to the office, the sound of voices had surprised them. The other three members of registry staff had had the foresight to take bags and jackets to the briefing with them and were probably off campus already, so who was in the meeting room? Cyan recognised Cyrus's voice the moment he spoke. When the woman spoke, Fayval smiled.

"See," said Fayval. "I told you Cyrus and Daniella were together. Here's the proof."

"Shh. Not so loud."

Cyan crept to her desk to pull the backpack from underneath it. She couldn't resist a peek through the blinds of the glass wall behind Dylan's desk. There was no romantic tryst taking place. Instead Daniella looked as if she had been crying. Cyan wasn't sure what to do. Cyrus wasn't a bad man, so what had happened? Then it came out.

"I don't understand—" said Cyrus.

"Well. You wouldn't. One moment of madness—"

"As said by all the best Victorian villains."

"—and it was all over." Daniella finished her sentence as if Cyrus hadn't spoken.

"It was hardly 'one moment'. That affair lasted for two academic years. That's not one moment," said Cyrus.

"Okay. It took a moment to decide to do it, all right?" Daniella sounded angry.

"No. It wasn't all right. You were supervising this student."

Cyan had never heard Cyrus sound so angry.

"Okay," said Cyrus. "Why didn't you tell the head of department—"

"I couldn't. I was married at the time. Plus you don't understand my family. It's all about favouritism and sibling rivalry with them. And an unhealthy dose of 'what will the neighbours think?' When it all came out I had to get away."

"So you came to a place you continually complain about?"

"Father has academic contacts everywhere," said Daniella. "This was the only place I could think of."

Cyan reversed away from her desk, backpack in hand. She nearly squeaked when she backed into Fayval. Fayval's eyes were as large as golf balls and her mouth was one big 'o'. Cyan kept her lips clamped together in a firm line. It was the only way she could avoid making a sound. They stood in this weird tableau, waiting for Cyrus or Daniella to speak so that they could open the office door undetected.

It felt like a long time before Daniella spoke.

"I had worked so hard to get there, Cyrus. I lost everything." Daniella's voice dropped to a whisper. "Everything."

Cyan and Fayval left the registry in silence and didn't speak again until they were off campus. Staff access to the registry and the office was changed shortly afterwards, so that only Zoe, Cyan, Dylan and Katherine could get in. Like Fayval, Cyan wished she had never been in the registry office that afternoon.

Cyan's mind returned to the present and from the look on Fayval's face it was clear that her mind had been on that afternoon.

"Have you seen Trevor?" she asked, more to break the silence.

"I went to the post room this morning. He's been signed off for this week."

"He did hit the ground hard when he fainted."

"He wouldn't be much good if the uni was under threat," said Fayval.

"Why should he be? He's a porter, not a superhero."

Fayval chuckled.

"About that day, Katherine asked an interesting question," said Cyan.

"That's a first."

Cyan ignored Fayval's sarcastic tone. "No, really. She wanted to know how Cyrus got into the Collection."

"Dayton stole the key and opened the door," said Fayval with a scowl.

"Sorry," said Cyan, "I meant, how did Cyrus know that Dayton would be there?"

CHAPTER 6

"Good afternoon, Cyan."

Cyan was sure that she rose vertically from the bench while still in the seated position. She landed with a dull thud. Judging from Fayval's laugh it must have looked hilarious. Cyan ignored her friend and looked over her shoulder into the beady eyes of Katherine, whose eyes became less beady when they spotted Fayval.

"Good afternoon to you," said Fayval after a few more chuckles.

Cyan looked down at a few pieces of pasta on her blue trousers and sighed. She picked up the pasta and dropped it onto the grass.

"Oh. Hello, Fayval," said Katherine after a pause.

Cyan tried not to smile. Katherine didn't enjoy any conversation she had with Fayval. It usually ended badly. Unlike Cyan, Fayval didn't have any patience with Katherine and would let her know. When Katherine deigned to talk to anyone on campus, the appearance of Fayval would stop the conversation dead. Actually the Christmas lunch worked well too, when Katherine chose to attend. Cyan looked up to see if Katherine was still there. She was. Katherine stood in front of them with her eye on the empty space between Fayval and Cyan. Fayval filled the space with her backpack and rummaged through it.

Katherine glowered briefly at the bag, fixed a smile on her face and raised her eyes towards Cyan. Her smile made Cyan think of Loki eyeing up a field mouse. "Did I hear you talking about Daniella?"

"Probably," said Fayval.

Katherine ignored her and turned to Cyan. "The police think she did it." Her smile became genuine and Cyan could have sworn that she saw a hint of a dance. "What if they arrest and charge her?"

Cyan opened her mouth to argue.

"I could have done with a little less relish," said Fayval.

"Sorry?" Cyan's head snapped around so quickly that she had to rub her neck.

"In my sauce." Fayval looked up at Katherine. "Did you say something?"

Katherine seemed to relax. "I would love to know why they think Daniella did it. I wonder if it's why she left England. Maybe academic. I hear she was caught plagiarising, or was it something more serious? Not good for a professor." Katherine smiled as she looked into Cyan's eyes and shifted her weight from one foot to the other. Cyan pushed an image of a cobra about to strike from her mind.

"Any university worth its reputation has to practise strict discipline," said Cyan. "No one is going to give a grant to a university that ignores plagiarism."

"Oh come on, Cyan. There has to be more than that." Katherine's eyes flicked towards Fayval and then back to Cyan. Cyan hoped she had her poker face on.

"Why should there be more than that?" Cyan held Katherine's gaze.

"Well. I heard that Daniella might have been called in for ... what was it called?" Katherine fished for the term. Cyan refused to help. "You know, a 'misconduct hearing'?"

"Really?" Cyan decided to follow Fayval's lead and went back to what remained of her own lunch.

"Do they have misconduct hearings here?"

Cyan's eyes watered, the last bit of pasta sauce burned as if it contained all the cayenne in her kitchen. The distraction caused Cyan's work brain to kick in.

"Academic misconduct. It's usually just a student's silly mistake. Inadequate referencing. After the formal hearing they never do it again."

"So," said Katherine with a wider smile, "there would have been a hearing for Daniella."

Cyan kicked herself mentally. "We don't know that. Anyway, if

Daniella was caught for plagiarism it would be more serious. She would never have got a job at Corner, as a professor she is supposed to know how to research and reference. Plus anyone she wanted to work with would have a lot to say about her appointment."

Cyan felt a slight dig in her side as Fayval stopped her flow. Cyan sighed. How many times had she explained procedures to Katherine? And what a waste of time. Katherine was only interested in what would keep her employed at that moment. Now, when it came to other people's business, Katherine was all over it until she believed she knew everything.

"Do you know what makes me really curious?" said Katherine.

Fayval snapped her lunch box shut. "No," she said.

"I have no idea how Dayton died. I mean, you two both saw the body?"

Cyan stared slack-jawed at Katherine.

"Where was he lying?" Katherine continued. "Cyrus won't tell me anything!"

How could you! thought Cyan. She took a deep breath and opened her mouth.

"I'll tell you what," said Fayval. "Why don't you come back to the Collection with me? You can stand between the two cabinets where Dayton lay and I can hit you in the back of the head with a stapler. That should give you a feel for it."

Katherine's smile evaporated like Corner Rise rain in summer. "You … oh!" She marched off.

"Yes, Cyan, before you say anything, I know I was rude. But all Friday, that woman," Fayval pointed her chin at Katherine's back, "was outside the Collection."

"Really?"

"Yes, and you should have heard her. Every time I went to the toilet or just needed to get out. 'Was he found here? Did you find the body? Was he already dead?' I nearly snapped when she asked what killed him."

"No!"

"The police asked her to give me some space and she did. She waited for me just out of their sight."

Cyan could see that Fayval was still furious. She gave her friend's arm a squeeze.

"Let's go back in, I'll buy us a treat in the cafe," she offered. As they packed up their lunch things a thought nagged at her. "Dayton must have known who killed him."

"Hmm?"

"Well. What you said to Katherine. Hitting her in the back of the head—"

"You know I would never," said Fayval.

"Of course. But Dayton must have thought that his murderer wouldn't, well, kill him. He turned his back on them."

Fayval paused. "That means his killer is someone here, on this campus."

Cyan stared ahead of her. Vee had hinted at this possibility, but she had denied it every time, no matter how good Vee's arguments had been. Now Cyan hated to admit that it could be true.

"Do you think it was Daniella?" said Fayval.

Cyan shook her head. "Like I said, not over a silly paper."

"Wow. Well, in that case, Dayton upset so many people."

That anyone could have killed him, thought Cyan. She knew that Dayton had upset, no, had angered and bullied her, but never enough to make her anger physical.

After cake, tea and lighter conversation with Fayval, Cyan's feet took her back to the registry. As she walked up the stairs to her office her mind was on Dayton. If he had finally got someone to snap, surely he would have been found in his office with a shocked look on his face, or the canteen drenched in tea. At most in the library under a book, probably alive. But dead in a closed museum? Cyan walked through the registry's main doors and stopped in front of the counter. Not only was the murderer on the campus, they had planned Dayton's death.

"Cyan? Are you okay?"

Cyan looked up. Dylan was on counter duty.

"Me? I'm fine," said Cyan.

"You don't look it. Did Katherine find you?" he asked.

"Oh yes."

Dylan rolled his blue eyes. "Bound to happen. Zoe had no reason to keep her here. Oh well. We tried."

"No, it was fine. Fayval was with me."

Dylan's eyes widened. "After Friday?"

"Fayval told me. You saw all that?"

Dylan nodded. "I swear, if it wasn't for the police Katherine would have been in intensive care."

By the end of the day Cyan praised Fayval's harsh words as Katherine didn't bother her again. In fact, Katherine went back to her normal behaviour of only speaking to Cyan if their jobs demanded it. Zoe raised her eyebrows at Cyan, who just shrugged back.

Later Zoe suggested that Cyan leave early. Cyan was doubtful as she usually made up any time missed by working late, but Zoe insisted. "Not only have you been through a lot more than I would wish on anyone, but you've been lucky with Katherine this afternoon. I'm sure she'll be on your back again tomorrow," she said.

Cyan could only nod in agreement to both points. Then she quickly scanned the office. "Where is Katherine?" she asked.

"I was wondering that," said Zoe. She looked at the coat hooks next to the office door. "Her coat's still here, so she hasn't gone far."

Cyan decided to leave quickly before Katherine returned, so she said her goodbyes and left the office.

"Well, it was really Cyrus who found the body."

The sound of Katherine's voice made Cyan stop at the top of the second flight of stairs.

Katherine laughed. "I hear say that Cyan threw up over the shoes."

A deep voice laughed with Katherine.

"How would you know, Katherine?" said Cyan. Her voice snaked between straight lips and her fingers wrapped around the banister. "You were behind police tape at the time."

"Of course," Katherine's voice lowered, but not enough to be discreet, "some people are pointing the finger at Cyrus."

Cyan was sure that her fingers had dug into the wood.

"Cyrus?" said the deep voice. "What about that other one? You know, the one who argued with Dayton all the time?"

"Oh Daniella?" said Katherine. "I don't see how."

"Why not? You said yourself that you heard them fight. From what I understood from you it was one big trouble and you were surprised that Dayton was still alive."

Cyan took a deep breath and rolled her eyes. If Katherine saw two people walk into each other and apologise, she would describe it as a war.

"I see where you're coming from," said Katherine. "It had to be Daniella. I mean, like you said, the arguments she had with him."

Cyan felt her blood pressure rise. She peeled her hand from the banister and bounded down the stairs. Before she reached the bottom she heard the door to the cafe open. She got there before it swung shut. Katherine was halfway across the cafe in the direction of the ladies toilets and didn't look back to see who had stomped down the stairs. Cyan ignored Katherine and spun around to search for the person with the deep voice.

There were a lot of people in the cafe and Cyan found it hard to spot who Katherine would have spoken to. A flash of red caught Cyan's attention. She saw a woman in a frothy, layered wine-coloured dress walk towards the main doors. But it was the wig that Cyan watched as the woman walked away – it was black at the crown, fading to the same shade of red at the ends, so it looked as if it was merging with the dress. Cyan watched in admiration. *Some people are just born with style*, she thought. Cyan's mind snapped back to the present and she scanned the cafe, but how would she find someone with a deep voice? She couldn't listen to every conversation in the cafe.

Then Cyan realised, to her horror, that she was more frightened of people hearing about her reaction to blood than any rumour being spread about Daniella. She felt shame rise in her cheeks. Then anger. There was no way she could find whoever had just told Katherine that Daniella was a murderer. She had no idea what they looked like. Cyan could have stamped her foot in frustration; she had read in the past how this kind of thing led to wrongful convictions or cases not being solved. She didn't want that.

No, thought Cyan, *I have to stop that before it gains legs*. She rearranged her backpack and marched out of the main door.

It was a mild afternoon and Cyan walked along the main path and in through the back entrance of the King Building. She followed the signs to KGFLT3, or the King Ground Floor Lecture Theatre, not a fancy name for a lecture theatre, but it was functional. A lecture theatre wasn't ideal for an ECC meeting, but it was the only room Cyan could book that week. At least it was smaller than the Hub's two cinemas.

Cyan walked through the door from the main corridor and along the short passage to the theatre's wide grey door. She read on the timetable next to the door that there was a class until five. She peered through the glass panel to see a lecturer at the lectern in front of rows of tiered seating. Cyan could see a laptop opened on the lectern and the lecturer was side-on to his audience as he gestured at the screen behind him. Cyan stood back and looked again at the printed timetable, then at her watch. She was five minutes early, so she pulled out her mobile phone to pass the time.

By the time the class had left Cyan had become worried – she stood alone outside KGFLT3. She pushed the thought of Cyrus in a police cell to the back of her mind and wondered if she was in the right place. She searched her work email. The grey door opened.

"Good afternoon, Cyan. Why didn't you wait inside?"

Cyan looked at Cyrus and smiled. *Of course*, she thought, *all lecture theatres have more than one entrance.* "Good afternoon, Cyrus," she added aloud.

Cyrus held the door open as she walked in.

"How are you?" she asked.

"I've been better."

Cyan tried to think of a subtle way to ask Cyrus the questions that Katherine had put in her mind, but she was unable to.

She heard the door behind her creak open and spun around to see a student in tight black jeans and a deep pink top.

"Good afternoon," said the student. She glanced at Cyrus.

"Good afternoon," said Cyan and waited.

"Sorry. I think I left something. Can I?" The student looked up at the blue-upholstered seats.

"Of course," said Cyan.

She watched as the student rushed up the stairs to one of the middle rows and smiled to herself. The student had to be in the first term of their first year, a second- or third-year student would have greeted Cyan as they walked up the stairs. Cyan glanced to her right to see Cyrus open his laptop and reach for one of the cables on the lectern.

"Got it." The student waved a pair of wireless headphones at Cyan. "Thank you."

"Glad you found them," said Cyan.

The student smiled as she slipped through the door. Cyan listened to the voices outside the theatre until the door to the main corridor silenced them. She walked towards Cyrus.

"Cyrus," Cyan said. "I have to ask. How did you—"

"Get into the King Collection that morning?" Cyrus looked up from his laptop to the theatre's seats. "Dayton," he said with a sigh.

Cyan blinked several times. "Really?"

"Oh yes," said Cyrus. "Dayton was his usual boastful self. He overheard me talk about wanting to look at teapots before the first class of the day."

"I'm sorry. Why teapots?"

"I had a bet with Michael Horsford. From SAS?"

"Oh," said Cyan. "The Tea Man."

"He's also the Teapot Man." Cyrus leant against the lectern. "Well, Dayton, in his usual immodest manner, told me that I didn't have to wait for Fayval to open the Collection. He could get in whenever he wanted."

"Fayval would never give him the keys."

"I knew that," said Cyrus before Cyan could say any more. "That's why I decided to meet Michael there. I had hoped we would walk in on Dayton and catch him with an open cabinet. Few things are nicer than watching a man like Dayton …" Cyrus inhaled deeply. "A man like Dayton getting a large dose of humility."

Cyan nodded. The thought of a humbled Dayton appealed to her too.

"So I was overjoyed to get there and find the King Collection in the dark." Cyrus combed a lock of dark brown hair out of his face with his fingers. "I didn't even try the doors. I looked at my watch, waited for a few minutes then walked into the cafe for some tea and sat down."

"And waited for Dayton?"

"I tried to. After five minutes I felt a bit daft looking at the door, so I read the news on my phone. I must admit that when it comes to the news I do prefer a newspaper rather than looking at a screen."

"And?" Cyan walked up to the lectern.

"And I got lost in a story from Brighton."

Cyan smiled. Cyrus had grown up in Brighton. She had visited there when she was in the UK and found the pebble beach exotic, especially when she saw it from a fish and chip shop as she ate a large cod in crispy golden batter and drank strong tea from a white mug.

"Sorry." she said. "You were saying?"

"Hmm?"

Cyan could tell that Cyrus had been lost in his own memories.

"Sorry? What? Oh yes. Well, when I looked up I thought that Dayton had slipped past. So I got up and walked back to the Collection. The lights were still out so I gave the door an angry thump." Cyrus shook his head. "With hindsight, I would have called security. The door should never have been open. But ..."

Cyan nodded. So many fails to be corrected with hindsight.

"So I pushed the door open, switched on the lights and called for him." Cyrus pulled off his glasses and squeezed the bridge of his nose. "And I found him."

The door behind Cyan opened and two members of the ECC walked in. They exchanged greetings and Cyrus went back to set up his laptop on the lectern.

The meeting didn't take long. Michael Horsford agreed to look after the food, and Cyan would let the club know if one of the cinemas in the Hub would be free. The meeting ended with the usual vote on which film to screen. Cyan was pleased that she had never heard of the film chosen – it was one of Ealing's later comedies *Who Done It?*, starring someone called Benny Hill.

CHAPTER 7

The next work day began awkwardly. The journey in was fine and Cyan was there long before Katherine. By nine thirty all the other staff were in before Katherine. Cyan looked at her computer screen and then at her watch, both confirmed the time. Cyan heard the office door open and saw Dylan walk towards his seat with a cardboard takeaway box in his hands. Cyan guessed that he had been to the King Canteen to get some breakfast. She gave him enough time to sit down before she leant to the right to talk to him, waiting until he had pulled a fork out of his top drawer.

"Do you know where Katherine is?" she asked before he could reach for the box.

"Hmm?" Dylan looked up briefly from his breakfast. "Dentist, I think. She should be in by eleven. Why?"

"Just wanted to ask her something. Thanks."

He had already opened the box before Cyan leant back. She breathed in the smell of dumplings with the tang of salted fish and tomatoes. Cyan could visualise the dumplings as they were browned in a heavy frying pan before they were steamed. Her mouth watered. She would happily swap Dylan's breakfast for the bowl of porridge she had eaten that morning, even though she had enjoyed it at the time.

Cyan had just straightened up when the registry door opened. "I'll get it," she said as she rose from her seat.

Dylan looked up and smiled gratefully.

"Good morning, Cyan."

Cyan smiled up at Cyrus. "And one to you too."

"We have a meeting? The student with multiple reassessments?"

"Oh. Yes." Cyan opened the office door to let the professor in.

Cyrus followed her over to her desk, his laptop held to his chest. He stopped and greeted Dylan. While they chatted, Cyan looked into the small meeting room behind her desk. The blinds were raised, and when she checked the room's timetable she was glad to see no one had booked it.

"Cyrus?" she said as she tilted her head towards the meeting room door. "It's free now, would you like to go in?"

Dylan smiled and lifted a loaded fork to his lips. As Cyrus walked into the room Cyan hunted through her letter trays. *I wouldn't keep student information in the open*, she reminded herself. She opened her middle drawer to see a Manila folder with a bright pink sticky note attached. The note read 'Too many reassm'ts' in Cyan's shorthand.

Cyan pulled the Manila folder out of her drawer, locked the cabinet and her computer, and followed Cyrus into the meeting room. Cyrus had his laptop open and looked up briefly when she entered. Cyan closed the door behind her and partially closed the blinds.

"How are you feeling?" said Cyan.

"I feel like a cliché."

"Sorry?"

"You know," Cyrus said. "I've felt better."

Cyan nodded. She went to the slate-grey security cabinet next to the door and punched in the code. After she had pulled out one of the spare laptops she closed the door with a click.

"Do you keep thinking about him too?" asked Cyrus.

"Yes," said Cyan as she sat down. "I do." She put the laptop on the table.

"After I'd called several times, I saw a pair of shoes. I thought, what a strange place to sleep."

Cyan nodded. She also had similar thoughts at the time. "So?" she said.

"Well. I did what anyone would do. I reached over to touch him." Cyan gasped.

"But I saw the back of his head first." Cyrus removed his wire-framed glasses and rubbed his face. "Then I leant over and saw Dayton's face. Like I said to the police, he wasn't scared or frightened. Just surprised."

"I couldn't look at his face," Cyan said. "What made you look further?"

"I wish I knew. And I wish I hadn't. I'm still seeing him in my sleep. I'd spent the previous week avoiding Dayton like the plague."

"Why?" asked Cyan.

Cyrus gave her a quizzical look.

"Oh yes," said Cyan. "His argument with Daniella."

"Daniella tried to be discreet, but Dayton had to fight at full volume. Everyone in the department knew how he felt, and that's all they talked about. Until the murder."

They sat in silence for a while. Cyrus put his glasses back on and tapped at his laptop.

"Okay," he said. "Let's start."

Cyan opened her laptop.

It didn't take Cyrus long to work out a new study plan for the student and Cyan was relieved when Cyrus said that he would contact the student to inform them.

"Well—" Cyrus started to say as he closed his laptop, but stopped to listen to the sound of footsteps outside the door. Both Cyrus and Cyan watched as the door was pushed. It bumped against its lock but stayed firmly shut. Outside, someone tutted. The door swung open and Professor Daniella Waldergrave rushed in.

"Cyrus! I went to your office and you weren't there!" Daniella said.

Outside, Cyan could see Dylan's puzzled face.

"That's because I'm here," Cyrus said.

Cyan was annoyed and didn't hide it when Daniella glanced at her. The golden rule of the meeting room was that if the blinds were partially closed, you knocked. They could have been having all sorts of discussions, from grade adjustments to disciplinaries, all confidential. Cyan closed the student records system on her laptop.

Daniella was in too much of a hurry to wait for Cyan to leave. "They think I did it! I know they do! I didn't … I couldn't … over some research?"

The professor's response was too slow. Cyan took her eyes off the laptop's screen and looked at Cyrus, who had his eyes on the desk in front of him.

"Y-you don't think I did it?" asked Daniella.

"I … we know you couldn't," Cyan said, but Daniella ignored her.

"Cyrus?" Daniella said.

"No … No. Of course not." Cyrus sighed.

"But?" Daniella finished the sentence for him. "It's Fayval isn't it? She just can't resist gossip. Even when there's no truth in it."

"No," said Cyan. "Wait!" she added to the empty air. Daniella had already gone back the way she came in. Cyrus stayed rooted to his chair. Cyan got up and raced after her.

The lift doors closed just as Cyan got there, which forced her to run towards the stairs. She slowed her pace to walk around two students and hoped that she looked more reserved than she felt.

"Hello," said one of the students.

"Can I help?" said Cyan, hoping that she didn't sound as impatient as she felt.

"Hi. Do you know when we can apply for the Charlotte King's scholarship? For the spring term?" he asked.

"Er?" The student support section of Cyan's brain kicked in. "You can apply now. The forms are available online." She moved to the student's left.

"When is the deadline?" asked the student, who also moved to his left.

"Sorry. I'm in a bit of a rush. The registry's open and one of my colleagues will be able to assist."

Cyan escaped and walked down the first flight of steps before she ran down the rest. She slowed herself to walk past a few more students in the Cinema Cafe and zipped through the open doors to the King Collection.

There were three students in the museum when Cyan rushed in. They no longer looked at the exhibits and stood, gazes fixed on Fayval and Daniella while Cyan surveyed the whole scene. Daniella stood there, her fists so tight her knuckles were beyond white.

"Please keep your voice down," Fayval said, her eyes on a point above the professor's head. Fayval's voice was deadly calm and she appeared to be on the very edge of control.

Cyan quickly scanned the museum; she was relieved that no one else was there, but she wasn't relieved when one of the students nudged another. This was social media material and the nudged student lifted her mobile phone to eye height. Cyan moved between the student, her phone and the angry duo while careful not to expose her back to anyone.

"Ladies," she said to the motionless staff members, careful to stand out of range of the clenched fists, "why don't we have some tea?"

"Tea," hissed Fayval. "A good idea." Her eyes lowered to Daniella's face.

Cyan wondered whether the venom in the curator's reply had caused Daniella to step slowly backwards.

"Not everything can be sorted with tea," the professor mumbled.

"No, but maybe we could step into the back for a bit." Cyan gestured discreetly towards the students, who were very silent.

"Yes," said Fayval, in a way that made Cyan regret the idea.

Cyan watched as Daniella and Fayval went into the kitchenette at the rear, then gave her attention to the students.

"I'm sorry," Cyan said as calmly as she could. "The King Collection has to close at short notice today. It will be open again after lunch."

Cyan wasn't surprised when the students left without a word of complaint, they probably couldn't wait to discuss the near fight they had just witnessed. She watched them giggle as they walked towards the cafe's bar. She thought about public relations and pictured the head of Marketing and Relations sending out an email about the 'Good name of the University'. Her thoughts were chased away by the dangerous silence from the kitchenette. Cyan turned the knob to lock the Collection's door, before taking two breaths and joining Daniella and Fayval.

When Cyan walked in Daniella and Fayval had their backs to each other.

"Well?" said Cyan, determined to know what took place before she arrived. Fayval reached for the kettle in silence while Daniella stared at the floor as if she would kill it had it been alive, arms folded. Cyan tried not to sigh.

"What happened?" she said.

"She started it," snapped Fayval as she slammed the kettle onto its base. She rested her hands on the counter.

Oh goody, thought Cyan, *just like my four-year-old nieces after a fight.* "Who," she said with restraint, "started what?"

Daniella shifted her weight and folded her arms tighter. Cyan could see the muscles flex in the professor's bare forearms.

Fayval spun around and pointed her chin towards the crossed arms. "Her! She came down here shouting rubbish, accusing me of telling everyone in Corner that she murdered Dayton."

"I did not shout," said Daniella, "there were students present. I only asked you why you were spreading lies."

"Me?" Fayval shrieked.

"Well the porters said that the news came from someone in the archives."

"What?" Fayval's voice got even higher.

Cyan stepped in quickly. "What did they hear?"

"That I was seen near the Hub the night Dayton died," Daniella said.

Fayval shook her head. "I don't know who they heard that from, but it definitely was not me."

"So you deny it?" asked Daniella.

"Yes," said Fayval. "I do."

A loud knock on the Collection's glass doors made all three women jump. Fayval hesitated until there was a second knock and then moved slowly towards the kitchenette's door, her eyes resting on Daniella. She opened the door and gasped, then left with more haste.

"I don't believe Fayval, but why am I telling *you* that," said Daniella.

Cyan refused to bite back, instead she thought for a moment. "Okay," she said, "which porter did you speak to?"

"I said I'd keep it quiet. Unlike Fayval, I know how to keep my mouth shut. Don't you dare look at me like that. The porters said she saw it all, from after I left the bar to Cyrus walking into the Collection the next morning—"

"Wait, what?" said Cyan. "Why would she be in the Cinema Cafe after hours? There were no films and the cafe was closed. I know, I was in an ECC meeting at the time."

Daniella's arms relaxed slightly and she bent her head forward. "Well ... I." She suddenly straightened her back and lifted her chin. "Fayval saw Cyrus discover the body."

"She wasn't there," said Cyan, amazed that she managed not to shout.

"What?" Daniella's arms uncrossed and hung loosely at her sides.

"Fayval wasn't there. She came after I'd seen Dayton."

"You would protect your friend." Daniella sounded doubtful.

"Ask Cyrus. Would he protect her too?"

Cyan and Daniella stood glaring at each other. They turned their heads when the door opened.

"This is Constable Peters," said Fayval.

"Good morning," said the police officer.

"Oh. Hello," said Cyan.

Daniella didn't reply, but out of the corner of her eye Cyan saw the professor shrink back slightly.

"I'm looking for Ms Cyan Butler?" The officer looked at all three Corner employees before he settled his eyes on Cyan.

"Yes, that's me."

"Ms Butler," said the police officer, "DS Brookes would like to ask you a few more questions. If you'd like to follow me."

Cyan nodded. "Yes ... yes of course."

The professor looked relieved as Cyan followed the officer towards the door. Cyan felt the first twinges of nerves.

"How did you know where to find me?" Cyan asked the officer in an attempt to distract her mind.

"One of your colleagues from the registry. They saw you and Professor Waldergrave just before they started work."

"Katherine Welman," said Daniella.

It was barely audible, but it made both Cyan and the police officer look at Daniella. She gave them her widest smile in reply.

Fayval led Cyan and the police officer through the Collection and they waited as she unlocked the door. Before they walked out, Cyrus walked in. He paused when he saw Constable Peters.

"Sorry," Cyrus said. "Is Daniella still here?"

"In the back." Fayval tilted her head towards the kitchenette.

"Excuse me." Cyrus walked past them into the kitchenette and closed the door behind him.

Cyan felt relieved. At least Cyrus hadn't abandoned Daniella.

As Cyan followed the police officer into the cafe she heard the door to the King Collection open. She looked over her shoulder to see Daniella, face like a thunder storm, walk through it.

"Daniella!" Cyrus called.

Daniella paused long enough for Cyrus to reach her. Cyan watched as they headed for a table. She was relieved that Cyrus had caught up with Daniella, he needed to apologise for his hesitation in the meeting room. *And I hope he calms her nerves*, Cyan thought. A wicked smile formed on Cyan's lips, maybe not too calm, it would be good for Katherine to be on the other end of Daniella's temper for a while. It might stop the rumours.

"Ms Butler?"

Cyan spun around to face the police office. "Sorry."

They stepped out of the building into a heavy downpour and the large umbrella the officer carried covered them both as they walked towards the King Building. Cyan was thankful for the weather; nobody on Corner liked the rain, which meant that there would be few people to stare both at Cyan and the black police uniform beside her.

The only people they did see on the path were two porters, who had just shared a joke, but the laughter seemed to go back into their mouths as Cyan and the police officer approached. Once Cyan and the officer had walked some distance past them, they heard faint, indiscreet whispers.

"Well," said Peters. "There's nothing we like more than gossip."

Cyan nodded in agreement.

It was a short walk to the small seminar room still being used by the police. The officer knocked, was called in and after a few words held the door open for Cyan.

Cyan recognised DS Brookes the minute she walked into the room. The detective sergeant stood next to a table that had been moved to the side, opposite the door and in front of the windows. DS Brookes bent down to read a file. Next to her was a laptop and Cyan could see the top of a person's head behind the screen. She looked at the close-cropped hair, black surrounded by a halo of salt and pepper. Then she admired DS Brookes's clothes – a black pleated top under a short-sleeved red jacket and a loose red skirt. On the detective's feet were sensible black closed-toe sandals. The detective looked up as Peters announced Cyan's arrival and she thanked the officer, who closed the door behind him as he left.

"Hello, Ms Butler. Please take a seat," she said.

"Hello," said Cyan. "I prefer Miss or Cyan."

"Of course. You've already said. Please take a seat Miss Butler."

The head behind the screen rose before Cyan could move towards the indicated seat, a pair of deep green eyes looking up at her. Cyan didn't recognise the face, but she knew the eyes. They had startled her on the day Dayton had been found dead. Cyan paused for a brief moment, certain that they had to be colour contacts, no one could have eyes as intense as those. To distract herself she looked around the room. Only three of the twelve tables were in use. The police officers were at one. Another two were arranged in a rectangle with two chairs on either side. On them, in the centre, was a black plastic tray on which sat two glass bottles of water, one still and one sparkling, and several glasses. The rest were on the right side of the room near the lectern, some on top of others with their legs pointing towards the ceiling.

"Please, help yourself to water," said Brookes.

Cyan sat down and reached for the still water. Her stomach felt like the drum in a washing machine on a slow spin and it had pulled all the water from her mouth. She poured herself a glass and concentrated on the bubbles in the neck of the other bottle as she drank.

Cyan heard chair legs scrape the floor and looked up to see DS Brookes approach.

"Sorry about that," she said. "Please let me introduce myself again, I'm Detective Sergeant Phyllida Brookes and this is Detective Inspector Andre Torrington. He'll be joining us this morning."

"Good morning, Miss Butler," DI Torrington said. He raised his palm. "Please, don't get up."

Cyan returned the greeting and sat back down in her chair. She noted that DI Torrington was dressed in the Corner Rise unofficial uniform of dark trousers topped with a bright polo shirt. His trousers were charcoal and the shirt was royal blue.

As DS Brookes explained the nature of the interview and that it would be recorded, Cyan felt relieved that she had decided to go directly to the seminar room and not to the registry to collect her handbag and backpack before the interview. Cyan knew that she would have kicked either bag about under the table or tried to seek refuge in her mobile phone.

Cyan listened as Brookes noted the time, date, location and the names of all present. She was glad to see both officers using notebooks, the recorder at the station had unnerved her and she had stumbled and stuttered through the first interview. She waited for the first question. Instead, DI Torrington nodded at her hands. Cyan looked down at her keys. They danced around her fingers with a nice jingle.

"Sorry." She pulled the key ring off her index finger and put the keys down on the table.

"Please describe your movements the night before Dr Dayton King's body was found," said Brookes. She had become as formal as her clothes.

Cyan's fingers moved automatically towards the keys. She lifted her hands off the table and put them in her lap.

"I was at the cinema on the ground floor of the Hub," Cyan said. She had been questioned before and signed a statement, so she was surprised to be asked this again.

"The Hub?"

"Yes. It's the unofficial name for the Portmore Building. We call it the Hub because all the central admin, administration, happens there. Well, it would if the central departments would transfer from the Main Campus." Cyan's hands trembled as she spoke. Opposite her both officers looked attentive but also relaxed, even Torrington's eyes no longer caused her alarm. Cyan knitted her fingers together.

DI Torrington broke the silence. "Please could you tell me what took place in the cinema that evening?" he said.

For the first time Cyan noticed his accent, there was a hint of Corner in it, but the rest came from somewhere in the USA. She stopped her mind before it pursued the thought further and answered Torrington's question.

"The Ealing Comedy Club," Cyan said. "Cyrus, Professor Cyrus Pepper, gave an introduction to *Passport to Pimlico*. The meeting started at six thirty, which was a bit late for us, but Humanities had it."

The detective inspector looked puzzled.

"Humanities had Cinema One booked. They showed a film, I think, which should have finished at five but ran over by about half an hour. Then we had to set up, put out the food and drinks left for us by Catering. Cyrus welcomed any visitors and introduced the film."

"How long was the film?" said Torrington.

"Not long. About an hour and a half."

"Thank you. Please go on."

"We always follow the film with a quick discussion, which we did that evening, and then we talked for a bit before packing up."

"And what time did your event finish?" said Torrington.

"Oh. About ten, after the social. I stayed behind to help Cyrus clear up, put all the glasses and crockery on the trolley for Catering to collect the next day. So we were probably done by ten thirty."

"And afterwards?" asked Brookes.

"I caught the same bus home as Cyrus. I live in Three Trees and he lives on the Centre Point, so we took 5B bus around the north of the Crown."

"And nobody heard anything strange?" asked Brookes.

"No," said Cyan. "The Cinema Cafe closes early on Wednesday, which is why we could use the cinema, so we weren't listening out for anything."

Torrington flicked through his notebook. "There are two cinemas in the Portmore Building? Why not use the other one instead of waiting for Cinema One?"

"Cinema Two had been closed for cleaning. There were no films scheduled that afternoon to allow for that."

Torrington nodded. "Would you mind telling me what you thought of Dr Dayton King?"

Cyan, who had managed to bring her hands under control, stared at the inspector. "Why?" she asked automatically.

"We would like to know more about Dr Dayton King's character," he answered. "To try to understand why he was killed."

They need a motive to find a killer, thought Cyan. She lowered her eyes to her lap. Although her fingers were together, her thumbs were free and were circling each other like birds in a fight. She willed them to stop. "I-I didn't get on well with Dr King."

There was an expectant pause. "In what way?" asked the inspector.

"It was his sense of importance. It felt like he wanted everyone to stop whatever they were doing and focus on him. Usually if you're busy, you indicate to whoever is next in line that you've seen them and you will be with them in a minute. It just takes a nod or eye contact and people nod in reply and wait. But not Dayton, he would tut loudly, or hold some exaggerated pose as he looked at his watch, and then just glare at whoever he had collared."

"Do you have any examples?" asked Torrington.

"Um. Yes," said Cyan. "First-year students arrive a week before the others. You know, for clubs and course admin – administration."

Both officers nodded.

"This term began in late September for the first-years, so I was tied up with student queries. Well, we were all really busy, even Zoe –

Zoe Mandeville, head of Student Services – was at the counter. I'd already smiled at Dayton to let him know that I had seen him and he glowered at me in return, so I just carried on with my job. I was with a first-year student, who couldn't make up her mind which options to take and we were nose-deep in the handbook. Dayton grew impatient and hit the registry counter so hard he made both of us jump."

"Why would Dr King do that?"

Cyan bit back a few harsh words before she answered. "I honestly believe that Dayton – Dr King – thought he was more important than that poor student. Can you imagine, your first day at university and that happens?"

"What happened next?" Torrington asked.

"The student went to pieces," said Cyan, scanning the officers' faces. "Oh sorry. Fortunately Zoe had just finished with her query and stepped in."

"Did you find out the reason for his urgency?"

"Oh yes. I made sure to ask Zoe. Dayton just wanted a class list. You know, how many students, uni email addresses." Cyan snorted. "Zoe tried to send him back to his department, where he could easily have got them. But he wouldn't go, said something about them being busy. You should have seen the look on Zoe's face. She gave him the list and left him at the counter without another word."

"And he would be allowed this information?"

"Yes," said Cyan. "It was his class. He was scheduled to teach it."

"So, he was sorry after this incident?"

"No," Cyan said with a wry laugh. "As he passed me on the way out he told me that next time I needed to get my priorities right and speak to him first. I was so angry. I pointed out that the student had been there before he arrived and that I had acknowledged him." Cyan crossed her arms.

"Sorry, Miss Butler."

Cyan jumped. She had almost forgotten about DS Brookes. Unlike Torrington, she had a rhythmic voice. She was born and bred on Corner Rise. Her familiar tone caused Cyan to relax.

"You said," Brookes referred to her notes, "'whoever he collared' referring to Dayton King. Please could you explain further?"

"Yes of course. All three of us in the registry offer exam and enrolment support to the different departments. I don't support Dayton."

"Who does?" asked Brookes.

"Well, at that time, Katherine provided support for SAS."

"Ah. The School of Agricultural Studies," said Brookes.

Cyan wondered whether the detective sergeant wanted to laugh.

"Dr Dayton King worked in that department," Brookes explained to Torrington who nodded.

She turned back to Cyan. "So Miss Butler, why didn't Dr King speak to Ms Welman?"

"Katherine always managed to be away from the counter whenever Dayton walked in. They've had some problems."

"Can you describe any of these problems?" asked Torrington.

Cyan stared at the table to hide her thoughts. She knew that Katherine was lazy and any 'problem' Cyan used as an example would just prove this. She took a deep breath.

"As I said, at the time Katherine supported SAS, but she always had trouble with the exam boards. The worst was when he, Dayton, I mean, told Katherine that she had supplied the wrong grades for the last one." Cyan raised her eyes from the table. "The examinations boards are where the grades are finalised before the students receive them. Anyway, it's a rule that two members of registry staff attend each board, so Dylan was with Katherine on that occasion.

"Another rule is that we double-check all course grades before the board, it's a hangover from when they had to be inputted manually, then we send them to the lecturers to approve. Well, Katherine didn't ask Dayton to approve the grades and Dayton didn't ask to see them. All lecturers check online anyway, but we need to keep a proper record of procedures in case of appeals. I can't prove this, but I have no doubt that Dayton had already checked the grades for his course.

"I'm still confused about what happened next. There are rarely last-minute changes, but when there are, the lecturers come straight to the registry to let us know, any one of us can make the amendments and ask a colleague to check. We can delay the board by a few minutes if we have to, everything has to be accurate. But Dayton didn't visit the registry, instead he emailed Katherine some last-minute changes. And, as usual, Katherine was late that morning. She came into the office, grabbed a laptop and went straight in to set up the meeting." Cyan looked at the officers. "So, when the wrong grades were presented Dayton shouted at her, in the exam board, in front of all the examiners. He even had the phrase 'the registry's poor administrative standards' recorded in the minutes. We were furious, both with Katherine and Dayton."

DI Torrington looked up from his notes. "Why do you think Dr King did this?"

Cyan shook her head. "I don't know. It just looked like Dayton simply wanted to humiliate her. Like he went out of his way to. Don't get me wrong, Katherine should have done her job properly, but Dayton could have sent any changes to the registry email address as well, then I could have seen it and let Dylan know."

There were a few more questions after that, but they were all about the Thursday when Dayton's body was discovered. The rain had stopped by the time Cyan walked out of the King Building, but she didn't notice. DI Torrington's questions about Dayton made her think. Why had Dayton humiliated Katherine in the exam board? It had been over a year since that exam board. Dayton had used that incident as a reason to get Katherine removed as support for SAS. Cyan remembered the way Zoe fought against it. Just as Cyan reached the place where the path split, she stopped. The exam board was held shortly after Katherine had spread the rumour that Dayton had asked her out, complete with Dayton quoted as 'being unable to live without her'. Although when questioned, Katherine admitted that Dayton hadn't said those words, but his body language did. And Dayton hadn't actually asked her out. But he would soon.

Katherine was wrong. He never approached her. In fact, he took it very badly when the rumour finally reached him, because Katherine had requested that people keep her romance a secret and the only person they kept it a secret from was Dayton.

"Excuse me, please."

The voice brought Cyan out of the past. She had stopped right next to a coned-off section of the path and had blocked it completely.

"Sorry," she said as she moved forward.

Cyan resumed her journey back to her office, her pace slowing. She realised that the exam board had been Dayton's revenge.

"And he called us pathetic," said Cyan.

Cyan wasn't surprised to see the King Collection open when she got back from her interview. She waved at Fayval to get her attention and mouthed the word 'lunch'. Fayval nodded and Cyan went up to the registry to collect her handbag and backpack. Katherine was nowhere to be seen and Cyan was glad.

Fayval was on the telephone when Cyan walked through the doors.

"Yes. The Collection is usually open from nine thirty to one and then from two until four." Fayval nodded at Cyan. "Any changes to the times are usually given on the King Collection website. Of course. Goodbye." Fayval hung up gently.

"How are you feeling?" asked Cyan.

"I'm okay." Fayval sounded surprised. "Would you believe Daniella apologised?"

Cyan blinked at Fayval. "Really?"

"Yes. Cyrus must have said something to her. She said she knew that I was a gossip. But, in her words, 'To be fair you aren't malicious or a liar.'"

"And that's okay? I mean. That's still a bit of an insult."

Fayval shrugged. "Well," she said, "Daniella's right about me being a gossip. My husband tells me that at least once a day." She chuckled. "Actually, the rest of the family do too."

"Um. Okay." Cyan still thought that Daniella had been blunt at the least. "How did they seem?"

"Who? Cyrus and Daniella?"

Cyan nodded.

"Oh they're friends again," said Fayval.

"Thank goodness."

Fayval got up from behind her desk and started to walk towards the kitchenette. "Hey. I've discovered a new tea. Want to try it?"

Shortly afterwards Cyan and Fayval made their way with steaming travel mugs of tea to an empty bench on the green behind the King Building. The green was the only lawn on the Crown Campus, a leftover indulgence from William King. In hot summers the grass was burned to brown, while the rest of the campus was covered in various shades of green from the large dragon tree to the many vicious prickly bushes.

After they sat down Cyan took a sip. "What's this?"

"Black tea flavoured with lychee," answered Fayval. "Like it?"

Cyan nodded. It was sweet without sugar and she was sure that it would go well with leftover fish curry. They both balanced their cups on the bench and ate in silence for a while.

"At least all the noisy work has nearly finished," said Fayval and nodded towards the Student Centre.

Cyan looked at the new concrete and glass building, empty of workmen. "I suppose it's needed," she said. "But I do miss the blue flower garden."

"Well, if Corner Uni wants more students."

More money, thought Cyan and she stared out towards the back of the King Building. At least she could still enjoy the sight of the vines trained up the walls. Not far away from her bench a poinsettia showed red bracts to the December sun.

"I would love to know who said Daniella was a murderer," said Fayval between forkfuls. "And then had the nerve to blame 'someone in the archives' for the lies. The archives! It's a museum. I studied part-time for five years to qualify for my job."

Cyan stabbed her fork into a chunk of fish. "There's only one person on campus who calls the King Collection the archives," she said. She put the fish into her mouth.

"Katherine," said Fayval.

Cyan nearly choked. She hadn't realised that she had spoken out loud.

"It's okay. I already knew that. I just wanted to ignore the fact for a while."

"Sorry?"

"I nearly had a fight with Daniella. Do I really want another one with Katherine? Anyway, Daniella will do that for me."

"What? Fight with Katherine?"

"Yep," said Fayval. "Like you said, Katherine is the only one who calls the Collection the archives, and the rumour about Daniella started there. She worked it out the minute that officer said 'one of your colleagues'. You heard the way she whispered Katherine's name."

Cyan shook her head.

"Katherine really did not think that through."

"No," agreed Cyan.

"And how did she guess that Daniella was near the Hub."

Cyan sat bolt upright. "I think she was told."

"What?" Fayval said. "Who by?"

"I don't know, but I heard them before the last ECC." Cyan then told Fayval about the snatch of conversation she had heard on the stairs.

"Did you find him?"

"It was a deep voice. Not necessarily a man's though."

"Oh. Okay."

There was no more to say so they listened to the voices of the workmen compete against bird song.

"Have you been interviewed by Inspector Torrington?" she said.

"Um hmm." Fayval swallowed her mouthful before she answered. "Yes. He's not originally from Corner Rise, but his mother is."

Cyan lowered her fork. "How did you find that out?"

"I asked about his accent. He only gave that much away. I was surprised to find out that his mother is a King."

"Is she a relative?"

"No idea. He got back to business pretty quickly." She looked at Cyan. "Stop smiling. I can't know every King on this island!"

Cyan glanced sideways at her friend. She knew that Fayval would know someone, who would know someone, who would know which branch of the King family the inspector's mother came from.

"So. Did he ask you about Dayton?"

"Oh yes. And you?"

"Yes." Cyan nodded. "But I feel a bit bad."

"Why?"

"I just couldn't find one thing I liked about that man. I mean, now I could come up with what a good lecturer he was. But at the time."

"Well," said Fayval, "I told it like it was. My opinion of him will not change, even after what happened."

"Many times I wished Dayton would just go away, usually to another country. But dead? Never."

As Cyan put the last of the fish curry into her mouth she caught a movement out of the corner of her eye. She followed it and saw Katherine attempt to reverse back up the path towards the King Building. Cyan then flicked her eyes towards Fayval.

"Good afternoon, Katherine," Fayval shouted in a voice that didn't wish Katherine any good at all.

Cyan watched Katherine, who had stopped in the middle of the main path. Her eyes bulged, then her shoulders hunched as if she wanted to sink into the ground.

"Who do you think she wants to avoid? Me or you?" said Fayval quietly.

"Who knows," Cyan said.

Fayval raised her voice. "Good afternoon, Katherine."

"Oh. Good afternoon," Katherine said, a fake smile forced onto her lips.

"How was the dentist?" asked Cyan.

"Oh. Just a check-up."

Katherine's eyes flitted to Fayval and Cyan swore she saw worry on her colleague's face. Fortunately for Katherine, Fayval appeared to be giving the last of her tea her full attention. Cyan noted the tension in Fayval's hands and for a brief moment wondered what would happen if the cup shattered. Cyan reached up and pulled at her wig. She heard her watch tick and checked the time.

"It's nearly time for me to head back to the registry," she said.

Fayval drained the last of her tea and nodded. Cyan put away her lunch box and glanced at her friend. No matter what Fayval had said, Cyan would not leave her alone with Katherine. Fayval's mobile phone rang and Cyan silently gave thanks.

"Sorry," Fayval said to Cyan as she pulled her mobile phone out of her skirt pocket. She answered on the fourth ring. After a few words Fayval picked up her cup, raised it in farewell to Cyan and headed back to the museum.

Cyan sat back in her seat and watched as Katherine puffed out a long breath. Katherine knew how lucky she had been, Cyan could tell from the look on her face. She wondered what would happen if Fayval did confront Katherine. Cyan shuddered, and pushed the rest of her thoughts about that part of the future from her mind.

Cyan slowly packed her lunch to give Katherine enough time to walk on ahead. Katherine didn't move.

"Hurry up. We'll be late back and you hate that," she said.

What do you want? thought Cyan, looking up with her head tilted to one side.

Katherine flashed an all-knowing smile. "I've got some news on your precious Daniella."

Cyan sighed. If Fayval were here she would have reminded Katherine that Daniella was neither precious nor belonged to anyone. Cyan wouldn't and pretended to ignore Katherine as she rose from her seat. They walked in silence for a few steps and Cyan was pleased to feel Katherine's impatience grow.

"Okay?" Cyan finally said. "What's the news?"

Katherine paused dramatically. "Your precious Daniella was seen near the Hub the night Dayton died," she said.

Cyan stopped dead and spun to face Katherine. Katherine stepped back.

"Who told you?" said Cyan sharply.

Katherine took another step back to steady herself and her gaze travelled from Cyan's face down to Cyan's shoes and back up again. "Wouldn't you like to know," she said.

"Yes I would, because up until last night the only person who knew for certain Daniella was outside the Hub *was* Daniella."

"What?" Katherine's eyebrows rose to her hairline.

"And probably the police," said Cyan, "but I'm not sure. Either way Daniella confirmed that she was outside the Hub."

Katherine's smile wavered. "She told you?"

"Yes she did."

"Oh." Katherine's gaze dropped to the ground.

"Yes, Daniella was there. So whoever told you must have been there too."

Katherine's eyes looked up towards Cyan's face. For a brief moment she looked worried, then she turned her face away from Cyan.

"I'd better get back," she said.

Katherine picked up her pace and walked away. Cyan jogged to catch her up.

"I'll walk with you," Cyan said.

Katherine gave Cyan a killer stare but Cyan didn't back down.

On the way they passed one of the prickly bushes planted at intervals beside the path and Cyan noticed a minty smell. She glanced at the bush and then back into Katherine's anxious face.

"Who told you about Daniella?"

Katherine slowed to a stop. "What?" said Katherine. "Look, Cyan. I didn't know, okay? I thought she was making it up. A joke."

"Who?" said Cyan gently.

"You know who. You caught us talking about Dayton's death. Remember?"

Cyan searched through her memories, her eyes staring past Katherine's left ear. "On the main stairs," she said. She focused on Katherine. "You ran to the toilet."

"And she went outside."

"But I didn't see her."

"How could you miss her?" said Katherine. "She's the sharpest dresser around."

Cyan's eyes and mouth opened into three wide circles. "Of course. The woman in the floaty wine dress."

"That's her."

"Wait," said Cyan. "Where does this friend of yours work?"

Katherine gave Cyan a puzzled look, then laughed. "She doesn't work here. She's a student."

"Dressed like that?" said Cyan. She thought for a few seconds. "Yes. Some students do have that kind of money."

"And she's one of those students." Katherine smiled to herself. "She does live in Brixton."

Katherine's voice made Cyan focus on her colleague again. Any concern was gone, instead Katherine's chin was in the air and she gave Cyan a sideways glance from narrowed eyes. Katherine was in full gloat mode. It made Cyan both angry and uncomfortable, so she decided to get back to the point quickly.

"How did your friend find out about Daniella?"

"Hmm?" Katherine replied with a musical hum.

"Katherine!"

Katherine lowered her chin and turned her head towards Cyan. The look on her face said that this wasn't the conversation she wanted. Cyan watched a scowl form and knew that Katherine was about to shut up like a safe.

"I think you're asking the wrong question. Daniella's the suspect. What was she doing there? I just remembered. I need to go to the Mann Building."

Katherine pushed her hair over her shoulder, spun on her heels and walked off.

Cyan suppressed a sigh and looked up at the sky. "Why were you there, Daniella?" she said to herself. "Probably the wrong place at the wrong time."

She took a deep breath and caught that minty smell again. It made her feel uncomfortable.

"Don't be silly," she said to herself. "It's only menthol."

She remembered the oil her mother still made her inhale when she had a cold. The smell passed. She shook that memory from her head and glanced at her watch. As she rushed along the path she knew she had to find out why Daniella was there that evening and wondered how to ask.

Cyan sat at her desk and logged in to her computer, then glanced sideways at Katherine's scowl while questions raised from their brief conversation bounced around her head. She needed to bounce them off someone else and decided to head down to the museum for a brief talk with Fayval. Cyan looked at Katherine, whose scowl had deepened, then got up and headed to the toilets. By the time she had got to the Cinema Cafe Katherine was there, a smile on her face, with a mug of something hot in her hands.

"Cyan," she said with a smile that Cyan didn't trust.

"Yes?"

"Could you come up and give me a hand? I'm on counter duty today, and you know how I don't enjoy that."

Don't enjoy? You hate counter duty, Cyan thought. "You'll be okay on the counter, and Dylan's in the office—"

"But I'd much prefer your help."

Cyan was aware of the people around them in the cafe, some of whom would be students. She stifled a sigh. "Of course," she said.

Katherine nodded towards the lifts. "Let's go up. There could be someone with a question."

Like you really care, Cyan thought and trailed after Katherine to the lift.

The rest of the afternoon followed the same pattern. Cyan was called to the counter every time Katherine had a query. If she went to the toilet Katherine would appear outside the doors as if to go in. The first time they stood outside the toilet door, Katherine waited for Cyan to go back to the registry and Cyan waited for Katherine to go into the toilet. A young woman had squeezed past, and exited a few minutes later. She had paused to stare, before she shook her head and walked through the doors to the stairs. Cyan felt like a fool and went back to the registry. After that Cyan gave up the fight. *Let's face it*, she thought, *Katherine can hardly follow me home.*

By the end of the afternoon Cyan wasn't sure whether Katherine wanted to annoy her, or if she had read her mind and wanted to make sure that she didn't talk to Fayval. The only relief Cyan got was when Dylan got up and walked to the counter to help Katherine. Cyan considered a quick bolt through the registry door at that point, but reasoned that Katherine would walk into the King Collection and interrupt anything said. Plus it would give Fayval an easy shot at

Katherine and Cyan would probably just stand back and watch.

Cyan was glad to see half past four displayed on the clock above the registry's door. It took Cyan less than four minutes to log out and shut down. She wished her colleagues a good evening and was out of the door. Fayval had locked the museum when Cyan reached the ground floor.

"Good," Fayval said before she looked into Cyan's face, "grief! What's wrong?"

Cyan told Fayval about her afternoon.

"Katherine just doesn't know when to stop. She's like a rat with a chicken bone. What's she so happy about anyway?"

"Self-satisfied, not happy." Cyan told Fayval about the brief lunchtime conversation with Katherine as they left work.

"I would love to know what's going on in that woman's head."

"I wouldn't," said Cyan. "I think we're best out of it."

"Maybe," replied Fayval. "So, how does Katherine know this 'friend'?"

Cyan shook her head. "I don't know."

"Okay. Does this friend have a name?"

"Sorry, I don't know that either," said Cyan. "But I wish I knew why she was around to see Daniella that night."

"On the way back to halls."

"No," Cyan pulled open the metal gate at the rear of the King Building, "Katherine told me, well it slipped out, that this student lives in Brixton." She held the gate open for Fayval.

"Thanks." Fayval used her ID card to open the arched double doors behind the gate. "Brixton, huh? Tell me, would you travel from Brixton to study here? She'd have to leave at dawn to get here for a nine o'clock start."

"Maybe she lives in halls on week days?"

"I doubt it," said Fayval. "The space is limited."

Cyan thought about this as they passed through a corridor into a courtyard.

"Why are we here?" she asked Fayval.

"They've replaced the tapestry and I want to have a look."

"Oh okay," said Cyan. They were both always early for the bus, which meant they could spare the time. Cyan hadn't walked through the courtyard for an age and slowed her pace. She scanned around her. The gravel in the courtyard had been replaced with large square slabs that looked like cream marble. There were also a number of chunky oblong tables scattered around the fountain and a number of cubed stools on wheels. Groups of students sat at the tables, some in conversation while others read and one was wheeling a stool over to join his friends.

"When did they replace the gravel?" she asked Fayval.

"Last year. You really should step out of the Cinema Cafe more. You get better drinks in the King Canteen."

"I'm not one for crowds."

Cyan focused on the sound of someone finishing a cold drink through a straw, iced tea would be perfect just now. Cyan felt her mouth water, maybe she would go to the main canteen, the only cold drinks the cafe served were fizzy.

A third of the courtyard was taken up by a concrete and glass extension in the same style as the King Building. They walked through open double doors into a space lined with artwork.

"Have you told the police?" said Fayval.

"About what?"

"About Katherine's student friend of course."

"I don't have a name."

"True? But how many students from Brixton would want to study at the Tech?"

Cyan thought for a bit. "I suppose I could have a peek," she said. "Not that it would help. It's not like I can tell the police anything."

"True," said Fayval. "But you can still call them."

"Really? What would I tell the police?"

"You might know who placed Daniella near the Hub when Dayton died?"

"Oh yeah. I can see it now. 'Officer, I heard it from a work colleague, who heard it from a student.' I'm sure they've had enough of that already. Anyway, unless the police ask, I can't say."

Fayval glanced at her watch and then stopped in front of a tapestry. It looked medieval at first, then on closer inspection laptops and mobile phones with multicolour screens could be seen.

"I really like this," said Fayval.

Cyan looked at it. The colours were bright and she was impressed. They stood in silence.

"Oh!"

"What?" Fayval leant in towards the tapestry to see what Cyan saw.

"It's the mobile phones in the tapestry."

"Good, aren't they?"

"Yes," said Cyan, "and they all display the time. I just realised, we don't know the exact time that Dayton was murdered."

"Sorry?" Fayval gave Cyan a puzzled look.

"Well. Was Daniella around before or after Dayton was killed?"

"Oh," said Fayval. "So how do we find out?"

"I have no idea."

Cyan looked at the tapestry phone closest to her. Then she looked at her watch. "We'd better hurry or we'll miss our buses."

CHAPTER 8

The next morning Cyan caught the 5B bus around the south of the island. She was near the end of her science fiction novel and the hero had reached the citadel on the hunt for a thief, which kept her nose buried in the book for the whole journey. Once her mind was out of the book it drifted back to Dayton – when exactly did he die.

Cyan sighed as she sat down at her desk. Dayton's death didn't feel so uncomfortable any more. As usual Katherine was the last to arrive and sat down with her usual scowl. She had just logged in when her mobile phone whistled. A young man walked through the registry door and Cyan went to the counter.

A short while later the young man, a postgraduate student, left and Cyan sat down to another whistle from Katherine's phone. There were few student queries that morning, which gave Cyan enough time to wonder how she could arrange to meet with Daniella. Cyan stared at the screen for a while. She hardly ever spoke to Daniella, which made her struggle to come up with a reason.

Cyan planned to spend lunch with Cyrus as they looked at the ECC web page. Could she invite Daniella as well? Recruitment to the ECC? Cyan sighed. She could see it now.

"Cyrus, why not ask Daniella to join us for lunch?"

"Why? She'd never join the ECC. She laughed when I suggested it. Remember?"

"But I'd like to know where she was the night Dayton died."

Cyrus would raise his eyebrows to his centre parting and Cyan would have a lot of explaining to do.

Katherine's phone whistled again. Cyan glanced sideways at Katherine to see her smile. She stopped and stared at Katherine.

"Oh it's nothing," said Katherine. She continued to smile and flicked her hair over her shoulder.

Before Cyan could answer her mobile phone chirped. She unlocked it to see a message from Cyrus and guessed that it had to do with lunch. She opened it. She was wrong.

Cyan leant back in her chair. "Daniella's with the police."

Next to her Katherine huffed. "You only know now?"

Dylan rose out of his chair and looked over at Cyan. "What?"

"She's been arrested," said Katherine.

Cyan read out Cyrus's message. "Daniella has been kept overnight by the police."

"Like I said, arrested."

Cyan was too shocked to respond. A second message chirped onto her phone. It was from Fayval, whose message started with the same topic in the same words. The rest of the message told Cyan that Fayval was on leave for the rest of the week, but to keep in touch with any news. The next half hour was filled with messages sent and telephones answered.

"Well," said Katherine when their mobile and desktop phones went quiet. "I told you it was her."

"No," said Cyan, "a student told *you* that Daniella was near the Hub the night Dayton died."

Dylan peered over the top of his monitor. "Why was she there?"

"She'd just killed Dayton." Katherine smoothed down her cerise hair.

"How do you know?" said Cyan. "The whole ECC were outside this building that night." Cyan shuddered. Dayton could have been murdered as they left the cinema. Then she brightened up. "Nobody spoke to Daniella!"

"What?" said Katherine.

"Well, some of the ECC members work with Daniella. At least one of us would have noticed her."

"Why can't you accept that she is a murderer?" Katherine sucked her teeth.

"Why are you so quick to?" Cyan said and thumped her keyboard to bring her computer back to life. She heard Dylan's office chair creak as he sat down.

"Cyan," he said, "I can't believe that Daniella killed anybody."

Katherine got up. "I don't believe you two! You," she glanced at Dylan, "come from overseas. And you," she gave Cyan a hard stare, "lived there. You came to Corner Rise because you thought it would be a nice, quiet, safe place. Well it's not a monastery! Things happen here too."

Katherine flounced out of the door.

Zoe walked in a split second later. "What just happened?" she said.

"We had an argument about whether Daniella killed Dayton," said Dylan. "Then I was told off because I was born in England and Cyan was told off because she lived there."

Cyan watched Zoe's eyes narrow as she looked at Dylan.

"This isn't the first time," Zoe said. "I will talk to Katherine about this."

"Do you have to?" said Dylan. "It's more about her than me."

Zoe opened her office door. "Well now it's about me too." She closed the door behind her and Cyan watched as she put a pile of papers on her desk and then closed the blinds.

"Oops," said Dylan. "I shouldn't have said the last bit. Anyway, Zoe can't do anything without a formal complaint."

"I wish you would complain," said Cyan. "Katherine blames everyone but herself, because she didn't travel when she was offered the chance."

"She was offered the chance?"

"Oh yes. By a rich ex-boyfriend."

"He really existed?" Dylan leant to the side of the screen and looked at Cyan.

"Yes? Why the surprise?"

"Well, she brags so much I can't tell fact from fiction."

Cyan smiled at him.

Dylan nodded towards the closed blinds. "I bet Zoe's heard the news."

"About Daniella?" said Cyan. "Of course she has."

Katherine walked back into the office. Cyan could smell the rich, spiced hot chocolate in her mug.

As Katherine sat down Zoe stepped out of her office and over to the counter. She leant back against it and crossed her arms. "You've probably heard the news about Daniella," she said.

"Oh yes," said Katherine in a smug voice that made Cyan want to knock the cup of hot chocolate over Katherine's keyboard.

"This is just to remind you that the SSC, Student and Staff Counselling, is available if you need someone to talk to." Zoe looked at her staff. "Well, I think you should take Katherine's lead and head to the cafe." She nodded to Cyan and Dylan. Cyan reached for her carry cup.

"What!" said Katherine. "Cyan's on counter duty!"

"Which is why we will be here to cover for a while." Zoe uncrossed her arms and sat on the chair behind the counter.

Katherine's scowl returned as Cyan and Dylan headed for the cafe.

Both Cyan and Dylan exhaled as they walked through the doors into the Cinema Cafe.

"Thank goodness," said Dylan. "After all that messaging I thought there would be people outside the museum."

Cyan nodded as she looked at the museum's open doors and then around the cafe. A handful of people were sat at tables and two waited at the bar.

"Katherine has inspired me with her hot chocolate," she said.

"The only inspiration you'll get from her."

Cyan chuckled in reply. A few minutes later they held cups of hot chocolate. Cyan nodded towards the cup in Dylan's hand. The chocolate was topped with cream. "There is no way a lid will fit on that," she said.

"Special treat!" Dylan smiled. "Anyway, we can take the lift up."

"True."

Dylan shifted his weight from one foot to the other. "Do you think Daniella killed Dayton?" he said.

"No. No, I do not."

"From all the stuff I read today I guess most people believe she did."

"Well," said Cyan. "The police will prove them wrong."

Zoe smiled when they walked back into the registry. "I thought you would be gone longer," she said.

"There was only a handful of people in the cafe," said Dylan.

"Okay." Zoe got up and walked back into her office.

"I bet Zoe's had a ton of messages about Daniella," said Cyan.

"Yeah. Plus some from Marketing," Dylan said. "Dayton's death was bad enough. But if he was murdered by another academic."

Cyan nodded slowly as she sat down.

What was left of the morning passed and Cyan was relieved to see it was lunchtime. She locked her desktop and reached for her backpack.

"I think I'll join you and Fayval for lunch," said Katherine. "You don't mind do you?"

Cyan froze briefly. They were the first words Katherine had spoken to her since the outburst.

"Er. Fayval's on leave. I'm off to see Cyrus. ECC stuff."

Katherine looked disappointed. She would have gatecrashed lunch with Fayval, but she wouldn't interrupt when an academic was involved, especially for anything social. She just about got on with the academic staff when it came to work. Cyan often wondered why Katherine remained at Corner; there were plenty of places to work that were student- and lecturer-free.

"Just remembered. I'm busy myself," Katherine said and walked away.

The brass neck of that woman, thought Cyan as she left the registry. *She shouts at me, scowls at me and expects to join me for lunch.*

By the time Cyan had walked to Cyrus's office she was calm. The professor's office was small, but at least he had one to himself. In the centre was his desk, which looked as if it was made of pine, and on the walls, shelves bulged with books. Behind the desk was a small two-seater sofa covered in wine-coloured fabric. Cyrus had moved his computer to the side to make room for Cyan's laptop and from somewhere he had found a spare chair. Just to the left of the door was a three-drawer filing cabinet. Cyan had wondered about the contents of the cabinet many times before. She looked up from her laptop's screen and nodded towards it. "What's in there?"

"Hmm?" Cyrus gazed idly out of the window beside his desk. "Oh. More books," he said.

Cyan smiled to herself and went back to the laptop's screen. She clicked to insert a picture. "How's that?" she asked.

Cyrus leant over her shoulder. On the laptop's screen Benny Hill burst through a sentence with a huge smile.

"It's good," said Cyrus. "but it's not a photo from *Who Done It?* I'm sure Benny Hill dresses as a woman at some point in the film.

That would make a better picture, don't you think?"

Cyan did a quick search and found a picture of Benny Hill dressed up in a hat, wig and fur scarf.

"Are you sure this time?" Cyan looked over her shoulder at the professor. She had lost count of the number of changes he had made.

He smiled. "Yes."

A few clicks later and the image was replaced. "Now?" she asked.

"Perfect. Where did you learn to use this software?"

"Online course. I had to learn fast for my mum's knitting group. They wanted a web page to attract new members."

"Did it work?" asked Cyrus.

"Actually, yes. One member said that the animation of needles and thick red wool really helped with her cable cast on."

"Her what?"

"It's a way to add a lot of stitches while knitting." Cyan looked over her shoulder at the professor's blank face, then at her watch. "Oh good. We still have time to eat."

Cyrus lifted his jacket off a paper bag and sat back in his chair. Cyan pushed her chair back and dug into her backpack. He waited for her to open her lunch box while he took a few mouthfuls of chilli noodles.

"That looks good." He nodded towards her lunch.

"Chicken stew with mixed beans and cassava bread. I thought I'd try a new recipe."

"I've enrolled on the traditional cooking class at the William King College of Technology. I've been here for six years so I should know more about the cuisine."

"Don't you eat out?" asked Cyan.

"Not the same as home-made."

Cyan nodded in agreement. They both ate in silence for a while.

"Have you heard anything more about the investigation?" said Cyrus.

"Hmm," Cyan replied through a mouthful of food. "Well, we're not really supposed to talk about it. Remember?"

"I know." Cyrus smiled. "But have you?"

"No." She chewed. "Not really. I was asked to confirm where I saw Dayton's body. Made me shiver."

"Me too," said Cyrus. "I had no idea that they used floor plans. But that did trigger a load of memories, so it must work."

Cyrus took another mouthful of noodles. Cyan looked at her laptop. The picture on her desktop was her idea of the perfect sea, coloured copper and gold from a gentle sunset.

"Do you want to know why I went to the King Collection that morning?" said Cyrus.

Cyan's fork hovered over her lunch box. "Yes," she said.

"I had a bet with Michael."

"Sorry?"

"You know, Michael Horsford. SAS."

Cyan nodded.

"Well," said Cyrus, "it was about tea. Actually, it was about eighteenth-century teapots."

"You don't know anything about eighteenth-century teapots," Cyan said. "Do you?"

"No. That's why I needed to get to the King Collection before Michael taught his nine o'clock class." Cyrus stared at the filing cabinet. "It's always something unusual, isn't it?"

"Sometimes," Cyan said quietly. She remembered the package that sent her to the post room that morning. "So how did you know it would be open?"

"Dayton. He must have heard about my bet. He just had to brag about how he could walk into the Collection at any time he wanted."

"Dayton could never resist bragging about anything."

Cyrus thought for a bit. "Do you know that I never asked him how he would get in."

Well, thought Cyan. *At least he didn't brag about how he got the key.*

She decided to keep that to herself. Fayval would speak about Dayton's theft when she was ready.

"If I had tried to ask Dayton how he could get into the Collection without Fayval, he would have just given me another patronising lecture on how I was still 'not focused enough'."

Cyrus slid the remainder of his lunch onto his desk. "That was how Dayton deflected any questions which required him to explain how he got what he wanted."

"I've had that talk too. How my 'not being focused enough' explained Dayton's rudeness, I'll never know." Cyan stopped herself.

"Uh huh. But recently that phrase just made me so angry."

Cyrus tore the lid from a bottle of water. He took a few gulps, followed by a few deep breaths. Cyan watched as Cyrus calmed himself down.

"Sorry," he said.

"No need to be."

Cyan's laptop started to go to sleep, so she touched the track pad to wake it up.

"Being honest with myself, I didn't go to the King Collection early that morning to win that bet," said Cyrus. "I went to watch Dayton fail. I just wanted him to be wrong. You know, him stood outside a firmly locked door, trying not to look embarrassed. I would have been pretty focused then."

Cyan chuckled. "I would have paid to see that."

Cyrus put down his bottle and reached for his lunch. They ate in silence for a while.

"You know," said Cyan, "what I really hated about Dayton was the way he tried to tell me what my job was."

"He did that to me too."

"What?" Cyan nearly dropped her fork. A piece of chicken bounced back into her lunch box.

"Oh yes. That's why I suggested that he work with Daniella."

"I don't understand."

"Neither do I now. Would you believe I used to be jealous of Dayton."

"Really?" said Cyan. "Why? You've got way much more experience than him. I've seen your module handbooks, they all have at least one paper written by you in the bibliography. Plus you get some of the best student feedback on campus."

"All the important stuff." Cyrus nodded. "But for a while I forgot all that and used Dayton's measure of achievement."

"And what was that?"

"Where he lived, his clothes. Most lecturers would struggle to rent in Brixton."

"Brixton?"

"Mimosa Gardens, Brixton."

"Stop right there." Cyan held up her palm. "Only the Vice Chancellor could even think about living in Mimosa Gardens."

"I know. Unbelievable. Dayton moved in two years ago."

"Huh." Cyan could imagine Dayton stretching the truth about that.

"No really," said Cyrus. "He had a very loud and long

conversation with an estate agent. He was standing in the corridor at the time."

"He was showing off."

"No, he wasn't. He asked me to witness his contract. It was Mimosa Gardens, all right."

Cyan shook her head. "How?"

"According to him, he was focused enough. That stopped my questions. Afterwards he used that phrase at every opportunity. He said it to everyone. When he decided that Daniella wasn't working hard enough on their project, 'You are not focused enough.' After my last relationship failed, 'You are not—' He drove me mad!"

"He was good at that," said Cyan.

"I should have stood my ground! I should have written that paper with Daniella, but along came Dayton."

"Daniella chose him instead of you?" Cyan's voice rose an octave higher.

"No. I backed down." Cyrus sighed. "I thought I was the fountain of generosity. Dayton wanted to leave SAS and work in Maths. He thought that this research would aid his cause. As much as I hated the idea of him in the same department as me, I thought I would aid his cause too."

Cyan smiled. "You are always helpful."

"Not this time. This time I wanted to avoid the 'not focused enough' jibe. In my mind Dayton repeated that phrase at every step of research. I ran away and left Daniella to him." Cyrus lowered his head and stared at the filing cabinet. "I should have stood up for myself. And then, when Dayton was killed. I should have given Daniella more support. I swear, if it hadn't been for *Passport to Pimlico* I would probably be the number one suspect!"

Cyan wanted to reach out and squeeze Cyrus's arm. Instead she scraped the last of the food out of her lunch box. She raised the fork to her lips, paused and said, "I used to think only the admin hated Dayton. How did he survive?"

"He wrapped himself in arrogance," said Cyrus as he closed the empty noodle box.

Cyan glanced at her watch. "Better go. I'll share the flyer with you." She switched off the laptop, packed up her lunch things and said goodbye.

She barely noticed her walk back to the registry. First she felt grateful that she never had to deal with Dayton much, then she felt guilty at that thought. Finally she tried to work out how Dayton could afford to live in such an expensive neighbourhood on a lecturer's salary. For the rest of the afternoon thoughts popped into her head at random and then accompanied her to the bus stop.

Cyan's mind switched from Dayton to Katherine's friend.

"Ugh! Of course," Cyan said, then looked around to see if anyone was looking at her when she realised that she had been speaking out loud. Fortunately the age of the mobile phone meant that most of those waiting for the bus were in their own worlds.

Cyan pressed her lips together to stop any other sounds leaking out. Katherine's student friend had to be Orlanda. Wealth was like an electromagnet to Katherine and it sounded like this student had a lot of money. From the clothes Dylan described to the exquisite combination of wig and dress that Cyan had watched float through the main doors before she had left for the ECC. Plus, not long afterwards Katherine had bragged that her friend lived in Brixton. Cyan shook her head. Did Katherine honestly believe that Orlanda's wealth would rub off on her?

Cyan boarded the bus, scanned her bus pass and sat down near a window at the back.

CHAPTER 9

Cyan spent far too long on her laptop that night. She had planned to look up properties in Mimosa Gardens, but once she started she was pulled down into a rich property internet rabbit hole. Loki sat on the sofa next to her for a while before she placed a paw on Cyan's arm. Cyan pulled herself away from the screen and tickled Loki's cheek.

"So, Loki. How does a man on an average wage afford to live in an expensive place? Loans? Credit cards?"

Loki purred and bent her head to allow for more of her ears to be rubbed.

Cyan glanced at the laptop. Mimosa Gardens looked like the perfectly manicured gated village, surrounded by tall metal railings and electronic entrances, decorated with squat palm trees and dark-leaved bushes.

Loki pawed at Cyan's arm again. Cyan got the message, closed the laptop and gave the cat her full attention. Once Loki was satisfied she stretched out on the sofa and started to wash her face.

Cyan reopened the laptop. She looked at houses that were more like mansions, complete with lawns that she guessed would cost a fortune to water if the summer was dry. As for the apartments, they would rival those in the richest parts of the world. She looked at swimming pools that shone on rooftops or hid in cool basements, large communal gardens and interior walls painted in shades of cream and white. To add to the minimalist opulence all the floors were in various shades of veined marble. Light came in through big windows and most of the properties had rooms so vast that Cyan's whole apartment could fit in many of the kitchens.

Her stomach growled loudly at the sight of the kitchens. In her haste to see where Dayton once lived she had fed Loki, but not herself. Cyan looked at her watch. It was too late to cook a proper dinner. She got up, walked into the kitchen and opened the freezer. There had to be something leftover that she could heat up.

Cyan started the next day determined to look up lecturer pay grades. She sat at her desk and fought with the HR system. Dylan arrived shortly after her.

"Hello. Early catch-up session?" Dylan said.

Cyan hummed in reply and glanced up at Dylan then back at the computer monitor. She checked herself, stopped and returned his smile.

"Sorry. Hello," she said. "Just personal stuff."

"No worries," said Dylan, never a man to be too nosy.

"It's about Dayton." Cyan was glad to share with somebody. She had not spoken to anyone the previous night.

"Oh?"

"Well, I just looked up his pay. He was a junior lecturer, right?"

"Uh-uh." Dylan shook his head and sat down. "He was recently promoted. He's ... was a lecturer."

Cyan tapped a few keys. "No way!"

"What?" Dylan sprung up.

"Cyrus told me that Dayton lived in Mimosa Gardens, Brixton."

"The expensive bit?" said Dylan. "I doubt it."

"So would I, but Cyrus was witness to the contract."

Dylan stared at Cyan then sat down again. A few seconds later she heard his fingers race across the keyboard.

"No way!" he said. "What was his side hustle?"

"Hmm?"

"What did he do, other than work?"

Cyan heard the sound of a gentle chime and checked the bottom right of her screen. No messages.

"Whoops. Meeting," said Dylan. "Zoe's probably already there."

Cyan listened to him open and close drawers then rattle his pen cup.

"I'll lock the registry on the way out." He bolted through the office door and reached the registry's door as Katherine sauntered in.

Cyan stifled a sigh as Katherine used her staff card to open the office door.

"Mornin'," Katherine said.

"Hello."

Cyan closed the browser and opened her email as Katherine hung up her raincoat, dumped her handbag on her desk and then sat at the counter with a cup of hot chocolate. She took a sip and turned on the counter computer.

Cyan was busy with student reassessments when she noticed that the conversation at the counter could reach complaint level.

"Cyan? Can you give me a hand?"

Cyan got up and followed Katherine to the counter. On the other side stood a student, arms crossed. Cyan guessed he was in his first year. She opened with a smile.

"Good morning. Can I help you?"

The student let out a deep breath. Cyan tried to ignore Katherine, who stared pointedly at the computer's screen.

"I went to the SAS. There was no one there," he said.

"I asked the student to go to his department," said Katherine.

Cyan waited for more information, but Katherine fell silent.

"Er. Why?"

Katherine shifted her weight on the stool and flicked her eyes towards Cyan. Cyan watched as Katherine considered several responses.

"A mitigating circumstance form is required," she said.

Cyan was impressed. At least Katherine gave a reason. On the other side of the counter the student sighed dramatically.

"Sorry to keep you," Cyan said to the student. "Why don't you tell me what happened?"

"I wouldn't have to if *she* listened!" The student glared at Katherine. Katherine's back stiffened.

Uh-oh, thought Cyan.

Fortunately the student focused on Cyan. "It's about my … our experiment." He sighed. "We can't believe it. Tara's in tears. It only had to be there until this afternoon. But some idiot broke it! They didn't even leave a note. What am I supposed to do?"

"Okay," said Cyan. "Sounds like you do need a mitigating circumstance form." Cyan was relieved when Katherine's fingers moved across the keys on cue.

"It would help if you knew when the experiment was broken."

"We asked not to have that Olivia in our group." The student uncrossed his arms and rubbed his forehead. "She never does any work and she should have checked that gauge while we did the other ones. But no. Today I go up to look at it and it's broken. Good thing the timer had stopped too."

"So, when was the gauge broken?" she asked when he had finished.

"Last week, Wednesday. I couldn't believe it. We'd put it off the path to avoid this. Mario, the other student in my group, had made the gauges. He did a great job with the timers. All we had to do was put out the gauges and set them for five days each. You know, one for each member of the group. So today I go to get the readings from the last one and notice that Olivia's gauge is broken. Stupid—" The student checked himself and didn't finish the sentence.

Cyan had fought hard not to interrupt the student, or dance on the spot, when she heard when the gauge was broken.

"Last week, Wednesday?" she managed to say calmly.

"Right. I know. Like I said to Olivia, that was ages ago. She should have checked."

"I mean, what time?"

"The timer says about eleven thirty, half an hour after the Student Union had closed. We had checked it just after the bar emptied and it was fine," he said. "That's why it was off the path, students walk up the path from the bar. Nobody walks across the grass unless they want to end up in those prickly bushes."

"By the Hub?"

"Yeah. That path." The student leant towards the screen that Katherine had spun around for him to see. "So what do we put on these forms?" he said.

"Have you told the police?" asked Cyan.

"What? Why?" The student pulled his eyes away from the display. "What's it got to do with them?" he said. Then his eyes bulged. "Oh my days. That's when that professor was killed!"

"Yes," said Cyan. Out of the corner of her eye Cyan saw Katherine sit upright.

"I'm not sure," said the student.

"You'll need evidence," said Cyan. "A letter from the police will be just as good as a medical certificate. You could ask Student

Support for further advice?"

The student thought a bit and then nodded. "I can find this form in the department?" he asked.

Katherine was silent until the student was gone. Cyan exhaled a long breath and shook her hands by her sides to calm down. She now had an idea of the time Dayton was killed, and thanks to that student the police would be able to have an idea too. This could be the break the police needed. Cyan smiled. The smile was removed by Katherine's voice.

"Did they see the murderer?" she asked.

"No. They saw their broken experiment."

"Then why have you advised them to go to the police?"

"Because it was near the Hub at the time of the murder."

"So they saw Daniella?"

Cyan was about to answer, but she guessed that Katherine would only hear what she could gossip about.

"Do be careful what you say to students," said Cyan. "So far you've been lucky."

"Is that so?" said Katherine. "How?"

"Daniella hasn't sued you. Yet. But students might and then where will you work?"

Katherine's silence gave Cyan enough time to head back to her desk.

"Hey, wait!" Katherine got up and followed her. "What did that student say?"

The bell on the counter rang. Katherine sucked her teeth loudly and went to answer it.

Cyan kept her eyes on her screen and away from Katherine, who, after the second student of the morning had left, went back to her slumped position in front of the counter computer. Cyan switched screens and checked how much lecturers were paid. She had just calculated how much Dayton would need to earn to be able to rent his expensive apartment, when Dylan walked into the office.

Cyan looked over the top of her monitor. "Dylan?"

"Hmm?" said Dylan, his eyes on his screen.

"The police searched the Hub after the murder. Right?"

"Of course."

"And outside of the Hub?"

"Probably," said Dylan. He looked up from his screen. "Why?"

"Just curious. Trying to find out the facts is almost impossible; the news is full of opinion pieces and hearsay."

"You can say that again," said Dylan. "Did you read that opinion piece in *The Crown Island Post*? Honestly, 'a huge leap in murder rates' proved that the government has lost control. Could one murder really be called a 'leap'? This island is not a hot bed of crime."

Katherine grunted and Cyan glanced at her.

"Whoops," Dylan said quietly. He raised his voice. "Okay, so there have been other crimes committed on Corner Rise."

"Yes," said Cyan. "But those did not involve people murdered in universities." She gave Katherine's back a hard stare. "Not even overseas."

Katherine slipped slowly from the stool. "Bathroom break," she said and walked out of the registry.

Dylan winked at Cyan and they got back to work.

After a while Cyan's mind switched back to Dayton. *His family must be loaded*, she thought. *But why is he an academic? Corner Rise rich kids go into business or politics.*

Cyan wondered if she should talk to Fayval, but decided not to. Fayval wasn't related to Dayton, nor had she liked him very much. Cyan scratched her head and switched her screen back to the student records system.

Cyan spent the rest of the day worried that the student wouldn't contact the police.

"Of course he will," she said to the computer screen. "He hasn't done anything wrong, and why fail because of someone else's mistake?"

When Cyan left the office at the end of the day she reached for her mobile phone and called the police information line. After a while she was put directly through to the incident room.

"Good afternoon, Three Trees Police Station. DS Phyllida Brookes speaking."

"Oh," said Cyan. "Good afternoon. I didn't think you'd answer the phone."

"I just happened to be here when it rang."

Cyan checked that there was no one nearby.

"Hello?" said Brookes.

"Hello. Sorry. It's Cyan. Cyan Butler."

"Hello, Miss Butler. How can I help?"

Cyan looked around again and decided to press on. "One of the SAS students came to see me today."

"SAS?"

"School of Agricultural Studies." Cyan went on to describe the student's visit.

"Hmm. Thank you. Do you have this student's name," said Brookes.

"Um," said Cyan. "Sorry, no. We ask for their student number, on their ID card, if we need to. But not usually."

"I see."

Cyan felt sympathetic. How many times had a student walked up and asked to know which room their class was in? Nothing about their course, just which room.

"I'm sorry. That was really daft of me. Like I said, I'm sure the student will contact you."

"Well. Thank you."

"Can I ask a question?" said Cyan.

"You can ask."

"I heard somewhere that Constable Peters took calls for the incident room?"

Brookes laughed. "Constable Peters. Yes. Well, he's been moved to other duties."

"Really?" said Cyan.

"You know how we love to gossip on this island?"

"Oh yes."

"Well for a while it felt like everyone wanted to give us information. A footprint here, a sound there. Usually of little use, but always with a few questions tacked on the end. Didn't take us long to realise that the majority of callers *wanted* information."

Cyan was glad that the detective couldn't see her smile.

"But we have to check the information given. Just in case," said Brookes. "Believe me when I say that we've been in more holes than the entire shearwater population of Corner Rise. And poor Peters had to file all these leads. I think one more story about crushed grass could have been the end of his career."

Cyan laughed. "Sorry!"

"Not a problem," said Brookes.

Cyan heard the laughter in her voice.

"But thanks for the tip," Brookes continued, "I'll ask the team to look out for a report of a broken experiment."

Cyan bit her lip. "Do you have a time? For Dayton's death, I mean."

Brookes paused for a bit. "We believe around twelve on the night before he was discovered."

Cyan nodded. "Well, the experiment was broken at about eleven thirty that night." She heard other distance voices at the officer's end of the call.

"Sorry. I have to go," said Brookes. "Please call back if you hear anything else."

"Yes, yes of course. Good afternoon."

"Good afternoon."

Cyan hung up. Excited was not the right way to describe the voices she heard, but they did give her hope that the student might just have contacted the police while she was on the phone.

CHAPTER 10

The rest of the week passed without any changes to Daniella's situation. Cyan watched the news and kept an eye out around campus, but there was no sign of the professor. On Friday afternoon Cyan called Cyrus.

"No," he said, "I haven't seen or heard from Daniella. I've heard about her though. It feels like the number of people who think she's guilty rises every minute."

"I know," said Cyan.

She looked up as Katherine sauntered through the office door to her desk and sat down. Cyrus had already hung up and Cyan released what had become a death grip on her phone's handset.

"No new news, eh?" said Katherine.

"No. Nobody has been charged yet," said Cyan.

Katherine opened her desk drawer and pulled out her mobile phone and laid it flat on the desk. Cyan glanced at it, then did a double take – not only was the mobile phone new, but the first edition of its kind and expensive. Cyan had seen it advertised everywhere and that particular model cost as much as a mid-range laptop.

"I really must get a cover for this." Katherine picked up the phone and walked back out of the office.

"Tell me, Cyan."

Cyan looked across to the counter where Dylan was on duty.

"Does Katherine actually work here?" he said.

"Well," said Cyan. "She gets paid." She looked at the time

displayed in the corner of her screen. Fifty minutes to the weekend. Cyan counted every second that afternoon and was out the door before Katherine logged out of her machine.

On Saturday Cyan woke to the sound of a loud purr and looked down from her bed into Loki's large green eyes. She rolled over to her other side to try for a bit more sleep, but she heard Loki meow and then felt her step onto the bed. The cat stretched and then moved along the edge of the bed towards Cyan's feet. Cyan took the hint and gently eased out of bed before the cat pounced. Once Loki was fed Cyan switched on the radio and headed to the bathroom.

A while later as the kettle boiled Cyan listened for news about Dayton, but the radio was full of preparations for the holiday season.

"Persons are advised to keep an eye on their belongings as they head to Bakersfield today," said the presenter. "There have already been reports of pickpockets in the area."

"Well," said Cyan. "Looks like Dayton is yesterday's news."

She almost laughed at her joke, but concern about the investigation took over. If the murder wasn't in the news, how would the police investigation fare? The police were still asking questions, but after a few loud headlines in *The Corner Gleaner*, and the one strongly opinionated column in the last edition of *The Crown Island Post* that Dylan had mentioned, there was no more news about Corner Rise University at all. Cyan made her tea and drank it while she pulled on some casual clothes and then walked to the news stand on the roundabout at the end of her road to pick up a copy of *The Weekender*.

Almost an hour later she nearly choked on her porridge. The paper was 'naming no names', but had it from a good source that the murder was 'professor on professor' violence.

"'Our source, a central student officer, had seen Professor Daniella Waldergrave argue with Professor Dayton King shortly before the murder.'"

Cyan rested the paper on the table and looked up at Loki, who lounged on the sofa.

"Can't they even get that right? It was Dr Dayton King."

She grabbed her dishes and carried them into the kitchen, where she dumped them on the draining board and yanked the tap open. It was obvious to Cyan who the source was.

"Really?" she said as she pushed a bowl beneath the detergent's bubbles. "'Central student officer' indeed. Also known as a student support administrator. Also known as Katherine Welman!" Cyan plunged her teapot into the hot water. The crack of china made her wince. She pulled at the teapot's handle and glared at the now spoutless pot.

A while later, after she had strained the dishwater, Cyan managed to gather most of the pieces of the teapot. She looked at the broken flower pattern that covered the cyan-glazed china – the description of the colour was the reason why she bought it. Cyan still remembered the small shop in Streatham, South London where she had first seen it in the window and wondered what the green-blue colour was called. She normally went for bright colours, but the flower pattern was almost like a lace cover over the thick teapot and she knew she had to buy it.

She laid out the pieces on a tea towel and wondered whether, with carefully applied epoxy cement, she could make it into an ornament. A search of her cupboards revealed no trace of epoxy, plus she now needed a new one-cup teapot.

"Now would be a good time to head for the shops," she said.

Cyan knew that she could pick up contact cement from the hardware shop in Trelissick, but she wanted more than a steel teapot. She opened her wardrobe and pulled a shoulder-length, deep brown wig from its hanger, then reached into her drawer for a wig cap. Not long afterwards Cyan left her apartment for the second time that morning and headed to the bus stop.

When the bus arrived it was almost empty, so Cyan was able to sit at the back in a window seat. She didn't bother to pull out her book as it would be a short journey to Centro Base, where she planned to take a quick walk around the small plaza. Instead Cyan looked out over trees and houses dotted along the side of the road and watched people as they got on the bus. This part of the route offered the occasional glimpse of the sea as it made its way to Centro Base, where the bus almost emptied. Cyan looked out into the busy square and thought about the department store that occupied the north side. Her teapot had been special, and although she planned to save it, she wanted another special teapot for everyday use. Well, it cheered her up at the start of the day. Plus a new wig for the holiday season and probably some new clothes.

"Well," she told herself. "I'll see a lot of family over the holidays, so why not?" So she settled back into her seat as the bus continued on its journey.

The bus route went out to Centro and then East peak, the three capes of the Crown. It then descended from the mountains and through small villages. By the time it reached The Bridge, the short isthmus that linked Crown Island to Main Island, it was full again. Cyan had often wondered how Main Island came to be called that. It was only slightly bigger than Crown and, to her mind, not as beautiful. But it did have Corner Rise's only port and capital city, Brixton. Cyan smiled. Sailors were not an imaginative bunch, they had named the capital after a village on the Devon coast.

As the bus crossed The Bridge Cyan strained to look over the sea wall to the sea, there were a few gentle waves, but not enough to suggest a strong wind. The bus route took it to the centre of Brixton and Cyan got off at Bakersfield, the island's biggest shopping area. She glanced at the back of the almost empty bus as it turned north towards the capital.

Cyan crossed the road and walked through the car park towards the Bakersfield. In front of the entrance was a square filled with shoppers brought out by holiday season preparations and the gap between winter showers. In the centre of the square stood an ancient dragon tree, decked out in purple and silver ribbon, and under its branches was a circle of food stalls. The smell made Cyan's mouth water, it was nearly midday, and as she walked past the stalls she tried to see what each sold. What she did see were long queues of people and a few spare benches to eat at. Her nose picked up barbecued chicken, fried fish and various curries. Cyan stopped to let a young woman walk past with a cardboard box heaped with fish curry with tomato rice and red cabbage coleslaw. Cyan forced herself not to stare at the box, but the aroma hung in the air.

Maybe I can get some food inside, Cyan thought.

She gave the woman's food a quick glance and managed to avoid the eye contact of one of the people seated at the table the woman walked towards.

Once inside the Bakersfield Cyan fully intended to go up the stairs to the food court, but the architects had thought of that and placed the stairs at the centre of the ground floor, which meant that she had to walk past a popular wig shop to get there. Cyan couldn't resist a quick peek at *Vera's Hair*. In the window wigs were displayed on crystal heads with long necks, others sat on wig hangers that floated in mid-air, and along the base of the window, in open boxes wrapped as presents, sat wig brushes and a multitude of other wig accessories. Cyan stood for longer than she had planned. The shop was empty, well almost, and if she got it now she wouldn't have to tangle with the crowd at lunch outside. Sometime later Cyan walked out the door with a box in her backpack. Her first ever ombré wig. It went from black at the crown to chestnut brown at the ends and was wavy rather than the usual spiral curls she favoured.

Before she reached the stairs Cyan had added a pair of sandals to her purchase. Well, they were on sale, she reasoned.

Cyan took a sip of water from the aluminium water bottle she always kept full in her backpack. She passed a few clothes shops, but had already decided to stop spending that day. She could always to go Centro Base if she needed to.

She stopped outside a shop called *Let's Cook* and looked in at bowls of all colours, stacked saucepans and the biggest pressure cooker she had ever seen. On the floor of the display, filled with baubles, were cups, bowls and egg cups. However, it was the teapot that stopped Cyan's gaze as it travelled around the window. It was the right size, but yellow was the wrong colour. Cyan opened the door and stood aside for someone to leave, and after they had thanked her Cyan walked inside. She smiled as she walked back out the door less than fifteen minutes later. She held a colourful paper *Let's Cook* bag that held her new, deep brick-red one-cup teapot.

Cyan's stomach grumbled loudly, reminding her how empty it was, so she went up to the first floor in search of food. To her dismay the chain restaurants were also packed. Cyan wondered if everyone on the island had decided to spend the day in Bakersfield. She would have to head to the exclusive part of the shopping centre and pay more to eat.

"Ah, why not?" Cyan said to herself. "I deserve a treat."

Plus she couldn't remember the last time she visited Bakersfield.

Cyan peeked into a few shop windows and the price tags gave her second thoughts. She turned to the food court. The first cafe was expensive and she began to think about tea and cake before a retreat back west for cheaper food. Or maybe there would be room in the square. She was about to leave the shops when one display made her stop. Cyan leant in close to look at a pair of brown shoes with tall square heels. She would love to be able to wear a pair like that, but her wide feet prevented her. She inhaled deeply at the start of a sigh and breathed in minty air. The scent made her freeze. Why did mint bother her so much? Then she remembered.

It was that morning in the King Collection. A minty, menthol smell had hung faintly in the air and was stronger as she approached the cabinets that Cyrus had pointed towards. It had clung to the clothes the late Dr Dayton King had worn. Cyan's blood pumped faster and she tensed. Behind her she could hear the crowds as they entered the shopping centre. All she had to do was move fast. She spun around ready for flight.

Gustavo, Cyan's neighbour, stepped back at her sudden movement.

"Good afternoon." Gustavo sounded as if he wasn't sure how his greeting would be received.

"Sorry. Good afternoon," Cyan said. "I must still be jumpy. I still imagine killers in cupboards."

"And in shopping centres," he added.

Cyan felt foolish, but also relieved and smiled up at her neighbour. Today he wore jeans and a cherry-red T-shirt and over his shoulder was a large reusable bag. The minty smell came from the gum he was chewing. He smiled back and stood next to Cyan.

"I couldn't afford a pair of those," Gustavo said. He nodded towards the display of men's shoes in the shop window.

Cyan looked through the window. "Wow," she said. "These are shoes for the super wealthy."

She was about to move away when she had a vision of Dayton's shoes. They must have been bought from this shop. All the footwear in the window had royal blue heels and soles. She walked behind Gustavo.

"Going in?" he asked with a grin in his voice.

Cyan shook her head. She was focused on the other display.

"Do you want a pair of men's shoes?" he asked. "Who for?"

"What? No!" Cyan said. "It's just that I thought Dayton had a pair of these shoes on when. You know."

Gustavo nodded and leant in for a good look at the shoes. "Wait. You're joking me. Wasn't he a junior lecturer? Those would be right out of his price range."

Cyan nodded. Gustavo was right. But Cyan knew what she saw.

"That said. They are distinctive," said Gustavo. He moved in for a closer look. "Cyan," he said after a few minutes, "you don't happen to know who *The Weekender*'s source is do you?"

Cyan looked at him in surprise.

"I ask because I think it was someone from the university. Am I right?"

"Not me!"

"I know that." He held up his hands to placate her. "Gossip is not what you do," he said. "But someone has a loose jaw."

Cyan's jaw tightened.

Gustavo lowered his arms. "Someone you really don't like."

"Katherine," Cyan said before she could stop herself. She checked herself, found not an ounce of regret in her body and continued. "Katherine Welman. I've no proof of course. But when I read that piece at breakfast I had to get out of the apartment."

Gustavo gave a dry laugh. "The one in *The Weekender*?" he said. Cyan nodded.

"I wish I could find out for certain who gave that interview," said Gustavo. "I know just who to ask, but I doubt they'll reveal their source to me." He paused, then asked, "Was Katherine there when you found the body?"

"No. She wasn't even inside the Hub. I saw her behind the police tape just before the police spoke to me."

"So how did she know?"

Cyan paused. "Katherine? I have no idea. But I do know that she's been at that rumour mill. She's said a lot of rubbish about how she heard from a porter who heard it from an archivist. We don't have any archivists on Crown Campus, so I doubt that."

Gustavo nodded and Cyan felt that he didn't quite believe her. Well, technically she hadn't lied.

"Nothing like Corner gossip," he said.

"But 'professor on professor'?" said Cyan. "How can they prove that?"

"And you believe it wasn't?"

"I do. But so many people think Daniella did do it, and I do blame Katherine for that." Cyan looked at the shoes. Her stomach gurgled so loudly she covered it with her free hand. "Sorry," she said with an embarrassed giggle.

"Hey," said Gustavo. "Would you like to join me for lunch? I know a really good place just off the square that does the best salt-fish and green bananas ever. I swear they start to roast the breadfruit at nine."

Cyan's stomach rumbled in agreement before she could answer. "As long as there is coleslaw," she said.

Gustavo smiled. "They have every coleslaw you can imagine."

"Oh I can imagine a lot."

She gave the shoes one last glance and hurried to join Gustavo who had started to walk through the now crowded Bakersfield.

After lunch Cyan smiled as she waited for the bus home. Gustavo had been right, that restaurant did have more varieties of coleslaw than she could imagine. This time Cyan waited for a 5A, she wanted the more direct and faster route home.

Once on the bus Cyan pulled her book out of her backpack and tried to read, but the large late lunch made her feel tired, so she put the book back and closed her eyes. Instead of sleep she got an active mind. The life Dayton had lived didn't make sense. Okay, she had to accept where he had rented, but the shoes?

"He must have racked up a lot of debt," Cyan said to herself in the half-empty bus.

It was the only way Cyan could explain the shoes. She wondered if the rest of his clothes were as expensive. She thought about the crisp suits Dayton used to wear, which he was at pains to point out were a linen and silk mix. He must have had at least three of them – silver grey, neutral sand and light blue. Then her mind moved to Katherine. If she was that paper's source, what could Cyan do? Tell her off? The rumours were now out there for everyone to read and she was sure that both Inspector Torrington and DS Brookes had heard them already. But she remembered Fayval's words, the police would be after the truth and Cyan didn't believe a word she read in that article.

The bus stopped at the small village on the other side of The Bridge. An elderly man got on and sat down in the seat in front of her and she absently watched as he settled and then reached into his pocket. She heard the rustle of a sweet paper as he unwrapped it and her heart thumped hard as the smell of mint wafted over his shoulders.

Okay, she thought, *this has got to stop. I'll run away from cups of mint tea next!*

She made up her mind to make herself a cup of that exact brew when she got home.

CHAPTER 11

The next morning Cyan went back to bed for a lie-in while Loki ate her breakfast. She was surprised at how well she had slept the night before, having fully expected her dreams to be filled with blue-soled shoes and the smell of mint. Cyan laughed at herself as she snuggled into her pillow, then dozed until her alarm clock woke her up.

At breakfast Cyan poured herself a cup of tea from her new teapot and checked her calendar. 'Dinner with Mum' it read. That would take her mind away from recent events. So there might be a few words about the murder – Cyan checked herself – there would be more than a few words, but she was sure that most of the conversation would be outside of the university. She looked out of her kitchen window at a clear sky and decided to leave early and walk from her apartment in Three Trees to her mother's house at Trelissick Top.

As Cyan had hoped the lunchtime conversation was all about Vee's church, her voluntary work at the library and how food prices had increased.

"Why do we import bananas?" Vee said. "We can grow them here."

"Mum, the fields are too full of pineapples."

"Then Corner Rise needs to diversify."

After lunch Cyan filled the kettle while her mother washed carrot strips in the sink. Cyan looked out of the kitchen window at a chain of four islands called the Rocks to the south. Around them the

Atlantic rippled like rich blue silk in the afternoon sun and in the distance there was nothing but sea. Cyan waited for the kettle to boil while in the background the radio broadcast a business programme. Cyan smiled. Her mother had always liked the sound of voices around the house, and Cyan had grown up with them.

"Is Beresford still on the radio?" Cyan asked as the kettle boiled.

"Hmm?" Vee said. "No, he stopped last year. He's on the TV. You must have seen him?"

"Really? I only watch TV in the evenings."

"You fall asleep in front of it in the evenings." Vee smiled and put the carrot strips in a sieve over a bowl. "Anyway," Vee said, "you should watch it now. There's news of some big depression."

Cyan handed her the kettle. "What? Financial?"

"No, weather," said Vee as she poured the boiled water into some glass jars.

"But the hurricane season's over? How—"

"Not a hurricane, a depression." Vee put down the kettle and tilted her head towards her youngest child.

"But everything was calm when I crossed into Bakersfield yesterday."

"Cyan," said Vee, "how long have you lived on this island. You know how fast the sea can change. Oven."

"What? Oh!"

Cyan quickly switched it off. She took the glass jars from her mother and arranged them in the oven to dry. Vee refilled the kettle, then she left the kitchen with an old biscuit tin and Cyan listened as she pulled crockery from the dresser in the dining room. The kettle boiled and soon Cyan and her mother were seated with tea and saffron buns. Cyan realised that her mother had been a bit generous with the saffron as the buns were almost a custard yellow.

Rich food, Cyan thought and smiled to herself.

The business programme was followed by a weather report.

"Tropical Storm Alpha is due to hit the islands before the end of next week," the reporter said. "The government has not issued any warnings so far, but persons are asked not to make any unnecessary journeys. Please keep tuned to Crown Island Radio for further information."

"What did I tell you," said Vee. "That Storm Alpha will bring nice seas with it."

Vee's house was high up on Trelissick Top, so she was safe from any storm surges. Unlike some of the early settlers who were dragged out to sea by storm-whipped waves, along with their slaves, houses and livestock. That was until they realised that the lovely flat rock base that skirted the fertile peak was not good to build settlements on.

"So," said Vee. "How did the papers find out about who killed that professor?"

"It was only in one paper yesterday."

"Well it's in every paper today."

Cyan tried not to sigh.

"Do you know, all they talked about in church was the murder?"

"There have been other murders on Corner Rise," Cyan said quietly into her tea.

Vee ignored her. "It took ages for me to leave. As for Miss Lenny. 'How is poor Cyan?' she said to me. I doubt she even knew your name before this weekend. I can't tell you how angry I was."

Cyan could guess by the way Vee glared at her tea.

"It was the first time I bought a Sunday paper in years." Vee looked at her daughter. "How did they know?"

"Huh?"

"The papers? All the police have given us is the dead man's name, Professor D King."

"Dr Dayton King," said Cyan.

"I listened to every police statement," Vee said. "They said when he died, how he died, but no suspects, no witnesses. Which makes me wonder, if the police said so little, how come I can read the names of everyone involved, including my own daughter, in today's paper?"

Vee put down her cup and went to fetch the newspaper from the small room at the back of her house. She handed it to Cyan.

"Mum, why do you read this nonsense?" Cyan held the copy of *The Weekender Sunday Special* as if it were infected.

"I get the *Sunday Gleaner* as well," said Vee. "I like balance. Anyway, you read these papers too."

Cyan had no reply to that. Truth be told she would have normally picked up a copy of the *Sunday Special*, but she was still angry about Katherine's interview.

Vee refilled their cups while Cyan read the Sunday scoop. It was worse than the Saturday edition. As Vee had said, everyone in the King Collection that morning was named. The only name absent was Katherine's.

After Vee had sat down Cyan told her mother, without hesitation, who she thought the guilty party was.

"You think so? Was this Katherine there when you found the body?"

"Cyrus found the body," said Cyan, "and no, she was not. Katherine's always late for work. She was outside, behind the police tape."

Cyan wondered how many times she would have to say that.

"So how did she know? You said the police gave instructions not to talk to each other or anyone else. Including your mother." Vee looked hard at her daughter.

"They didn't tell Katherine," said Cyan. "And why would we talk to her? Cyrus has no reason to, Katherine doesn't deal with his department. Fayval would rather see Katherine drop down a well and Trevor was carried off in an ambulance. Which leaves me. And I was in no state to gossip."

"Well she must have heard it from someone." Vee looked her daughter in the eye. "Who?"

"Katherine told me. A very glamorous student." Vee listened as she told her about the wine-coloured dress.

"Sounds like she had a red meringue on for clothes," said Vee.

"It looked like a very expensive red meringue," said Cyan.

"I suppose you can't tell me her name?"

Cyan shook her head and reached for a second small saffron bun.

"So, was she inside the building?" said Vee.

"What?" Cyan stared at her mother for a while, then blinked. She thought of the cafe that morning. "There were only two members of bar staff," Cyan said. "But nobody else."

"Could she have been in the building? What about one of the cinemas?"

"I doubt it," said Cyan. She took a bite of the bun and thought as she chewed. Vee sipped her tea.

"No," Cyan repeated. "The cinemas are locked until classes start or films are shown. There was a huge mess in one of them when they first opened and half that day's films had to be cancelled, they've been kept locked outside of use ever since."

"So she could have been somewhere else?"

"She could have been on the first floor," said Cyan. "But the security cameras in the foyer would have seen her arrive. Plus it was before the cinemas open, so she would have had to swipe to get in and her student card would have been logged. The police must have viewed both the logs and any videos by now."

"So," said Vee. "If this student was outside, how did she know?"

Cyan looked at her mother. Then down at the bun she held in her hands. She took another bite. Vee had asked a good question. Cyan wondered why Katherine's new friend Orlanda had suggested Daniella. She tried to remember the snatch of conversation that she heard when she caught them at the bottom of the stairs. But the only words she could remember were, 'It had to be Daniella.'

"Did you read about the court trial?" said Vee.

Cyan looked up. "Which one?"

"Which one? It was all over the news before your place."

"No? Oh yes!" Cyan nodded.

"So you do remember that woman from the Peck Gang?"

"Peck Gang?" Cyan looked out of the dining-room window and onto the drive that separated Vee's house from her neighbour's.

"You do know. The gambling gang," insisted Vee. "Oh, what was the woman's name? Dancia Dunaway, or Dinah Delany. Some kind of double-D name."

Vee had raised a saffron bun to her mouth and took a bite, and while she chewed the case came back to Cyan. The woman's name was Dancia Dunway and she had convinced a lot of people to invest in a new online casino. Dunway had assured them that the whole enterprise was backed by this Peck Gang, which carried a lot of weight because of the gang's financial activities. In the end, a very bitter one for most of the investors, the casino didn't exist beyond a few images and the gang had never heard of it.

"Oh. Yes. I remember. Dancia Dunway was arrested for fraud."

"Fraud indeed. How did those people think that they could make something out of thin air?"

Cyan shrugged. "They didn't know it was thin air," she said.

"Well, she was sentenced on Thursday," said Vee and took a sip of her tea.

"Pecunia, not Peck."

"Sorry?" said Vee.

"The gang's name was Pecunia," said Cyan. "And I remember more. There was a delay as the police had information that some members from Pecunia were on the islands. I think they were after Dunway." Cyan thought about the picture of the small, scared woman she had seen in the papers. She had no doubt that Pecunia had wanted all the money that she had made.

"Yes!" Vee lowered her cup. "One of them was this young man. Oh I remember him. He was tall and they had his picture on TV."

"They? You mean, the police?"

Vee nodded.

"So they must have caught one of them," Cyan said.

"No," said Vee. "In the end the police thought he had got off the island with his mate. How they missed him at the airports I'll never know. Plus the cruise ships were on their winter break, so he didn't get on one of them."

"But his picture was public, surely someone would have recognised him," said Cyan.

"Maybe not. I mean, it wasn't a real photo, it was just one of those new computer-generated pictures that the police use now and it really made him look handsome. I had to ask myself why such a tall, handsome young man would throw his life away on some gang."

"Easy money."

"Hmm! The only easy money is inherited. And you have to be the only relative alive for that to work." Vee drained her cup. "The jars should be cool enough now," she said.

Cyan followed her mother into the kitchen and pulled a jar of vinegar from one of the cupboards that were carefully positioned to be out of the sun. At the bottom of the jar floated a few mustard and coriander seeds and a few tiny, bright-red chillies. Cyan thought about Pecunia, but after a while the familiar process of making pickles with her mother, along with all Vee's comments and jokes about the world in general as reported on the radio, chased all thoughts from Cyan's mind.

The sun had set by the time she left Vee's house, so Cyan decided to take the bus home. It was a long wait at the bus stop and as she watched a few cars pass by she thought again about the Pecunia Gang. She had not paid much attention to the trial and wondered how much money was involved. Maybe some of their clients made money from a few bets or games, but Cyan knew a lot of lottery players and they never made more than a few dollars. She spotted a bus in the distance and held out her hand.

CHAPTER 12

When Cyan got out of bed on Monday she was half asleep and reluctant to go to work. She was only fully awake by the time she was at the bus stop and that was when her thoughts focused on Katherine and Orlanda. Mainly Orlanda. Her mother had a made a good point. If Orlanda wasn't in the Hub, why would she spread rumours? Once again she tried to remember the conversation she had heard at the bottom of the stairs. Whatever had gone on, Cyan knew that it began with Katherine.

As Cyan approached the Hub she reached into her handbag to pull out her purse. She couldn't find it. She stopped in front of the main doors and dug deeper into her handbag, then walked into the Hub and rested her bag on the first cafe table she came to and put down her travel cup. She had looked through her small shoulder bag and was now deep into her backpack.

"Good morning."

Cyan paused, and looked up to see Cyrus.

"Hello," she said and dug deeper into her backpack in the hunt for her purse and knocked over the travel cup, which fell onto its side and rolled towards the edge of the table, but Cyrus caught it before it reached the table's edge.

"I hoped to catch you. Do you have time for a quick cuppa?"

"What?" Cyan said. She was concentrating more on her search than on Cyrus.

"Of course. If you're busy?"

"What, no. Sorry," said Cyan, at last focusing on Cyrus. "I think I left my purse at home."

"Do you need to borrow some money?"

"No. I've got my cards, I keep them separate. Of course I'll join you for a tea."

Cyrus headed to the bar while Cyan continued to root through her bag. She retrieved her purse from the bottom of the backpack just as Cyrus sat down with two full jewel-coloured mugs.

"I must have put it there on Saturday," she said. "I went to Brixton, well, Bakersfield. How was your weekend?"

If Cyrus had enjoyed a good weekend it didn't show on his face. Cyan stopped the smile that came naturally to her. "What happened?" she said.

"I went to Brixton yesterday," said Cyrus. "Daniella wanted to see me and we met at a cafe. Ridiculously early."

"Oh. How is she? How are you?"

"Daniella is in a bad place and I'm exhausted."

Cyan sipped her tea and waited.

"She started to cry. I mean, what am I supposed to do about that? I can hardly put my arm around her?"

Cyan searched for a response. Nothing appropriate presented itself. "What happened?" she asked instead.

"It went wrong from the start. I greeted her in the traditional Corner way and she told me, quite forcefully, why it was not a good morning for her.

"Daniella believes that the police will charge her with Dayton's murder. And she blames Katherine for that. When she gets back on campus we had better keep them apart."

"I'll try," said Cyan. "At the moment I'm the only reason Fayval hasn't ripped Katherine's head off."

"Ah yes. Katherine's rumour originally came from 'someone in the archives'. I bet Fayval didn't take long to work that one out."

"Not long at all," said Cyan.

Cyrus shook his head. "I could remove Katherine's head myself. Daniella swears that her dad will believe the police and never speak to her again. She barely speaks to him now anyway. You know," Cyrus leant in closer, "after the affair."

Cyan nodded and looked down at her cup.

"And then Daniella produced a copy of the *Sunday Special.*" Cyrus sighed. "Oh boy. Well. We all know who that anonymous source is."

"She read that too?" Cyan's shoulders sagged.

"Oh yes," he said. "And now so have I. And what a title, 'Murdered for Mathematics'. Were they after a literary prize? At least they didn't have a picture of Daniella."

"They didn't have to," said Cyan, "just look up Professor Daniella Waldergrave and Corner Rise University. Then choose."

Cyrus hummed in agreement.

"Is she being held by the police?" said Cyan.

"Nope. She had hoped to be here today. But she can't come back right now. It was bad enough with the gossip, can you imagine after *that* article?"

"Oh come on. Nobody believes that trash."

"But they will believe there's some truth in it. Daniella's scared and I don't blame her. If this story continues, or Katherine opens her mouth again, a bunch of journalists might dig around and find out about why she left the UK."

Cyan twisted a spiral strand of hair around her finger. She suddenly had a lot to say to Katherine and none of it was nice.

The Hub's doors slid open and a group of students walked in. Cyan glanced at her watch. "Nine o'clock. I have to go!" Cyan paused. "I hope you have a better day today."

"So do I. Thanks," said Cyrus.

They rose from the table and Cyrus walked towards the main doors while Cyan headed for the stairs. Fuelled by anger she bounded up the stairs and reached the registry without loss of breath. The shutters were raised and she could see Dylan at his desk.

"Good morning," she said. "Sorry I'm late."

Dylan looked over the counter. "Hello. One minute is hardly late."

Cyan unlocked the door and, after a quick check to make sure no one was behind her, let it swing back in place. Dylan went back to his keyboard.

"I had a quick chat with Cyrus," Cyan said as she hung up her jacket. "He met with Daniella on Sunday morning."

"Oh. After *The Weekender* story?"

Cyan nodded. She put down her empty paisley mug, sat down, put her bags away and logged in to her machine.

"Well," said Dylan after a while. "We all know who that source was."

"Katherine," they both said in unison.

A livelier version of this conversation took place when Zoe arrived. Even though Zoe stood next to the counter they didn't see Katherine until the office door bleeped and opened. Cyan, Dylan and Zoe went silent at the sight of Katherine, who froze like a stranger in a local bar.

"Hello," said Dylan in a monotone voice.

"Good morning," said Katherine. "I have just walked into Professor Cyrus Pepper and he had a lot to say to me."

"And I bet none of it was good or even remotely complimentary," said Dylan.

Katherine bristled. "So I really don't need any more from anyone else," she added.

Cyan didn't care. Katherine always wanted attention and today she would have it. Cyan took a deep breath. Zoe stepped in quickly.

"Okay. Well, we do need to check student registration for the January intake. Do you all have the class lists?"

Cyan and Dylan mumbled an affirmative. Katherine ducked down behind her screen.

Zoe walked over to the small noticeboard attached to the pillar between the counter and the office door. "Cyan. You're on counter duty today?" she asked.

Cyan switched her screen to the registry calendar. "Yes. Yes I am," she said.

"Well," said Zoe. "There shouldn't be many enquiries today. Okay."

Two hours later Zoe gathered some paperwork and left the registry. Cyan decided to count to twenty before she tackled Katherine. She got to ten before Dylan rose out of his seat.

"Did you speak to anyone unusual this weekend?" Dylan said.

Katherine stared at her screen and didn't reply.

"No? Any reporters?" he added.

"I told you!" said Katherine. "I have already had this out with Dr Cyrus—"

"Do you see Cyrus here?" Cyan said.

"Ooh Cyrus," Katherine teased.

"And," Cyan ignored her, "we are not supposed to talk about Dayton's death."

"*You're* not supposed to speak about the case. Nobody told me not to."

"Because you weren't there. You were not even in the building!"

"You didn't have to be in the Hub to know what happened." Katherine smiled smugly as she looked at Cyan.

Cyan could only blink back. "What is wrong with you?" she said.

Katherine's eyes flared up like sudden flames.

"Just tell us if you spoke to *The Weekender*," said Dylan, any patience had left his voice.

Katherine's smile was replaced by thin lips.

Cyan switched screens. "Let's see. 'Professor Dayton King was slumped in the corner of the museum, arms raised to fend off blows, his face fixed with the last emotion he would ever feel. Fear.'"

Dylan snorted.

Cyan swivelled her chair to face Katherine. "Regular little purple prose writer, aren't you?" she said.

"Oh and you saw better?" said Katherine.

Cyan opened and closed her mouth. She felt as if she had been slapped hard.

"Not much to say now?" Katherine smirked and raised an eyebrow.

"How can she?" Dylan's voice filled the registry. "She was one of the people who found the body. Or maybe you just forgot?"

Katherine looked at Cyan and then her eyes flickered briefly towards Dylan before she returned to her screen. Dylan took a few slow, deep breaths as he sat down, Cyan followed his lead.

The registry door opened. The three student support administrators looked up to see a young man enter.

I wonder how much of that he heard, thought Cyan. She took another breath, smiled to make herself better and went to the counter. "How can I help you?"

Zoe opened the registry door just as the young man said his thanks. She held it open for the student as he left. Cyan headed back to her desk, Katherine stared at her screen and, opposite Cyan, Dylan thumped his keyboard.

"Is everything okay?" asked Zoe.

"Fine," said Cyan and Dylan in unison.

Cyan heard Zoe take a deep breath. It was obvious that there had been some form of argument. Zoe walked into her office and wedged the door open. Cyan picked up her telephone's headset and called

Fayval.

"Are you free at lunch today?" she asked.

"No. Some nit has called a lunchtime meeting. I plan to scowl at a presentation while my lunch sits in the fridge."

"How about a quick tea at the Spice Shack after work?"

Cyan was relieved when Fayval agreed and they arranged to meet later.

She put down the headset just as her computer pinged. A message flashed up from Dylan, *I don't think Katherine fully understands the situation.*

Oh she does, Cyan replied. *She just wants to be in the centre of it.*

The centre of a murder? With the murderer still about? My first statement stands, Dylan typed.

Cyan could only agree. She glanced sideways at Katherine, who had a face more thunderous than usual. She kept one eye on Katherine and the other on the clock, hoping to catch her before she bolted. At eleven forty-five Cyan found a discrepancy between the number of students registered on a foundation module and the number of students enrolled. By the time she had untangled the figures it was one minute past twelve and Katherine had gone.

"Crikey," Dylan said in response to Cyan's expletive. "She was fast."

Cyan shook her head and reached for her bags, then she leant to the right of her screen. "Dylan?"

"Hmm?" Dylan replied, his eyes on the screen as he typed.

"Doing anything at lunch?"

"I plan to eat." He smiled up at Cyan. "Want to join me?"

Grey clouds huddled in groups in the sky and Cyan imagined them in discussion about how hard to rain. Dylan sat down and pulled a sandwich box out of his bag while Cyan reached for her tub of home-made tuna and potato salad.

"What is wrong with Katherine?" she asked.

"Where do you want me to start." Dylan looked at his sandwich. "She treats life like a game," he said. "Like a long game of chess. She always tries to be the queen." Dylan bit into his sandwich.

"Well," said Cyan, "her story in the papers didn't help her."

Dylan shook his head. "I don't agree. Katherine didn't get what she wanted from us, but I bet she's lapped up the attention from family and friends elsewhere."

Cyan nodded. "I guessed it was her when I read the made-up job title," she said.

"Yeah. 'Central student officer'? That's obviously student support administrator," said Dylan. "Katherine is *The Weekender*'s source all right, and she wanted everyone to know it."

Cyan watched as he took another bite of his sandwich. She forked some more salad into her mouth. "Have you looked up her student friend?" she asked.

Dylan snorted. "Only because I had to, for work," he said. "I've recently had to send Orlanda an attendance letter. She wasn't around last week."

Cyan stared at Dylan. "But I saw her on campus."

"Oh?" said Dylan. "They didn't see her in class. What was she doing?"

Cyan shook her head. "I don't know," she replied, "I really don't."

The rest of the afternoon passed slowly. No matter what Cyan did she could not get Katherine alone, and she really wanted an answer to Vee's question: who did tell Orlanda to implicate Daniella. It didn't help that neither Zoe nor Dylan hardly left the office that afternoon and Zoe's office door remained open. By four thirty Cyan was heartily fed up with student numbers and registration. Dylan had gone down to the cafe and Zoe had closed her door, which meant that the call was probably confidential. Cyan turned her head towards Katherine, but before she could speak Katherine had switched screens and got up from her desk.

"Where are you going?" said Cyan.

"To the toilet," said Katherine. "Am I allowed?"

Cyan sat open-mouthed as Katherine left. Then her brain regained control of her jaw, closed it and she walked through the office door. She couldn't leave the registry empty so she stood there and waited for Katherine to return.

Katherine glowered at Cyan when she walked back into the registry. "Waiting for someone?"

"Yes, you." Cyan darted to the office door before Katherine got there. "Who told Orlanda that Daniella murdered Dayton?"

The bluntness of her question took Katherine by surprise. She looked Cyan in the eye for the briefest of moments. "What rubbish—"

"This isn't rubbish," Cyan said quickly. "If, when Daniella is cleared she could sue you for libel, so your friend had better have her facts right."

"*My* friend has her facts right, and Daniella will be too busy in prison to sue anybody." Katherine smirked. "I'd like to get back to work, please."

Cyan stood aside. What else could she do? She could hardly hold Katherine in the doorway until she provided an answer.

By the time Cyan reached her desk Dylan was back. It felt like a few seconds before Katherine spoke again.

"See you tomorrow."

Then she was gone. Cyan looked up in time to see Katherine's heel as she walked through the registry door.

"She moved fast," said Dylan. "I swear she must have jumped over the counter, I definitely didn't hear any doors open."

Cyan could only look at the empty doorway. "She must have been desperate to get out," she said. "I bet we weren't the only ones who read that article, maybe she'll think twice before she talks to the press again."

"Course she won't," said Dylan.

Zoe's door opened. She looked at Katherine's empty desk. "Where's Katherine?" she said.

"On her way home," said Dylan.

"Well I guess we'd better all follow her lead. It's been a long day," Zoe said. "Have a good evening."

She walked back into her office and Cyan logged out instantly. She really wanted to talk to Fayval.

It was a short walk from the campus to the Sweet Orchid Spice Shack. Cyan walked past the tables arranged outside and Fayval waved from the bar as she walked through the door.

"What will you have?" said Fayval after Cyan settled.

Cyan looked at her friend's tall glass of iced tea. "One of those."

"Shall we grab one of those tables at the other side of the grill?" said Fayval once Cyan had her drink.

Cyan thanked the bartender and they walked through the half-empty restaurant, past the burnished bronze-roofed open grill to some tables in the corner. The reed blinds had been raised to let in the sunset and Cyan watched as all the flat surfaces outside the window reflected the golden colour of the late-afternoon sun.

"So," said Fayval after they had settled, "what's happened?"

"Where to start?"

"The beginning usually works for me."

Cyan began with the reason she broke her teapot and ended with Katherine's swift exit from the office that day. Fayval sipped her tea slowly and put down her glass.

"I would have paid good money to hear what Cyrus said to Katherine," she said. "But I did hear Katherine and Trevor."

Cyan's glass stopped in front of her lips. "Trevor?"

"Oh yes. You know I had that lunchtime meeting today?"

Cyan nodded and took a sip from her tea.

"Well, it was on the second floor of the Hub, so I used the side stairs. Anyway, I walked into the stairwell and heard them. Trevor asked Katherine, right up front, if she had spoken to the papers. I didn't hear her reply, but it must have annoyed him because the next time he was louder and more forceful."

"I can imagine," said Cyan, who had been on the end of Katherine's drawn-out reply of 'Maybe,' more than once.

"So she shouts, 'Yes, it was me, so what?'"

"She could hardly deny it," said Cyan. "What did Trevor say?"

"He reminded her that Dayton was dead."

"And," said Cyan, "the murderer still not found." Cyan put her glass on the table.

"He didn't say that straight away," said Fayval.

"Really?"

"No. He just wanted to know who had told Katherine to blame Daniella."

"And?"

"She didn't tell him. She just said, 'Wouldn't you like to know,' in that awful fake sing-song voice of hers. It felt like an age before Trevor spoke again. He told her that the murderer was free and could be anywhere. Katherine didn't say a word after that. It must have hit home.

"I was about to walk up the stairs when Trevor spoke again. He must have put some thought into what to say. He said, 'Let me warn you now, a pinky mouse has no business playing with a tom cat.' Katherine shouted that she wasn't a baby mouse and he told her that she was never a tom cat."

Cyan sat back in her chair. "I bet that scared her."

"I don't know, but no words came out of her mouth for a long time. As far as I'm concerned that woman needs to tell the police whatever she knows. And now. Then afterwards she should just leave everything else well alone."

"Yes she should." Cyan sipped her drink. "So what did you do?"

"I was lucky, I stayed in the doorway so they couldn't see me and fortunately they hadn't heard the door bleep open. So I slowly opened the door and slipped outside. Then I buzzed myself back in again. They didn't make another sound, so I stomped up the stairs as hard as I could.

"Trevor bounced down and gave me one of his smiles, that's how I knew it was him. I don't know why, but Katherine was having trouble with the door, so I caught her up and buzzed her onto your floor."

"Her pass doesn't work on the side staircase," said Cyan. "I have no idea why. I keep telling her to go to security and have it set up."

"So Trevor must have let her into the stairwell."

"Nah. She probably followed him in. She does that to me sometimes. Anyway. How was Katherine?"

"A bit shaken, but she recovered quickly enough. She barely managed to say hello."

Cyan drained her drink and set down the empty glass. "What has Trevor got to do with Dayton's death?"

"I don't know," said Fayval. "But I have no intention of being anywhere alone with him at the moment."

"But he found the body with us."

"Maybe. But where was he the night before?"

Fayval's question kept popping into Cyan's mind at different times on her journey home and her head ached by the time she opened her front door. She fed Loki and then herself and settled in front of the TV. She needed something else to concentrate on.

CHAPTER 13

Cyan started work with her mind more on Trevor than the information on her screen. Her plan for that day was to contact absent students and warn them of possible suspension, but her plan had changed. She now wanted to take any post back to the post room as a ruse to speak to Trevor. Of course, nothing was delivered and so she had to think of other excuses.

Cyan's calendar popped up a reminder about a meeting in the afternoon at the tech college. She was only there to make a quorate, which for her meant ninety minutes of trying to look interested. Cyan could hear both Katherine and Dylan type on their keyboards. Katherine was a picture of unhappiness, so Cyan decided that it was best not to talk to her, and Dylan was probably working on last-minute items for the meeting, so Cyan got up and headed to the cafe. Maybe a quick break would get her back into work mode.

Cyan had just joined the short queue at the cafe's bar when she saw Trevor on his way to the security door that led to the basement. Cyan left the queue and thanked her lucky stars.

"Good morning," she said.

Trevor had just raised his identity card to the electronic lock. He turned his head towards her. "Hello, Cyan," he said with his usual smile.

Cyan forced herself to smile back. "I heard you were signed off last week," she said. "How are you now?"

"I'm fine," he said, then looked around him and leant forward. "Actually, I'm really embarrassed. I mean, I fainted?"

"At least you kept your breakfast."

"I didn't expect to see Dayton like that."

"Who did?" said Cyan. "And to think that you had words with Dayton the day before."

"Over a stupid package," said Trevor. He looked back at the door.

"It must have been a really important package then," said Cyan.

"Yeah. You'd think it was made of gold. Well—"

"Hmm." Cyan nodded. "But still, it's not like the post is always labelled correctly. But he was really angry and a trip to the post room would have sorted that."

Trevor's reply was fast. "He also said that I made a fool of him in front of his students."

"Oh yeah, that would do it. But how?" asked Cyan. "Were you in his lecture?"

Trevor faced Cyan. She took an involuntary step backwards.

"He was unhappy with the way Portmore C1 was set up," he said.

"Really?" said Cyan. "Oh." From the look in his eyes Cyan guessed that Trevor knew she wasn't convinced.

"It was the audio equipment. I needed to sort it out."

Really, Cyan thought. "Oh," she said aloud. "Oh you mean the desktop. Dayton would have needed a computer for his lecture."

"Yeah. Yeah. That was it. The audio on the computer wasn't working. I fixed it, but he wasn't grateful."

Cyan gave what she hoped would appear as a real smile. "Sounds like Dayton."

"Well I'd better get back," Trevor opened the door, "afternoon post and all."

"Well, hopefully your evening was better. I'm really into sci-fi and a friend recommended a great book." As Cyan paused for breath she hoped Trevor would speak soon, or she would have to give him the whole plot. To her relief he seemed to relax.

"You've told me plots before but I really don't get science fiction. I had to work overtime. I helped Greg to rearrange the desks in one of the King Building's large seminar rooms and had to rush to meet my friends near The Bridge." Trevor smiled and slowly shook his head. "It must be your influence. We went to the Bakersfield Cinema and I suggested we watch that new science fiction comedy."

"I know the one. Well, it's more a superhero movie, but I've been told that it's very funny."

"Oh it is." Trevor's radio crackled into life and a voice called for him.

"Sorry to have kept you," said Cyan.

"No worries," said Trevor. He had unhooked his radio from his belt.

"Glad to see you're back," Cyan said.

"Thanks."

Trevor dismissed Cyan with a nod and she smiled and left him to join the queue. Behind her Trevor spoke into his radio before his voice was silenced by the security door as it swung shut.

Trevor had lied to her about Dayton, she knew that, but what about the way he said he spent the evening? She glanced over the shoulder to make sure that Trevor was gone, left the queue and walked to the King Collection just as Fayval walked out and locked the door behind her.

"Sorry," said Fayval as she walked past Cyan, "washroom break. Back in a bit."

Cyan stood outside the closed door of the King Collection for a few minutes until she remembered the real reason she was on the ground floor. Fayval was back in the Collection by the time Cyan had bought her a hot chocolate.

"Sorry about that," said Fayval. "Honestly, I can understand why they wanted the Collection here, but it takes ten minutes for the library staff to get here from the King Building. I'd have to use a crystal ball to get them here for when nature called." She looked up at Cyan. "You look confused."

"I am. Did I tell you about Trevor and Dayton?" Cyan said.

They walked into the Collection where Fayval listened without questions.

"Do you know why they argued?" she said after Cyan had finished.

"Well. When I asked Trevor what the problem was he said Dayton was mad about a package."

"I don't believe that."

"Neither did I, and it must have shown on my face because he added that Dayton was probably angry about the sound in C1."

"What?" said Fayval. "Trevor's a porter. They have audio techs to fix the sound in the cinemas, Dayton could have just called them."

"I know," Cyan said. She took a sip of her hot chocolate. The taste was smooth enough to make her pause. "Trevor's got a big secret to hide," she said.

"You don't think Trevor—"

"Murdered Dayton?" said Cyan. No—"

"Why not? After what he said to Katherine. And where was he when Dayton was killed?" said Fayval.

"But."

"Yes. I know Trevor was flat out cold when I saw him the next morning."

"If he did murder Dayton then that was quite a performance," said Cyan. "He would have to be a multiple award-nominated actor."

"So you don't think so?"

"No," said Cyan. "He just told me that he helped rearrange some furniture in a seminar room with Greg and afterwards met up with some friends."

"Did he now?"

"I believe he did. Don't forget, the police would have interviewed him too. And they could check his story, just like they probably checked that the ECC had a meeting that night. Trevor can hardly lie about going to the cinema with friends if the police track down his friends."

"And what if they lied for him?" said Fayval.

Cyan thought quickly. "Data from the ID cards," she said. "Each swipe is logged. Security would have the records. Plus there are cameras outside the Hub's main entrance – they would have recorded him too."

"Maybe he wore a disguise."

"Can you see Trevor in a catsuit?" said Cyan with a chuckle in her voice.

Fayval laughed out loud. Cyan finished her chocolate.

"Seriously," said Cyan, "I have no idea what to do now. I …" Her voice faded as she looked up to see the scowl on Fayval's face. Cyan looked over her shoulder.

"Hello, Katherine," said Fayval.

"Fayval. I've been sent to see where Cyan is," said Katherine.

"Well. Now you've seen. So all good," said Fayval.

Katherine backed out of the door.

"I'd better get back to the registry," said Cyan. "Thanks for listening."

"You're more than welcome." Fayval smiled at Cyan.

Cyan followed Katherine towards the side stairs and watched as Katherine stepped aside. Cyan wondered if Katherine would ever get her staff card reprogrammed.

"So," she said to Katherine, "why does Zoe want me?"

"I don't know."

"I'll just have to ask her why she sent you." Cyan held her card up to the lock.

"Sh-she just wanted to know where you were."

"So she didn't send you?" said Cyan.

She wasn't surprised, if Zoe ever started to monitor staff movement Katherine would be in deep trouble. Cyan held the door open for Katherine and glowered at the back of her head. She had wanted to ask Fayval's advice. It was obvious that Trevor had lied. Okay, so he didn't murder Dayton, she was sure about that, but he was up to something.

Or, she thought, *maybe he's like me. Too interested.*

Katherine walked up to their floor and turned to Cyan. "So," she said. "What were you and Fayval talking about?"

Cyan nearly tripped on the next step. What was with Katherine? Obviously she had completely forgotten the miasma from the day before.

"Sorry?"

"I heard you mention Trevor?"

"Yes," said Cyan as she opened the door to their floor, "you did."

Automatic politeness caused Cyan to hold the door open for Katherine, who ignored Cyan's expression as she stopped in the doorway. "Anything we all need to know?" she said.

The door began to bleep rapidly.

"There will be if I don't close this door," said Cyan. "It's alarmed and will soon let everyone know that it's still open."

Katherine's gaze travelled around the door frame then to Cyan's face. Cyan looked back passively. The bleeps got faster. Katherine stepped out from the doorway and Cyan let the door close behind them. The bleeps stopped and Cyan walked around Katherine and into the registry.

Fortunately Katherine didn't have another chance to ask. Cyan braced herself at lunchtime but Katherine was gone before Cyan had locked her computer. Cyan sent up silent thanks for whoever

Katherine had arranged to meet.

After lunch it seemed that Katherine had forgotten all about Cyan's conversation with Fayval, and Cyan was happy to leave it that way.

"Ready, Cyan?" said Dylan as he rose from his chair.

Cyan looked at her watch, it was three o'clock. "Yep," she said and pulled a reporter's pad from her desk.

"It would be best to shut down too. And take your stuff," said Dylan. "These meetings take ages."

"Where are you going?" said Katherine. "I thought we could walk to the bus stop."

"Meeting at the tech college," said Cyan. "I'm making up the numbers."

She smiled to herself as she followed Dylan out of the office, then looked back over the counter at Katherine's furious face.

"It's on the schedule," Cyan said. "The registry is closed for this afternoon, so I'll lock the door. Have a good evening."

"Mornin'," Katherine said as she walked into the registry the next day.

Cyan fought to keep her eyes on her screen and slowly reached for her tea. "Hello," she said.

Cyan squared her shoulders. Her calendar was empty for the day, Dylan would not be in until later and Zoe wasn't in her office, although a new cardigan hung in view. But for the moment Cyan was alone with Katherine.

Out of the corner of her eye Cyan watched Katherine take off a leaf-green raincoat.

"So. What did you say to Fayval about yesterday? I heard something about Trevor."

Cyan looked up. "Wow. Straight to the point," she said.

"Like a laser." Katherine smiled down at Cyan.

The registry doors opened and Zoe walked through with a laptop in her hand. "Good morning!" she said.

"Zoe," said Cyan. "Hello."

Cyan tried not to smile as the look of surprise in Katherine's eyes changed to annoyance before she straightened herself and replied to their line manager.

"I thought I saw a new cardigan," said Cyan.

"Yes," said Zoe. "Although I don't know why my cousin sent me a black and cream one. But hey."

Zoe rested her laptop on the counter and went back to unlock the registry's door. She picked up her laptop and had barely closed her own office door before Katherine leant across her desk towards Cyan. "So?" she said.

"So what?"

Katherine exhaled loudly. "Why did you mention Trevor to Fayval yesterday?"

The counter bell rang.

"Better crack on," Cyan said before Katherine could open her mouth. She picked up her cup and walked to the counter.

"Good morning. Can I help?"

"Hello," said a young woman in a red raincoat.

Behind her Katherine tutted and a few moments later she walked out of the registry. The student's query was short and she left shortly after Katherine.

Cyan took the opportunity to log out of her desktop and on to the counter's computer. She opened the first of several emails.

"Hello?" The voice deep and richer than a good chocolate mousse.

Cyan looked up. "Can I help you?" she said.

Then she noticed the clothes. This young woman wore a semi-transparent teal blouse with a high-necked, frilled collar. Underneath she wore a deep blue strappy vest. On her shoulder was a tan backpack. Her hair was shoulder-length and black with a dark blue tint. None of the ensemble looked cheap. Cyan felt certain that this was Katherine's student friend, Orlanda.

The woman gave Cyan a smile that shone like a galaxy, but was also strangely familiar. Orlanda appeared aware of Cyan's glance. She lowered her eyes as she reached up and patted her hair. Cyan was puzzled by the student's hand. It was the colour of caramel, which was much lighter than her face. Cyan checked herself.

"Good morning," she said. "How can I help?"

"Can I see Katherine?"

"Katherine?" said Cyan, surprised.

It wasn't unusual for students to ask for individual support administrators by name, but it was unusual for them to ask for administrators who didn't support their department. If this was Orlanda, she should have been more familiar with Dylan.

"Yes. Katherine Welman," the student said.

"Er. She's just gone out for a bit. She should be back soon."

"Can I wait?" She turned and gestured to the chairs lined up against the wall opposite the counter.

"Yes, please do," said Cyan.

Cyan watched as the perfectly dressed student slowly walked towards the chairs. She sat in the one furthest from the door. For the second time Cyan struggled to keep her eyes on the screen. She was sure that she recognised that smile. She quickly looked across at the student, who was busy with her mobile phone.

Of course, she thought. It was Trevor's smile. *Maybe Orlanda's related to Trevor.* Cyan sneaked another peek. The student shared no other features with the porter, just the smile.

Cyan was so wrapped up in this thought that she didn't see Katherine until she was near the counter.

"Now," said Katherine in a drawn-out fashion.

"You've got a visitor," Cyan said quickly. "Your friend Orlanda?" Cyan nodded to the student who had lowered her mobile phone.

"What?" said Katherine. She looked over her shoulder as the student stood up, then glanced at Cyan. "So Orlanda told you her name?"

Bingo, thought Cyan.

"Anyway, why aren't you at your desk?"

"I'm on counter duty this morning," said Cyan. "Remember?"

Katherine glared at Cyan before she spun around to face Orlanda. "Hello, Orlanda," she said.

The student flicked her eyes towards Cyan, who tried to hide behind the computer's monitor. But she stayed at the counter, she wanted to know why Orlanda was there, and slowly moved the mouse around the screen as if occupied. Cyan guessed from the silence that followed that the two women in the registry wanted her to move, which was daft as only a counter separated Cyan's desk from them. Cyan slowly locked the screen, slid off the stool and returned to her desk. She quickly logged back in to her desktop.

"Hello, Katherine." Orlanda's voice had lost the cheerful tone used earlier.

Cyan kept her head down. There were a few hissed words then

Katherine walked into the office. Cyan's eyes flicked towards the counter to see Orlanda staring at Katherine. The Look made Cyan return swiftly to her screen and she sank into her chair.

"Cyan," said Katherine.

"Yes."

"I'm off for a break. See you in a bit."

Cyan was about to argue when she was distracted by the sound of a bag thumping onto the counter. She looked up into Orlanda's face. The look the student gave Katherine was so sharp that it made Cyan's insides try to run for safety. Cyan hid behind her screen again. She didn't move her eyes from the monitor until Katherine and Orlanda had left the registry.

She got up and quickly locked the registry's door, then returned to her desk. She had a lot of questions to ask Katherine about that brief exchange.

She was pulled out of her thoughts by Dylan's arrival.

"Good," he checked his phone, "morning."

"Hello," said Cyan. She watched as he hung up his blue jacket. "How was the dentist?"

"Easy," said Dylan. "Just a check-up. Keep brushing and flossing and all will be well. You must be the only one in the office who hasn't been to the dentist lately."

"I went in September."

He nodded at Katherine's empty chair. "She not in?"

"She had to go out," said Cyan. "I think Orlanda came for her."

"What?" said Dylan. "Why Katherine?"

"I have no idea why. But it didn't look good."

Dylan put his backpack on his desk and then went to unlock the registry door. There was no sign of Katherine for the rest of the morning.

It had started to rain heavily when Cyan went for lunch, so she sat in one of the empty blue leatherette sofas near the Hub's box office. She was lucky enough to be in front of one of the picture windows by the entrance. She looked out as people moved quickly around the campus. Some were lucky enough to have umbrellas and Cyan's attention was drawn to a brightly coloured umbrella which, unlike the others, had stopped on the main path to the Hub. There was a prickly bush between it and Cyan, so she put her lunch box to one side and stood up for a better view. Underneath the neon pink fabric stood Orlanda. Cyan could also see the back of someone else's head. It was covered by a green hood.

Well, thought Cyan, *whoever is with her will be drenched by the time they get here. Wait.*

Cyan leant closer to the window. She recognised the raincoat as the one Katherine wore when she walked into the office that morning. Plus it was the only leaf-green raincoat that Cyan had seen that day.

Katherine didn't face the student and Cyan could see why. The two women didn't appear to be engaged in a friendly chat, instead Orlanda slowly wagged a finger while Katherine barely moved. Although Cyan couldn't see below Katherine's shoulders she could picture her fists firmly on her hips.

Katherine turned her face away from Orlanda and towards the Hub and Cyan sat down quickly. She waited for a few minutes, her eyes on the door as if Katherine would burst in. After a few deep breaths Cyan reached for her lunch box.

"Hello, Cyan."

Cyan jumped.

"Oops," said Dylan. "Didn't mean to startle you."

"No. I'm sorry," said Cyan. "I was ... miles away."

"I wish I was. Just saw Katherine with that absentee student." Dylan gestured towards the window. "It was not pretty. I can see a disciplinary over that."

"Really?" said Cyan.

"Oh yeah. Raised voices. Well, voice. I don't know what Katherine's done, but I doubt she'll get away with it this time."

"Katherine shouted at a student?"

"No. The student shouted at Katherine. She told Katherine to mind her own business, in no uncertain terms. And I definitely heard the phrase, 'You got what you wanted.'"

"Really?" said Cyan. "I wonder what that was."

"Who knows. But for an absentee student, that one," he nodded towards Orlanda's umbrella, "has done very well in her last test."

Cyan's eyes flew open. Dylan nodded. She made sure no one was close. "You don't think Katherine—"

"Gave her the answers?" said Dylan. "I don't know. But I will be asking Katherine a few questions this afternoon. See you upstairs."

"See you."

Cyan watched Dylan head for the main staircase and then checked her watch – she still had a few minutes before she had to get back to the office. Cyan stood and looked out through the window, but the pink umbrella was gone. Out of the corner of her eye she saw Katherine enter through the main doors. Cyan watched her colleague walk towards the stairs and briefly saw the thunder in Katherine's eyes.

What, thought Cyan, *did you get from that student?*

She had a few questions to ask Katherine as well; any gifts from students had to be either refused or declared and usually the former. And what if Dylan was right? Katherine would be disciplined, and probably sacked, Orlanda would be expelled. Whatever followed, it would not be good for Katherine.

CHAPTER 14

Dylan smiled at Cyan across the counter as she walked through the registry door. She stopped behind the counter and gave him a puzzled look while she mirrored his smile.

"Have you heard the news?" said Dylan.

"No?"

"Daniella's off the hook."

"What? Daniella?"

"Yeah. Zoe told me as I walked into the office, then Fayval popped in and confirmed the news. It must be all over college by now. She's no longer a suspect."

Cyan's smile broadened. "I am so relieved to hear that." She pressed a hand to her chest and gave silent thanks to the student with the experiment.

"Most people will be."

"Most people?" said Cyan. "I thought everyone would be. Okay, Daniella is not always the easiest—"

"*The Weekender?* The secret source?"

"Huh?"

Dylan looked Cyan in the eye and leant his head to one side.

"Ooh," said Cyan. "I bet Katherine feels like a fool right now."

"I hope so," Dylan said. "That said. Where is she?"

Cyan looked over at Katherine's desk. "She walked into the Hub before I had finished lunch. She's not here?"

"Nope."

"Maybe she already knows," said Cyan. "She did look pretty mad after lunch."

She walked into the office, hung up her jacket and settled at her desk. She had just logged on when Katherine arrived with a face that told her colleagues not to bother her. Cyan glanced up at Dylan who raised his eyebrows. Suddenly she wanted to warn him not to ask any questions about class tests.

Zoe stepped out of her office the minute Katherine sat down.

"Cyan. Great," she said. "Hello, Katherine."

Zoe walked to the end of Katherine's desk and Dylan rotated on his stool to face them. She smiled, oblivious to the tempest that raged on Katherine's face. Cyan scooted her chair away from her colleague.

"Heard the news?" said Zoe.

"Yes I have!" Cyan said.

Katherine looked from Cyan to Zoe and back again. Their smiles were infectious and soon she smiled too. "What news?" she said.

"Daniella is no longer a suspect," said Zoe.

"What?" said Katherine. The smile fell from her face.

"Daniella?" said Cyan. "She's no longer a suspect."

"But I heard she was here by the Hub!" said Katherine. She looked as if she had just been kicked.

"From whom?" said Zoe.

Cyan felt as if the temperature in the room had dropped to below zero. Katherine's eyes flitted from Zoe to Cyan to Dylan.

"I just heard." Katherine's voice had gone quiet.

For a moment nobody spoke. Zoe cleared her throat. "Extensions and deferrals for the coming exams," she said. "If you could put together a report on your programmes and let me know? Thanks." She slipped into her office and left the door open.

Cyan tilted her face towards Katherine. "So. Have you informed *The Weekender* of your mistake?" she said.

Katherine glared at Cyan, a stare that would normally cause Cyan to back down. "When I told them, I thought it was the truth."

Before Cyan could open her mouth to reply Dylan spoke.

"Well," he said. "If you're speaking the truth you can tell me how a student, who is rarely seen in the tech college, let alone any classes, manages to get ninety per cent on her test."

"Your students are your problem!" said Katherine.

"Not when it's your friend."

"Huh?"

"Orlanda?" said Dylan.

"What have her tests got to do with me?" said Katherine.

If she was concerned it didn't make it to her face.

"Those multiple choice things are what? Five years old or something," she said. "You can probably buy the answers online." Then her eyes grew to the size of golf balls. "You think I gave her the answers?"

Dylan crossed his arms and leant back against the counter. Katherine looked at Cyan, who stared back blatantly.

"Do you think I'm mad?" Katherine said.

"No," said Cyan truthfully.

"So what did Orlanda pay you for?" said Dylan.

Katherine's head whipped back to Dylan so fast that Cyan thought it would fly off. It took a few minutes for Katherine to compose herself.

"Y-you listened—"

"Overheard," said Dylan. "As did a lot of people. Orlanda really bawled you out."

Katherine glanced around the room. "I don't even look at your programmes."

Cyan agreed, Katherine barely looked at the programmes she was responsible for.

"I believe her," she said to Dylan.

Dylan's eyes flicked towards Cyan. He nodded, uncrossed his arms and perched on the counter stool with an eye on Katherine. She turned to her screen and placed her hands on either side of the keyboard. Cyan watched the skin tighten across Katherine's knuckles.

Cyan's telephone rang.

"You've heard the news?" said Fayval.

"I have! What happened?" said Cyan.

"You'll have to ask Cyrus for the details, but basically she overhead someone say experiment and her memory flooded back."

"So they have evidence to prove that she couldn't have done it?"

Katherine inhaled sharply. Cyan ignored her.

"The police kept quiet about that," said Fayval. "But they must have. How's the snitch?"

"Not good."

"You know," said Fayval, "Katherine is going to need three-sixty-degree vision when Daniella's on campus."

"And the rest," said Cyan. "Are you free after work?"

"Not today. I've been invited to dinner."

Cyan hid her disappointment, she had hoped for a good chat about Daniella on the bus home.

After Cyan hung up she wondered if Cyrus would catch the bus towards Three Trees after work. She wrote an email to him and tried to go back to work.

"Hey, Cyan," said Dylan. "Daniella's made the news again."

Cyan pulled up a new site. It was a small article about the murder, which mainly warned that nobody had been arrested yet, but it did have a good picture of Daniella at an awards ceremony.

"Finally," said Cyan. "They've got it right. *Dr* Dayton King, *Professor* Daniella Waldergrave."

The silence next to Cyan became too much to ignore and she looked at Katherine, who sat as still as a rock, her bottom lip pinched between index finger and thumb. For the first time she looked worried.

No, thought Cyan. *She's scared.* A drop of concern formed in Cyan's mind. "Katherine?"

"You warned me about libel, and I've just read up about it," said Katherine. "The news mentioned Daniella and legal advice. She'll get a lawyer on to me. I'll be in the news again. They'll be all over me."

The drop of concern evaporated. "Oh," said Cyan. "So it was okay to do that to Daniella?"

"It's not my fault," she said.

Katherine pushed her chair back and grabbed her bag from under her desk. Cyan felt like a compressed spring. She was about to open her mouth, but no words came out when she saw Katherine's bag. It was tan with a sapphire-blue flap. Cyan watched as Katherine slung the bag over her shoulder and walked out of the registry. Dylan acknowledged her departure with a grunt.

Cyan waited until Katherine was out of the registry and looked online for the bag. She wished she had noted the name of the shop, it would have made her search easier. It took her a few minutes to find.

"Dylan?"

He twisted the counter stool around to face Cyan. "Hmm?"

"Have you ever heard of Terrance Warru?" she asked.

Dylan thought for a while. "What does he do?"

"Very expensive shoes," said Zoe from her office doorway. "More than I would want to pay. Why?"

"Katherine's got one," said Cyan. "One of the bags anyway."

"Probably fake," said Zoe. "They've got knock-off ones all over Centro Base market." She tilted her head towards Katherine's chair.

"She just went out," said Dylan.

"Probably needs a break," said Zoe. "When she comes back could you ask her to see me?"

Cyan nodded and Zoe returned to her office.

"I could do with a bit of a break," Cyan said. "You okay for a while?"

Dylan surveyed the empty registry. "I think I can hold them back."

Katherine wasn't in the cafe when Cyan got there, so she joined the queue at the bar. She picked up snatches of conversation and heard Daniella's name several times. She smiled and pulled out her mobile phone to distract herself.

"Cyan!"

Cyan looked up as Trevor approached.

"Good afternoon," she said.

"Yes it is. What great news. It's all over the campus."

As the queue shrank they both described how they found out about Daniella.

"Did Greg put out a radio call?"

"Oh yes," said Trevor. "He was in the Mann Building and let every porter know."

"Really? I was joking when I asked that."

"Oh come on. We've got to get our news from somewhere. Anyway, you going back to the office?"

"Yep."

"Can you take this up with you?" He pulled an envelope out of his post bag.

Cyan pretended to struggle under the weight of the envelope. "I'll try," she said.

Trevor's response was his usual sunshine smile.

"I met someone who smiles exactly like you," said Cyan.

"I doubt it. This is one hundred per cent original."

"Well, maybe not exactly." Cyan moved up the queue. "Do you know someone called Orlanda?"

Trevor thought for a second. "Nope."

"Oh." Cyan was surprised. "She dresses like a celebrity. Expensive clothes, perfect make-up, perfect hair. She has the figure for it all."

Trevor shook his head and Cyan knew that to be the truth. She looked at the cakes on display, which included her favourite Pastel de Nata, and decided she should pass.

"How do you know this person?" said Trevor.

"Hmm? Oh. Katherine knows her." Cyan's mind was on whether to swap her hot chocolate for herbal tea. "Why?"

"Well, if there's someone on campus with my smile I should take a look at her." Trevor's eyes twinkled.

Cyan fought the urge to make any further comments. She remembered how many heads turned when Orlanda walked through the Hub's doors and wondered how Trevor would have missed this student. The person in front of Cyan stepped aside and the barista looked at her then up at Trevor.

"I'd better be off. Have a good afternoon." Trevor left the queue and headed for the Collection.

"How can I help you?" said the barista.

Cyan handed over her travel mug. "Can I have a cup of tea and an orange cupcake, please?"

There was no sign of Katherine when Cyan got back to the registry. Dylan was back at his desk and looked up as Cyan walked in. He eyed the cupcake in her hand and chewed his lower lip.

"Can you hold the fort?" he asked.

"No problem," she said as Dylan rose from his chair.

Cyan took a fork from her desk and started on her afternoon treat. She was lost in the orange smell and bittersweet taste of the cupcake when her computer chimed at her. Cyan took a sip of her tea and opened her email. At the top was one from Cyrus.

Hi, Cyan,

Excuse the late reply. I have been in tutorials most of this afternoon.

I cannot tell you how pleased and relieved I feel about Daniella, I was on the phone to her as soon as I heard. That shut up some of the gossips around her straight away. I was about to lose it with these loose-lipped people I work with.

I will finish at five today. Meet at the Gatehouse?

Kind regards,

Cyrus

Cyan answered yes and went back to her cake. She was halfway through her sweet treat when Dylan walked into the office with his own. It was a while before Katherine returned and she didn't look happy. Katherine's mood didn't change as the afternoon ground on and Cyan was glad to logout and leave at the end of the day.

CHAPTER 15

"I told Katherine that Zoe wanted to see her. She didn't thank me for the message," Cyan said to Cyrus as they waited at the bus stop that evening after work. "I've no idea what was said, but Katherine wasn't smiling when she eventually sat down at her desk."

"I'm not surprised. Over an hour. Where was she?"

"I don't think it was about that," Cyan said. "We had a bit of a … an altercation before Katherine left the office. About that article."

"The first of many," said Cyrus. "Did she honestly think she would get away with that? And why Daniella? I have never seen Daniella and Katherine so much as nod to each other."

Cyan realised that one of the people in the bus queue behind them had stopped talking on their phone. She walked away from the stop, Cyrus following.

"I doubt that person knew who we were talking about," said Cyrus.

"They had a college staff pass and would have had to be living under a rock to avoid the news. People pointed at me for days after Dayton's body was found."

Cyrus nodded. "Me too," he said. "Now they'll do it to Katherine."

"That's one bit of attention even she won't like."

A woman in the queue raised her arm and Cyan looked down the road to see their bus. She began to walk back towards the bus stop but Cyrus stopped her. He nodded towards the Gatehouse. Daniella had stepped out and was about to walk in the opposite direction when Cyrus waved. She waved back and walked over to join them. Cyrus moved further away from the bus stop and towards the iron railings at the front of the campus. Cyan followed.

"All's well?" said Cyrus.

Daniella sighed. "Yes it is," she said. "Good evening, Cyan."

"Er. Good afternoon," said Cyan.

"Afternoon? One day I'll get the hang of Corner Rise times."

"I haven't seen you since—"

"Since *that* article. I heard it was Katherine?"

Cyan and Cyrus stared straight ahead in a desperate bid to avoid catching each other's eye.

"Hmm," Daniella said. "I can tell from both your faces that it was. Well. I haven't found her yet. But when I do she'll need an army of lawyers to protect her from me."

Daniella glared at the floor, which Cyan thought was fortunate as Katherine had just walked out of the Gatehouse. She saw Cyan and raised her chin, looked Cyrus up and down as if he had climbed out of a bin and then she saw Daniella. Katherine's eyes bulged and Cyan managed not to laugh as she backed slowly out of sight. Cyan gave her attention back to Daniella.

"Oh he was very understanding," Daniella was saying.

Cyan wondered what she had missed, but she didn't want to interrupt.

"I always thought he was a good man to have as head of the department," said Cyrus.

"Yes, Paul is. He's let me have time off," said Daniella. "Funny that, when I was under suspicion I just wanted to work, but now I just need to rest. Fortunately I've covered all my topics, I can do any revision online. I spent all afternoon with IT."

Cyrus nodded.

"So," said Cyan cautiously, "when did the police let you know?"

"Late this morning. That DS Phyllida Brookes told me, what did she say, 'no longer needed with our enquires'. New evidence had turned up. At first they didn't want to say what the evidence was, but I pressed them. I mean," Daniella looked at Cyrus, "I had been called into that police station so many times I should have been given a staff pass."

"What was this new evidence?" said Cyrus.

Cyan kept quiet, this was Daniella's moment.

Daniella looked at them both. "It was a student experiment, broken at the time when … whoever killed Dayton left the Hub. It was then I remembered. After speaking to him I decided to settle my nerves with a drink in the Students Union. I was just so angry with the man, I thought a glass would relax me." Daniella snorted. "But after, goodness knows how many glasses, I was even madder than before. I knew what I wanted to say to him and I was so focused." Daniella smiled. "Dayton would have liked that."

"What happened next?" asked Cyan.

"I nearly walked into the prickly bushes to get to him, that's what happened next. I realised my mistake and walked back towards the path and to the dragon tree near the Hub. I felt a bit woozy and leant on the tree to steady myself."

"How did you know he would be there?" asked Cyrus.

"Dayton planned to meet someone that night. He boasted about how he had easy entry to the King Collection. Goodness knows how he got that. He couldn't charm anybody, let alone Fayval. Oh," Daniella looked up, "your bus."

Cyan glanced at the bus.

"I'm okay. I need the 5B," said Cyrus. "It goes to Centro Base. You okay, Cyan?"

"Yes. Of course. I can get either bus," Cyan said. She faced Daniella as the 5A bus slowed down and stopped to collect passengers. "Did Dayton say who?" she asked.

"No," said Daniella. "He just gave that secretive smile of his. It made me want to slap him."

Cyan remembered that smile and tried not to grind her teeth. Dayton used it when he thought he possessed secret knowledge.

"Sorry," said Daniella. "You both must have places to get to."

"No rush," said Cyan.

"We could go back to the Cinema Cafe or the canteen?" said Cyrus.

Daniella shook her head. "I only came in to sort out online tutorials. Don't get me wrong, people are so kind and patient with me. But I'm a bit embarrassed by it all. I would rather be back when it's calmed down a bit."

For a moment Cyan felt like she understood what Daniella meant, but then she hadn't been accused of murder and repeatedly questioned, so couldn't know for sure. She decided now was time to let the professor go.

"But it has been good to talk," said Daniella. "Maybe we could go somewhere else?"

"How about Vincent's?" said Cyan. "It's not far."

Daniella caught the eye of two people who had just left the Gatehouse. They did a double take when they saw her.

"Okay," she said.

They waited for a gap in the traffic and crossed over to a small piece of parkland, then they walked in silence until they reached the Spice Shack. They picked a table as far from the door and bar as possible.

"Drinks?" said Cyrus when they were seated.

"Beer," said Daniella. "Any kind. Mini bottle, please."

Cyan asked for the same.

Cyrus went to the bar and Daniella asked Cyan a few questions about her day. Cyrus rejoined them with drinks and a wooden spoon with the number five painted on it.

"You ordered food?" said Daniella.

"Just some spiced potato wedges," he said. "Cheers!"

They clinked glasses and sipped at their drinks. Cyan hoped Daniella would mention more about the night Dayton died, but didn't want to press her.

Daniella smiled as if she had read Cyan's mind. "I keep thinking about it. That night. I thought I was the last person to see Dayton alive. Well, I wasn't. But I was the first one to see the murderer though." She shuddered.

"What?" said Cyrus. Cyan's fingers covered her mouth as she gasped.

"Well I was. While I was behind the dragon tree when I thought I saw Dayton near the bushes." Daniella stared past them as if she could see the scene again. "But it wasn't him. The person I saw left the path, then I heard the crunch and they tripped and landed hard. I tell you, that person was on their feet like a stunt man, and they cursed all right. The voice could have been Dayton's, it was deep enough."

"Another man?" said Cyrus.

"Must have been," said Daniella. "To grab that statue from the top shelf and whack him hard enough to kill him?"

Cyan nodded.

"I must admit, when I thought I saw Dayton fall, I smiled. I wanted to ask him if he felt focused enough."

Opposite Cyan, Cyrus put his glass down hard. Daniella carried on as if she hadn't noticed.

"Instead I watched as they took really wobbly steps and stopped to rub their shin. It must have been the drink that made me think it was Dayton. I actually smiled as he – they – hobbled back towards the path.

"Then the person looked at me." Daniella leant back in her chair as if she had been poked in the chest. She took a large breath and continued. "That look could have penetrated a nuclear bunker. It made me jump back behind the tree. Then I heard someone behind me. I turned to see torches and realised it was the nightwatchmen. I was relieved, I can tell you. I nearly called to them too, but they headed off towards the technical college. By the time I looked back at the Hub the person had gone."

Cyan glanced at Cyrus, who swallowed hard.

"I am so lucky," said Daniella.

"Really?" said Cyan. "How can you say that?"

"Daniella didn't shout, or call to anyone," said Cyrus.

"Which meant that the murderer had no idea I was there," said Daniella. "They didn't see me. Now I know who that person was, I ask myself, what they would have done if they knew I was there?"

Cyan exchanged a look with Cyrus just as the potato wedges arrived. They thanked the waitress and looked at Daniella.

"I'm not all right," she said. "But I will be. The only people I've told that to are the police, and you two now. Thanks for listening." She reached for her fork. "Those wedges look good."

Cyan looked at the wedges and realised that she was hungry. "Yes they do," she agreed.

Cyrus nodded and they all tucked in.

CHAPTER 16

Cyan and Cyrus spoke about future ECC meet ups on the bus journey home. They tried to talk about Daniella, but the idea that Daniella's silence had saved her life made them both shudder. As Cyan walked the short distance uphill from the bus stop to her apartment she thought about what the police had to go on. Someone tall with a pair of eyes that could startle a professor. Not much really.

Cyan stopped at the apartments' letter boxes and checked for post, as there was nothing there she pushed past the overgrown bushes to the front door.

"Good evening, neighbour."

The sound of Gustavo's voice brought her back from her thoughts. She looked past the bushes as he stopped at the letter boxes.

"Good evening. How are you?" Cyan said.

"Not as preoccupied as you." Gustavo smiled. He looked inside his box. "Any chance of a story?" He pulled out an envelope and locked the box shut.

"Probably not." She slid her backpack from her shoulders to the floor and told Gustavo the latest news from the campus. "I don't understand why they wasted so much time on Daniella."

"By they," said Gustavo, "you mean, the police?"

"Sorry, yes. But really? Daniella?"

"Hmm. Was there any clue about the type of person the police were after?"

"Well." Cyan looked at her backpack. "All I've heard was that the person had to be tall. The statue used to kill Dayton was up on a high shelf and there were only his footprints on the kick stool. Well, smudged ones – Cyrus sat on it for a bit."

Gustavo nodded. "That would be the offender profile. I guess Daniella is tall?"

Cyan stared at Gustavo. "Of course," she said. "Daniella is at least a head taller than Dayton. When they fought he either had to stand well back or look her in the throat."

"Then that's why."

Cyan sighed. "Well, that's two weeks gone since the murder. What will the police do now? The crime scene has been cleaned up. People have walked through the Hub and sat on the grass around it. Any other clues have to be gone by now."

"I can ask the police," said Gustavo.

"How?"

"I can call them. I'm a journalist remember?"

"Gustavo," Cyan picked up her backpack, "you write celebrity gossip."

"So. This is a big story. Plus celebrities go to university too. Even Corner Rise."

Cyan was tempted to ask which celebrity, but instead she shrugged. "Why not," she said.

"I'd better get to it before *The Weekender*'s secret source gives up another piece of useful information." Gustavo winked.

"Oh I doubt that will happen," said Cyan as she opened the front door. "Daniella knows that Katherine was the secret source."

"Ouch."

"And, to quote Daniella, 'an army of lawyers', will not keep Katherine safe."

Gustavo whistled.

"See you later?" said Cyan at the foot of the stairs.

"Whether I have news or not," said Gustavo.

Cyan walked up the stairs to her apartment and Loki mewed loudly as she opened the door. Loki twisted around Cyan's legs and she bent down to lightly scratch the cat's head. Loki, apparently satisfied, led the way to the kitchen with her tail in the air.

Cyan fed the cat and kept one eye on the clock as she prepared her dinner. She rushed to the door and opened it on the first knock. Behind her a pot bubbled on the cooker.

"Hi," she said to Gustavo, "would you like to come in?"

"Thanks, but I've got the oven on." Gustavo glanced at his watch. "Anyway, I spoke to the police and they spoke to me."

"What did they say?" said Cyan.

"The police did have another suspect," he said, and leant against the door frame, "but they had a solid alibi."

"Oh no."

"But I did do a bit of research when I got off the phone. I called them back to ask about Pecunia."

"Who?"

"That gambling organisation."

"Oh yes. My mum reminded me of them," said Cyan.

"When we saw those shoes in Plaza Verde you said they looked similar to the ones Dayton had on. You know. Brown uppers with different coloured soles."

"I'm sure they were. That's what I saw first."

"They were." Gustavo nodded. "I reread it in the early reports, but remind me. Where did Dayton live?"

"Mimosa Gardens."

"So how did he afford all that?" said Gustavo.

Cyan shook her head. She really didn't know how.

"Think about it," said Gustavo. "Lecturer salary, apartment in Mimosa Gardens, Terrance Warru shoes? I can't help but think that there is a link between Dayton and Pecunia."

Cyan could only blink in reply. "I doubt Dayton would gamble," she said.

"You don't sound too sure."

"I won't believe it. The way he used to boast about how well he was doing. I mean, he got Cyrus to witness the contract on his apartment."

"I bet he did. Hide everything in plain sight. Did anyone ever ask how he could afford all this."

"Only one person. A colleague. He took one look at Mimosa Gardens and wanted to know what Dayton's side hustle was."

"Hustle is right," said Gustavo. "Come on. You pointed out those shoes to me. You saw the price of them."

"So he used a credit card?" Cyan knew she sounded weak.

Gustavo shook his head. "Then how does he pay for his apartment?"

"Oh."

"I don't think Dr King was all he seemed to be," he said. "And I don't think the police do either."

"But he ..." Cyan trailed off.

"A man on his salary would have to get himself into a load of debt to live the way he did. And without a promotion, how would he get out of it?"

"He'd need more than a promotion." Cyan chewed her lower lip.

"Would you have ever described Dayton as dumb?"

"What? No."

"So, he knew if he kept spending more than he earned he would end up in trouble. He had to make money somehow."

"What?" Cyan almost laughed. "He got himself into debt and had to find a quick way out of it? Sorry, no."

"Or," said Gustavo. "He made a lot from his first try with Pecunia. Liked what he got and kept on going."

Cyan bobbed her head slowly. "Yes. That would be Dayton. I bet he believed that he couldn't get hooked."

They stood in silence for a few seconds.

"They've had another look at the CCTV footage," said Gustavo. "They reckon the murderer knew the campus."

Cyan stared at him for a few seconds. "What? Are the police sure?"

"Yes. They've just released that information. The murderer left the Hub by the fire doors at the side, without so much as a peep."

Cyan raised her hand to her lips. "Those doors only sound an alarm when they are forced from outside," she said through her fingers.

Gustavo nodded. Then he sniffed. "Is there something burning?"

"Oh no!"

Cyan wished Gustavo a hasty goodnight as she closed the door and ran to the kitchen. Fortunately her chicken stew was not too badly burned, as long as she didn't scrape the bottom of the pot. She took her dinner through to the living room and looked through the window, down the hill to the main road. It was already dark and the clouds reflected the light sweeping across the bay from the lighthouse. Cyan watched the light for a while, then put down her plate and closed the curtains.

She turned and got to her plate just as Loki walked into the living room. Raising the plate, she smiled at the cat. "You've had yours."

Cyan sat down. She didn't want to admit that Gustavo was right. Dayton must have been involved with Pecunia, how else could he have paid for those shoes and lived in Mimosa Gardens? She tried to ignore the thought that Pecunia probably had a lot to do with why Dayton was dead. She got up to switch on the radio, chose a music station and sat down to eat.

CHAPTER 17

The next day Cyan sat at her desk in silence. Both Dylan and Zoe had taken the day off and Katherine had barely managed to greet Cyan before she sat at the counter. There she swapped her attention between her mobile phone and the counter's computer. Cyan had tried to call Fayval but only got through to voicemail. She thought about Cyrus, but with end-of-term exams on the horizon she knew that he would be busy.

Cyan stared at her desk, maybe she should give it a clean. She looked over the counter to the empty registry, her mind wandering back to the previous day and Katherine's absence from the office.

Katherine doesn't have to answer my questions, Cyan thought as she left her desk and walked past her towards the kitchenette. She opened a cupboard and pulled out a bottle of spray cleaner and a cloth. Cyan paused on the way back to her desk. Katherine had her eyes on celebrity news and didn't bother to switch the screens when she heard Cyan behind her.

"Oh. Hello, Cyan. Again."

Cyan watched as Katherine switched to an article about some singer's new baby boy. She fought the urge to retreat.

"How are you?"

Katherine looked up from her screen to the empty floor in front of her. "Quiet," she said.

Outside the registry, the lift doors opened. There was a murmur of voices, a laugh and the lift doors closed again.

"Got anywhere with your investigation?" Katherine said.

"Sorry?" Cyan nearly dropped the bottle.

"The murder?"

Cyan sighed. She put the bottle and the cloth on the counter, pulled out another stool from under the counter and adjusted the height.

"Well?" said Katherine.

"I only asked a few questions."

"Is that so? Well," Katherine twirled a long, thin, blue-tinted plait around her finger, "now so am I."

"Really?"

"Yes, really," said Katherine.

Cyan stared at Katherine, who seemed to look through the screen in front of her, her lips as thin as a sheet of paper. Cyan changed her mind about the stool.

"Well," said Cyan. "Better get back."

"I've been made a fool of." Katherine's voice was metallic. "I was lied to about Daniella and then encouraged to go to the press. They even gave me a contact to speak to."

Cyan sat back down. "Did you know about Daniella before Zoe—"

"No. I did not."

"So why did you argue with that student about Daniella?" Cyan said to herself.

"We didn't argue about Daniella."

Cyan jumped, landed badly and just managed to balance herself on the stool. "Sorry. I didn't mean to say that out loud."

Katherine smiled at Cyan's acrobatics. "Well you did," she said. "I was angry because Orlanda believed that she could tell me what to do, just because she's rich and thinks she's important. Do you know that she paid someone to log in as her and take that test she scored so well on? She actually bragged about that!"

"Oh."

"Oh indeed. It's not like I can accuse her without evidence." Katherine grunted. "She probably knew that Daniella had been cleared before she met me and she didn't even say." She threw the plait over her shoulder. "Well," she continued. "That will change soon."

"Why?"

Katherine smiled. "I know who murdered Dayton."

This time Cyan gripped her stool. "Really? Who?"

Katherine remained silent.

"No," said Cyan after some thought. "Don't tell me. Tell the police."

"Why? What will they do?"

Cyan stared at Katherine in disbelief. "Lock the person up?"

"Not before I speak to them." Katherine raised her chin.

"Katherine! This is a murderer!"

Katherine's eyes shot towards the registry's open door. "Keep your voice down."

"But—"

"It was an accident. It wasn't meant to happen. They—" She shut her mouth suddenly.

"They? Only one person was seen near the Hub that night. Who's they?"

"Toilet break." Katherine slid off her chair and walked towards the office door. "Cover the counter will you?"

"Katherine!" said Cyan.

She stood as Katherine walked through the office door. Cyan chased her – this time Katherine would answer her. She opened the office door as two people walked into the registry, behind them Katherine smirked and left in a flash of blue and red. Cyan suppressed a sigh and put on her work face.

"Good morning, how can I help," she said.

Their query took less than five minutes to answer and after they had left Cyan followed procedure and closed the registry door. She went back to her seat and glanced over at Katherine's desk. Katherine's new handbag leant against the wall.

"Hmm."

She put her mobile phone in her desk drawer and locked it. Then she followed Katherine to the toilets.

Cyan was soon back in the registry. Katherine wasn't in the toilets, she wasn't in the cafe either and Cyan had no desire to walk around the Hub in search of that woman. She sat at her desk and waited.

"This," said Cyan to the empty office, "is why we need more registry staff."

She wrote an email to Zoe, read it through, decided to wait until the afternoon to send it and saved it as a draft.

By eleven thirty Cyan was furious. This time she would complain, formally. She didn't care what happened to Katherine. At twelve noon she closed the counter's shutters and went down to the King Collection.

"What is wrong with that woman?" Fayval said as she filled the kettle in the archive's kitchenette. "You don't mess with a murderer."

"I know. I think Dylan was right, Katherine treats everything like a game. I would have been scared witless."

Fayval flicked the switch at the base of the kettle. "Katherine isn't scared. Sounds to me like she thinks she's in charge."

Cyan sighed. She turned towards the kitchenette's window and looked at the small holly bush outside. A tiny bird popped out briefly from between the deep green leaves.

"So," Fayval said. "I guess you have to tell the police."

Cyan looked at Fayval. "What? Again?" she said.

"Again?"

"I told them about the experiment. Remember?"

"True," said Fayval, "but it looks as if Katherine has turned fool. You can't play games with someone who's killed before—"

"We only have Katherine's word for it," Cyan said quickly, "just like the story she told that reporter."

"You think. You sounded pretty convinced to me."

Cyan pressed her lips shut. What would she say to the police? My colleague knows who murdered Dayton? Why not? Last night she was worried that the case would never be solved, today she'd heard news that could do just that.

"Fayval, you're right, I will phone the police," said Cyan.

"Good. Before you do, did she say more when she got back?"

"That's the cheek of it," said Cyan. "I was stuck behind the counter for the rest of the morning. By the time it reached midday I was pretty mad, so I closed the shutters and left the registry."

"I hope you've made a complaint," said Fayval.

"It's drafted and ready to go." Cyan looked at the bush outside again. "Actually," she said, "that's really weird, she left without her bag."

"Is that unusual?" said Fayval.

"Very, especially a new one. That's why I thought she would only be a few minutes. Not the rest of the morning."

Fayval handed Cyan a mug and she inhaled the sweet smell of

cinnamon spiced tea. "Should I talk to Katherine before I call the police?" she said.

"I don't see why. Let the police interview her, they've had more practice."

They spent the rest of lunch talking about holiday preparations. Cyan was planning a quiet Christmas with her mum, her brother would handle Christmas Eve, while Fayval would be cooking up a banquet for her family. Cyan's phone rang – she pulled it out of her bag and read the screen, it was Cyrus. Cyan apologised to Fayval as she answered it.

"Where on earth are you?" he said.

Cyrus's tone made Cyan pull the phone away from her ear and look at it. Fayval gave Cyan a quizzical look.

"In the King Collection?" Cyan said. "What are you so excited about?"

"The police have been called in again."

Cyan lowered the phone from her ear and looked up at Fayval.

Once again Cyan found herself on the wrong side of blue police tape. She sat at one of the square wooden-topped tables in the cafe and watched as a member of security staff swiped open the door next to the lifts that led to the main stairs. He held it open for two police officers. A few tables away from Cyan another uniformed police officer sat with Fayval – Cyan had just given a statement to the same man. The door next to the lift opened again and in walked Inspector Torrington. It was the palm-green polo shirt in a cloud of black police uniforms that made him stand out. The inspector gestured to the police officer, who nodded to Fayval and went over to speak to him. Cyan briefly caught Fayval's eye before she gave her attention to the pattern in the woodgrain on the table top.

"Good afternoon."

The voice made Cyan jump. She looked up into the face of Inspector Torrington, then down at his shoes. Soft black leather and almost as silent as a feather.

"Good afternoon," said Cyan. "What's happened?"

"Well," said Torrington. "I'm here to find out. But I do know that I'm back in Corner Rise University with you, Mrs King and Professors Pepper and Waldergrave. Oh, and a very disturbed senior porter." He flicked through his notepad. "Mr Gregory Thomas?"

"Greg? What happened to him?"

"Do you mind if I sit down?"

"No. Please do," said Cyan.

"It's to do with Ms Welman."

"Katherine?"

"Yes. Mr Thomas found her, she's in one of the meeting rooms on the second floor."

"What's she doing there?"

Torrington didn't reply.

Cyan's gaze slipped towards the floor. She blinked and fumbled in her bag for a tissue. Torrington sat next to her in silence.

"Sh-she's dead?"

"The medical examiner is not here yet, so I can't say right now. I'm sorry."

Cyan nodded, to her, he did sound sorry.

Inspector Torrington flipped open his notebook. "You work with Ms Welman?"

Cyan was glad that he used the present tense. Maybe Katherine wasn't dead.

"Yes. In the Crown Campus Registry. She left the office sometime before lunch."

The interview was short. Torrington didn't have to ask many questions as Cyan quickly told him all that she remembered from that morning. Torrington's face displayed little emotion as he closed his notebook.

"I should have called you straight away." Cyan unfolded the tissue for the umpteenth time. "If I had just said."

Torrington shook his head. "No," he said. "Ms Welman could have known who murdered Dr King long before she told you. She could have called us herself. Instead she decided not to."

The tissue started to come apart in Cyan's hands. Another flash of colour made her look up. DS Brookes, this time dressed in dark crimson with a grey jacket, headed towards them.

"Do you need anything?" asked Torrington as he rose from his seat.

"No. No thanks," said Cyan.

Torrington led Brookes away from where she sat, and for a brief moment he looked grave.

"You okay?" said Fayval as she slid into the seat next to her.

"Can I say no?" said Cyan.

"Yes you can. It was a silly question." Fayval looked over at the bar. "The staff have gone. I could really do with something right now."

"Miss Butler, Mrs King," said Torrington. He pulled out a chair opposite them and sat down. "I'm afraid that Katherine Welman has just been pronounced dead."

Once again Cyan felt as if she was in deep, thick fog. A police officer escorted her to the registry where she shut down her desktop before she joined Fayval in the foyer. They walked out of the Hub together. Fayval sighed as they walked past the blue police tape, while Cyan was glad to see that there wasn't much of a crowd, it made it easier to spot Cyrus. She was surprised to see Daniella with him. All four walked over to the King Building and into the canteen. Cyrus offered to buy hot drinks while Fayval and Cyan found two white-topped round tables away from the sandwich bar.

"Well," said Fayval after they had sat down on pale orange plywood seats, "the PR team will be having a million fits. 'Come to Corner Rise University, excitement is what we do best'. I'm surprised some parents haven't told their children to leave."

"Yes they have," said Cyrus. "The parents might want them to go, and some will, but so many will just hang around. Excitement is the word. Have you read some of the staff blogs recently?"

"No," said Cyan.

"You should," said Cyrus. "The prose could come out of any Victorian Gothic novel. Bestsellers all."

Daniella snorted. "When I heard the police cars arrive I was so glad that I was in the library. They can't blame me for this." She took a swig from her mug of coffee.

"True," said Cyrus, "but Katherine is now dead."

"Saved me the lawyer's fees," said Daniella. She looked around at their surprised faces. "Oh come on. The damage she did to my reputation?"

"Nearly did. You were released, right?" said Fayval.

"*I* was never arrested. Even though my name was all over the front pages." Daniella looked out of the window.

Fayval watched the professor for a while, her mouth a tight line. Cyan flicked her eyes towards Cyrus who just shrugged and looked out of the same window. Cyan lowered her head and tilted her cup towards her. Another member of staff that Daniella wouldn't mourn.

Daniella pulled her gaze from the window and looked at Cyan. "You two were in the Hub for long time."

"I know," said Cyan, "more questions. It's a good thing you called me," she said to Cyrus. "If the police had hammered on the door I'd have leapt six miles in the air."

"I wouldn't have," said Fayval. "The closed sign on the Collection must be invisible. People knock on the door when I put it up for even a few minutes."

"Well, here's some good news," said Daniella. "I've been given permission to publish the paper. Of course, because I did most of the research I get authorship."

Cyan wasn't sure what to say. She looked at Fayval, who appeared to be very interested in the contents of her dark blue mug. Then at Cyrus, who looked shocked.

"Don't all congratulate me at once," Daniella snapped after a few minutes. "Well. I'd better be off." She rose from her seat and flounced out of the canteen.

"Well," said Fayval. "She did manage to wait until Dayton's body was cold, I suppose."

Cyrus gave a dry chuckle. "No love lost there," he said. "That has to be the first time Dayton didn't get his own way."

"The second," said Fayval. "If he had got his own way he would still be alive."

Cyrus finished his tea. "More tutorials," he said. "I guess HR will be in contact with us soon. The counselling service will be busy."

Cyrus was right, first Cyan's mobile phone sounded with an email from HR, then Fayval's.

"Oh, poor Zoe," said Cyan.

"Hmm?"

"HR have called her in." Cyan's thumbs flew over her mobile. "I've just arranged to meet her in here."

Fayval nodded. "Looks like I'm off to the library," she said. "They've found a spare desk for me, but I doubt I'll get anything done there. Can you imagine the questions waiting for when I arrive?"

Cyan laughed. "You'll spend the rest of the afternoon drinking tea," she said.

"What about you?" Fayval nodded at Cyan's phone.

"No idea," she said. "I'll probably find out after I've spoken to Zoe."

Fayval nodded, then reached out and squeezed Cyan's arm.

"I should be okay," Cyan said.

"You worked with Katherine."

"True. If I need to leave I'll let Zoe know."

Cyan watched Fayval leave.

Yes, Cyan did work, had worked with Katherine, but Katherine only made friends with anyone she considered advantageous. Cyan was neither rich, in any position of power, or glamorous. She had never been Katherine's friend. She didn't even know if Katherine had family. Cyan suddenly felt sad.

She pulled herself out of her seat and went to the King Canteen's bar. She bought herself another tea and had just seated herself when she saw Zoe. She raised a hand and Zoe waved in acknowledgement. Cyan's line manager got straight to the point.

"I can call HR. You don't have to work today."

"No. No thanks. I'd rather be here than at home," said Cyan. "I'd only just sit and listen to the news."

"Hmm," said Zoe. She didn't seem to agree.

"I'll be fine," she said.

"Sorry, Cyan, but you don't look fine to me."

Cyan looked into the steaming travel mug cradled in her hands. "I knew nothing about Katherine."

"Nobody did," said Zoe. "Well, HR probably had an emergency contact on her record. But." Zoe shrugged. "We all tried. But she just wasn't interested in us."

Cyan thought of Katherine's sullen looks at the team's first Christmas lunch. Katherine had complained that it was pointless with only three staff. Then, when they were invited to the Estates party Katherine chose to stay away.

"Cyan?" Zoe's voice brought her back to the present.

"Yes."

"I don't believe you should stay, but I can't force you to go home. Do me a favour, if you change your mind, just leave. Then let me know, I'll contact HR for you."

"Yes. Yes of course. Thanks, Zoe."

"Okay," she said. "Looks like you've been allocated a room in the Gatehouse."

Cyan screwed the lid onto her travel mug, gathered her possessions and rose. Zoe stood up.

"I'm sorry you had to come in," said Cyan.

"What else would I do?"

They said their goodbyes and Zoe headed for the back of the King Building while Cyan walked towards the main entrance.

She stepped out of the King Building into the afternoon sun and walked along the main drive to the Gatehouse. Cyan liked this building more than any other on the Crown Campus; it was made of two square towers held together by a Tudor arch. The towers were topped with crenelations, and she still liked to imagine a guard in a Tudor doublet and hose planted, feet wide apart, in the archway with the question, "Who goes there?"

After all, the Gatehouse was used by campus security.

When Cyan got to the Gatehouse she felt as if most of the security staff were there. Jennifer sat at the reception desk flanked by three other members of security who nodded their greeting and went back to their own conversations. When Jennifer welcomed Cyan by name the conversations stopped and one member of security staff spluttered into his mug.

Yep, thought Cyan. *The campus grapevine must be on overtime.*

Cyan nodded and stumbled her way through a few questions after she was buzzed into the Gatehouse. Jennifer managed to get Cyan past the curious group and she was glad to be shown to her temporary office.

Jennifer waited until Cyan was seated. "How are you?" she asked.

It took Cyan a few minutes to answer. "I think I'm still stunned. I mean, this morning Katherine was, well, Katherine."

"We can call HR? You should really be at home."

Cyan shook her head. "I've already spoken to my line manager about that. No. Not this time," she said. "Do you know that I haven't cried once over Katherine?"

"Katherine wasn't the most," Jennifer searched for a word, "amiable of people. I must confess, although I hate that she's dead, it's more the fact that she is the second person killed on this campus. That really bothers me."

Cyan nodded. Jennifer said what Cyan imagined most people felt.

"How is Greg?" Cyan said.

"I didn't see him," said Jennifer. "But several of the other guys did. He nearly had to be carried back here. HR sent him straight home."

For a while Jennifer stood still and Cyan sat, both with their own thoughts. In Cyan's mind Katherine had a smug expression as she toyed with her hair. She stifled a sigh.

"Well. If you're okay?" said Jennifer.

"Yes," said Cyan. "And thank you."

Jennifer smiled in reply and closed the door behind her.

Cyan turned to the old desktop computer and logged on. It took an age to come to life, which gave her a chance to look around the room – she had never been inside one of the Gatehouse's towers before.

The door that Jennifer had just closed wasn't the heavy oak of Cyan's imagination but a regulation fire door with a single tall, thin window above its handle. It stood in contrast to a room that looked as if it hadn't changed in centuries. Heavy wooden beams held up the whitewashed ceiling and the walls were of cool clean stone. The four windows around her were all deep set and beneath her feet a wine-coloured rug covered the dark wood floor.

Cyan opened her email and thought about work, but after a few attempts stopped. Outside her window she could see the King Building, which was taller than the tower she sat in. She looked at the plain walls and large Georgian windows and tried to figure out how much work it took to convert an old colonial house into a lecture space.

A delivery truck brought Cyan back to the present and she tried to work again, but her mind went back to Katherine. She gave in and looked up the news. A murder had been reported and the victim was identified as 'another staff member at the Crown Campus, Corner Rise University', but that was all. There were no details of how Katherine had died, so Cyan's mind began to fill in the gaps. Katherine had been found in one of the meeting rooms. Cyan logged in to the room booking system to check on the equipment in each room. Dayton had been murdered with a statuette from the King Collection, so maybe the killer had, once again, used whatever was to hand. Or. Cyan stopped herself.

"Katherine is dead," she admonished herself.

She switched back to the student records system and pulled up a class list. She closed it and went back to her email. An empty inbox greeted her. She switched to her pending file, looked up the emails that needed replies and started to send out reminders.

A knock at the door made her jump. Cyan switched screens and looked up to see Trevor smile at her from around the doorway. Cyan reluctantly mirrored his smile – she wasn't sure she wanted any company. They exchanged greetings and went back to silence. Cyan looked down at her screen, she wanted to look busy. She glanced up at the porter through her eyelashes. Trevor's face was turned towards the window.

"Bad business," he said. "How are you?"

Cyan looked up and exhaled quietly. "Not good. You?"

"It's all so strange." He continued to look out of the window. "What's really strange is that Daniella was there again."

"What?"

"In the Hub—"

"No she was not!" said Cyan indignantly. "She was in the library with Cyrus. And was outside the Hub when I left it with Fayval—"

"Oh. So you were in the Hub?" said Trevor.

Cyan resisted the temptation to remind Trevor that she worked there. "Yes."

A voice in Cyan's head shouted at the porter to leave. She looked back down at the dark wood table.

"Funny way to go—"

"Look," Cyan said. "I worked with Katherine, so this is not what I want to talk about right now."

He looked at her. "Of course." He then looked at the floor.

Cyan's shoulders tightened like a loaded catapult and she pressed her palms onto the table. A sudden bleep from Trevor's radio made her raise her head sharply and she felt her whole body complain at the rapid movement. Trevor unclipped it from his belt.

"Hello?" said Trevor.

"Trevor? It's Steven."

The voice from his radio gave Cyan hope. Surely the porter would have to leave now.

"Yeah? Trevor here."

"Where are you?" said Steven.

"In the Gatehouse?" Trevor wandered from the window back to the door.

"I thought you were on your way down to the Tech? I'm already in three-oh-six."

"Sorry, Steven," said Trevor. "See you in a bit."

He nodded to Cyan and left.

Cyan didn't move until she heard Trevor walk down the stairs.

"I'm going home," she said to the empty room.

She sent an email to HR to let them know that she was still shaken. She didn't add that she was ready to bite off the head of the next person to speak to her. "Daniella was in the building indeed."

The computer began to install updates and Cyan drummed her fingers on the desk as she waited for it to shut down. Her anger increased at the sound of hushed voices outside the office window. "Get a grip," she said to herself, "people talk in universities."

"Who you call fool?" a voice shouted.

Cyan jumped. Someone else was as angry as she felt.

She got up and went to the window, hoping that the ledge would keep her hidden from sight. She leant forward slightly and could see Trevor on the path below her, but she couldn't see who he was with, but whoever it was had made him very angry. Cyan could see that underneath the neck of his black polo shirt the porter's shoulders were like strong knots about to come undone. In a violent way.

"I knew you'd be trouble," he said. "I had it all sorted here."

Cyan only heard a buzz in reply, she was sure that someone spoke, but they were not loud enough for her to hear words. Cyan tried the window, it wasn't locked and didn't creak, so she slowly pushed it open.

"You were sent for nothing!" Trevor raised a pointed finger. "You were supposed to keep quiet until called."

"I've waited three months!"

Cyan had heard that voice before, but couldn't place it.

Trevor sucked his teeth. "You should've kept yourself quiet," he said. "So what happens now?"

Cyan leant further towards the ledge. She had just got a glimpse of a blue headscarf when a pigeon flew past the open window, close enough for her to hear its wings beating. The sudden movement and sound made her gasp. Trevor held up his palm for silence. Cyan backed away from the window.

She didn't bother to see if the computer had finished its updates. She switched off the monitor, grabbed both her bags and jacket and raced out of the door.

Jennifer wasn't behind the security desk so Cyan said a hasty goodbye to the security guy behind the desk to avoid any further questions, and left. She walked quickly to the bus stop, ears ready to pick out the sound of footsteps behind her, and she looked over her shoulder more than once. She wasn't sure if Trevor had heard her, or who he had shouted at, and what did he mean when he said 'sent for nothing'?

Cyan didn't feel safe until she locked her apartment door behind her, and even then she watched for anything unusual out of her kitchen window. She filled the kettle and pulled her new teapot out of a cupboard. Then she switched on the radio and moved it to a music channel while she concentrated on the pot of red bush tea. The music and familiar actions eventually calmed her down and she sat on her small balcony with a large cup held in both hands.

Her mind went from Katherine's words about who killed Dayton, to Torrington's announcement of Katherine's fate, then to Trevor. Last weekend Gustavo had mentioned another suspect, which had to be Trevor. But Trevor had a solid alibi. Loki leapt up onto the grey metal chair next to her and she reached across to stroke the cat.

"What did Trevor mean, 'funny way to go'?" Cyan asked Loki.

Loki purred in reply.

Cyan had been so angry with Trevor that she had cut him off. She sat upright. Trevor must have been about to say what happened to Katherine. She shuddered. How would he know? This time she didn't hesitate, she reached out and picked up her mobile phone. Maybe this would go nowhere, but she had to tell the police.

CHAPTER 18

The police thanked Cyan for her call, but even as she spoke she knew that it hadn't provided them much information. Trevor had an alibi for the first murder, but when Katherine had said the word 'they' it brought Trevor back into the frame. He might not have picked up the statuette that killed Dayton, but he knew who did and Cyan had no doubt that he was there when Katherine died. Maybe this time it was him. Perhaps it had always been him. There had to be someone prepared to lie for him. The other gang member?

Cyan's head began to throb, so she picked up a new book to give her mind a rest. She put it down after she realised that she had read the first sentence of the third paragraph multiple times. She switched the TV on and briefly watched the news. Katherine's death was mentioned, but as the police had only released the location and time the reporter didn't have much to work with and quickly moved on.

Vee called before the news had finished and Cyan told her mother what had happened earlier that day.

"Did she know who the person was?" asked Vee.

Cyan went silent. She hadn't planned to tell her mother that.

"She did, didn't she?" said Vee after a few moments.

"Yes," said Cyan. "I think she did."

"It's a bad business."

"Yes," she said.

Cyan managed to move the conversation onto the holidays before she let slip about the words she heard through the Gatehouse window. The call ended with Vee's offer of her spare bedroom and afterwards Cyan sat down to watch a superhero movie. She needed the loud soundtrack and action sequences to take her mind of the day's events.

Cyan fell asleep in the early hours of the next morning and Loki gently woke her up with a loud purr. She got up and switched radio stations to one that played music with a five-minute newsflash on the hour followed by traffic updates. The updates warned her of sudden roadworks along the west coast road, so Cyan rushed her breakfast, jumped into her clothes, bid Loki a hasty farewell and raced out of her front door. Gustavo walked out of his apartment as Cyan stepped off the stairs.

"Hello. You look like you slept in a tree," said Gustavo.

"I had a bad night."

"I'm not surprised. You worked with Katherine?"

"Same office," said Cyan.

"I'm sorry, but I have to ask. What do you all get paid by the university?"

"What?" said Cyan.

"Well, another member of university staff dies in a pair of Terrance Warru shoes."

Cyan blinked at him. "I saw her bag," she said. "But I never looked at her shoes."

"She had a bag too? This just gets worse."

A car horn sounded.

"That's my ride. I'll have to catch up with you," said Gustavo. He trotted off down the path towards the main road.

Cyan hesitated for a moment then saw a flash of red through the trees. She ran to the bus stop and got there just as the bus arrived. She sat at the back of the nearly empty bus and her mind went back to Katherine's shoes. Katherine was paid the same as her and Cyan knew that neither of them would be able to afford either the shoes or the bag without a huge credit card bill. Her mind went back to that rainy lunchtime when she watched Katherine and Orlanda out of the window. What had Dylan overheard? Something about gifts? Cyan's head started to ache.

The bus drove along the High Road, named for its position high up on Crown Island. It left the coast to avoid the roadworks and turned through a field of pineapples. Cyan closed her eyes and inhaled deeply, the sweet smell was faint, but it still made her mouth water. At each stop she glanced at the passengers as they boarded or left the bus. One of the passengers was Fayval. Cyan was in half a mind to let Fayval sit down so that they both could enjoy a peaceful journey, but at the last moment she waved. Fayval seemed not to notice her at first and headed for the first window seat she saw. She nearly sat, then stopped and defied gravity to rise and take the seat next to Cyan. For a while they complained about road closures as the bus tried to navigate a narrow street.

"So," said Fayval. "What about the hurricane?"

"Hurricane?"

"Where have you been? It's all over the news. There's a late season hurricane due to hit these islands soon."

Cyan shook her head. "Surely Alpha must still be a tropical storm, it's too late in the season for a hurricane," she said. "Anyway, its energy should have been burned up before it reaches us."

"Yeah," said Fayval. "They said that about Pearl. Then that thing picked up more energy over the sea and slapped us hard."

"Pearl was actually a hurricane."

"Exactly."

"It was a really hot year. Remember?"

"Well, hurricane or tropical storm, I don't care," said Fayval. "We've taken tomorrow off and will be at home with the shutters closed. My boys on the main island are doing the same."

The bus stopped and several people got on. A man walked to the back of the bus and sat down next to Fayval.

"I'll be in. There's a film club tomorrow," said Cyan.

"Is that so? Bad weather is nothing to mess with."

The man next to Fayval agreed. "My sister lives on The Bridge and she's due to join us in Trelissick," he said. My wife doesn't get on with her, but Sis is by herself and I couldn't leave her down there."

"The Bridge should be okay," said Cyan.

"Nope," the man said and hugged his satchel. "When I was a child we lived just east of The Bridge and I remember back then when another hurricane hit in December. They said that was a tropical storm too."

Cyan wondered at this. The man must have seen the look on her face.

"True thing," he said. "The water came up to us knees. My

parents pushed us up the stairs." He shook his grey head. "Straight through a wall it came, carried away Mum's dresser with all her fancy plates on it."

"Oh," said Fayval.

"Fortunately rest of the house stood." He chuckled. "We moved to Crown Island after that. Land was still cheap."

The man was interrupted by a song.

"Excuse." He reached into a trouser pocket and pulled out his phone.

Cyan looked out at the sea. In the past she had watched it go from as smooth as a newly made bed to thunderous grey fists in less than an hour and then watched as it calmed down just a quickly after the strong winds had passed.

"The uni's not on the water's edge," she said to Fayval.

"Uh-ha," said Fayval. "Remember when they used to say, 'When sea water looks to walk on land, stay high'?"

Cyan chewed her bottom lip. It wouldn't be the storm surge that worried her, it was the wind. Cyan's only way home from any other part of the islands involved coastal roads, and in bad weather they were always shut. Cyan decided to wait for guidance from the government and checked her phone in the hope of an official 'stay at home' message.

"Did you listen to the news?" asked Fayval.

Cyan's mind was still on the weather. She put her phone away, shook her head. "Has Alpha been upgraded?"

Fayval blinked at her. "No," said Fayval. "The news was about how Katherine … How she died."

Cyan kept quiet, she waited for Fayval to finish her dramatic pause.

"She was hit with a full-sized flip chart easel," Fayval said.

Cyan sprung upright and looked at Fayval as if a single silver horn grew from her forehead. "Say again?"

"I know," said Fayval. "A flip chart easel!"

Cyan slowly leant back into the seat. What could she say to that?

The grey-haired man had just finished his call and appeared to have no problem with what to say next. "You knew that woman?"

Fayval looked away from Cyan to answer him, and Cyan stared out at the sea. She didn't see, or hear, much else for the rest of the journey, her mind working on the image of a piece of very large stationery in flight. A nudge brought her back to the bus.

"Well it was good to speak to you," said Fayval as she reached out to ring the bell.

"And you," said the man. "Keep safe in the next two days."

She got up and Cyan followed. They paused briefly to wish their fellow passenger well.

"Yes," said Fayval as they stepped off the bus. "A flip chart easel."

"But how? How can you slap someone around the head with that?"

They showed their passes to security and walked through the Gatehouse.

Fayval nodded in agreement. "You'd have to be both tall and strong to get some swing on that thing."

"Good morning!"

Trevor's voice made them both jump. Cyan looked into one of the brightest smiles on campus.

"Um. Hello," she said.

"Oh hi," said Fayval.

They walked into the King Building. If Fayval harboured any suspicions about Trevor, they never made it to her face or voice. Cyan marvelled at her. For Cyan, it felt awkward, especially after her call to the police.

"More bad news about this place," Trevor said. "I might have to get a new job."

"Can you imagine?" said Fayval. "The whole of Crown Campus leaving en masse." She laughed with the porter.

Cyan half smiled as something tugged at the back of her mind. It was something that Trevor had said the day before, but she couldn't remember what it was. She had been too angry to listen and now she wished that she had.

"What do you think?" Fayval looked directly at Cyan.

"Sorry?"

"About the campus being closed tomorrow?"

Of course, the storm, Cyan thought. "If it's really serious we'll be warned," she said aloud.

Cyan stepped through the main building's back entrance.

"You're braver than me," said Trevor. "I'm staying home tomorrow." He adjusted his full post bag.

Fayval nodded and glanced at her watch. "Oh!" she groaned.

"Those roadworks have made me late! I've got to show some new library staff around the Collection before it opens. Have a good day."

Cyan watched as Fayval sped off ahead of them along the path to the Hub.

"So, how are you after yesterday?" she said.

"Not good," said Trevor. "At least I can joke about a new job now. But. How are you? You worked with her. You must have known her well."

"Nobody knew Katherine well. She only spoke to us if she had to. But still." They stood in silence. Cyan took a deep, quiet breath. "Why did you think Daniella was there?" she asked.

"I just heard she was." He shrugged. "Some people said so."

"Island gossip. Actually, about gossip. What was a funny way to go?"

"What?" said Trevor.

"Just something I heard yesterday."

Trevor's intense stare made Cyan uncomfortable.

"From whom?"

Cyan lost her nerve. "Maybe the radio. I can't quite remember," she said. "Too much information, not all good."

"True." Trevor nodded, but his eyes stayed on her. "Better be off. People want their packages."

Trevor waved a farewell and walked towards the technical college. As Cyan walked to the Hub her legs trembled and her ears picked up every sound, from distant chatter to the rustle of leaves and birds landing in the branches. Corner Rise University continued to prepare for the day and Cyan took comfort from that. Even if Trevor was the bad guy, he wouldn't be bad enough to do something in front of so many people.

Once inside the Hub Cyan's thoughts returned to Storm Alpha. She pulled her mobile phone out of her bag and sent Cyrus a message with the suggestion that the ECC meet should be cancelled. She put back her phone and pulled out her travel mug, but because she had arrived later due to the bus's change of route, the queue in the cafe was longer than normal. Cyan glanced at her watch. It was nearly nine so she decided to head straight for the office instead.

The first thing Cyan noticed as she walked into the registry was Katherine's desk. It was empty. The police had taken everything from the computer to Katherine's notebook. Cyan guessed that everything in the drawers had also been removed.

She inhaled deeply for a sigh and instead got the strong smell of industrial-strength cleaner. She put down her bags and opened the window next to the empty desk.

"Katherine would never have allowed me to do that." Cyan's shoulders dropped. Did she not possess one good memory about Katherine? She picked up her travel cup, remembered it was empty, put it down again, and looked out of the window at the sky while her computer went through its start-up. The registry's door opened and Cyan glanced over the counter as she usually did. Then her head whipped around towards the door.

Trevor walked in with a package and Cyan froze. He nodded at her, put the package on the counter and left. Cyan breathed again once the door had closed behind him. She composed herself and lifted the package from the counter – it was addressed to Dylan. She placed it on his desk.

It wasn't long after that Zoe arrived, wearing an interesting Fair Isle cardigan in red with a black and cream pattern around the neck and shoulders. It made Cyan's blue raincoat seem plain.

"How are you?" asked Zoe.

"Me? Fine."

Zoe nodded towards Katherine's desk.

"Not fine," said Cyan. "At least the news is fairly quiet this time. And my mum called, she was concerned, but she managed to lift my spirits. My brother just made me laugh."

"I'm here with Dylan today, so if you need to leave just say."

"No," said Cyan. "I'd rather be here at the moment. I'd only sit at home and think about everything. At least I was with Fayval. Poor Greg."

"Yes. I heard about him this morning." Zoe leant against the counter with her arms crossed. She glanced at Katherine's desk and then stared out of the window.

"How about you?" asked Cyan.

"I've had better days. Paul, my brother, has started to give me grief and last Sunday's dinner with the rest of the family was no joke."

"I bet they think this campus is a dangerous place."

"Oh yes. But, to be honest, I've started looking over my shoulder." Zoe shook her head. "I know that sounds stupid."

"No it doesn't," said Cyan.

Cyan thought about how much she had found out about Dayton's murder and was glad that she hadn't shared any of it with either Zoe or Dylan. Cyan sighed. She hadn't really thought about her safety until Katherine was murdered too.

The registry door opened.

Zoe spun around and rested her hands on the counter. Cyan shot up out of her seat.

"Sorry," said Dylan. "I didn't mean to startle you."

"Don't worry," said Zoe. "Right now everything makes me jump. So if you need to print anything let me know first, or you might find that I've jumped clean through the ceiling!"

They all laughed.

Dylan unlocked the registry door.

"I don't know how you wear those cardigans," he said to Zoe as he hung up a very light raincoat. "It's so hot!"

"You've only been here a year," said Zoe. "Once you've acclimatised you'll do the same."

"I doubt it," said Dylan. He reached for the package on his desk. Cyan remained on her feet to see what it was, and smiled when he pulled out a new laptop cover.

"Are you in tomorrow?" she asked Dylan.

"No," he said.

Cyan braced herself for another warning about the storm.

"I've booked the day off to go shopping."

"Of course," said Cyan, "you're going back home for Christmas. You'll need a jumper then."

"Don't remind me. At least Cornwall is milder than the rest of the UK."

Cyan wished she had seen more of the UK when she lived there. She had never travelled to the West Country, or much outside the South East. Every time Dylan spoke of his home she thought about a visit. But it would cost a fortune, and that was just the airfare.

"Cyan," said Dylan. "Sorry to ask, but what happened yesterday?"

Dylan's question burst through images of a green coastline and grey-blue seas. Cyan didn't have to ask what her colleague meant. Behind him Zoe leant back against the counter. She obviously wanted to find out as well.

"If you don't want to answer," he said quickly.

"Don't worry," said Cyan. She believed that her colleagues should know, at least this time. "Not much really. Katherine sat at the counter and the registry was empty. Then she went on a toilet break." Cyan frowned. "She left her bag behind, it was on the floor under her desk instead of locked in her drawer."

"She thought she would be back soon," said Zoe.

Dylan looked over his shoulder at Zoe. "Why do you think that?" he said.

"Because I either lock my bag away, or take it with me," said Zoe.

"Me too," said Cyan.

Dylan nodded.

Cyan told them about the rest of the morning, and for once Dylan didn't roll his eyes at Katherine's extended absence.

Well, she thought, *how could he?*

Cyan said nothing about her conversation with Katherine. If she were honest it was beginning to scare her. It meant that Katherine, like Dayton, had gone to meet her murderer. Zoe went back into her office and left the two of them with their thoughts.

"If you need me to cover anything today," said Dylan as he sat down at his desk.

Cyan nodded. She appreciated his gesture. "It should be quiet today," she said.

Cyan looked across Katherine's empty desk. Then back to her screen. She wasn't sure how many times she had read the first two lines of the same email before she heard Dylan get up.

"I'm heading to the canteen," he said. "Do you want anything from there?"

"No, thanks," she said.

She watched Dylan leave.

"Wait," she said to herself quietly. "He's not in tomorrow."

Cyan didn't want to be in the office by herself. She got up and walked to Zoe's office. She had barely tapped on the door frame before Zoe looked up.

"Yes," said Zoe as if she had read Cyan's mind, "I'm in tomorrow. There's been little advice from the government, so." She shrugged. "If we stayed home every time there was a threat of bad weather, nothing would get done over the hurricane season."

Cyan smiled. "That's true."

She went back to her desk, logged in and opened up the morning's emails.

A short while later Dylan walked back into the office with a brown box containing his breakfast. Cyan inhaled deeply.

I should have skipped breakfast, caught an earlier bus and eaten here, she thought.

She listened as he opened and rattled around his desk drawer. After a while he closed it and Cyan could picture the fork in his hand. The smell of hot food got stronger as he opened his breakfast box. Cyan reached for her travel mug, remembered that she hadn't stopped in the cafe that morning and mentally kicked herself. She should have asked Dylan to get her a hot drink. *Oh well*, she thought, and read her first email of the day.

Cyan's telephone rang, it was Miranda from HR, who called to check that Cyan had made an appointment with the university's counselling service. Cyan apologised and promised to make one then wrote a reminder on a sticky note and stuck it to her screen. An event flashed up in the bottom right-hand corner telling her of a meeting at nine forty-five that morning. She glanced at the time on her screen: it was nine thirty-five. *This is going to be a long day*, she thought.

"Cyan," Zoe called as Cyan hunted for her copy of the agenda, "ready?"

Dylan was already on his feet, his new Cornish black-and-white flag laptop case already fitted. Cyan put her handbag into the bottom desk drawer. Then she grabbed her mobile phone, lowered the shutters, closed the registry door behind her and headed for the stairs. She paused at the door to the second floor. It didn't open when she swiped her staff card and through the window she spotted someone wearing a face mask. They glanced up at the door and Cyan nodded, then she climbed the last flight of stairs.

It took Cyan some time to find the room booked for the meeting and was shocked when she saw it. It was small and looked more like a storage cupboard – it smelt musty and the floor was a standard grey vinyl that felt strange when she stepped off the hallway carpet. There were only four tables and both Dylan and Zoe were seated with their laptops open. Cyan closed the door behind her and was relieved to see a monitor on the pedestal opposite the door. She put her papers down and walked over to it. When she reached down to turn on the room's computer her finger met with empty space. She looked at the hole where the machine should have been.

"It was the only room we could get at short notice," said Zoe. "The booking. Erm. Slipped."

"This meeting was scheduled at the beginning of term," said Cyan. "Who waited until the last minute to get a room?"

Dylan and Zoe lowered their eyes in silence.

Katherine, Cyan thought.

She looked at the disconnected screen and the four tables. "I-I'll just go and get an office laptop," she said and left quickly.

CHAPTER 19

Cyan took the stairs back down to the first floor.

She slipped through the empty registry and straight to the small meeting room where she collected a laptop from the security cabinet. Cyan didn't notice how much her hands shook until she tried to punch the combination into the security cabinet's lock. It usually came automatically. She stood upright and rolled her shoulders then her head. Through the blinds Katherine's empty desk tugged at Cyan's gaze. She sighed and went back to the keypad. She gave the 'C' a hard push and tried the combination again. This time she was rewarded with a click as the cabinet opened. Cyan grabbed a laptop, paused, took a charging cable, locked the cabinet and left. She headed for the main staircase, but the sound of talking ahead of her changed her mind. Cyan didn't want to hold up the meeting any longer, which would happen if she tangled with students, so she headed down the corridor to the fire escape.

Known as the 'side stairs' it had swipe card access and led staff to either the fire exit at the side of the Hub or a fire door between the King Collection and the cinemas. The staircase had a yellow tubular metal banister and each step was fronted with a yellow strip. There was a narrow landing on each floor, which meant that the flight of steps below could be seen clearly, but not those above. Cyan remembered fire drills where she could look up and see the hands of those behind her as they followed the instructions to hold on. Sound bounced off all the hard surfaces in the stairwell, and Cyan wasn't surprised that Fayval had heard most of Trevor's and Katherine's tense conversation. So she was not surprised to hear the clang of feet above her, but she did pause to listen, then shrugged. It was probably a member of staff or perhaps one of the few research students that visited Crown Campus.

Cyan continued to climb upwards. She had hoped to ignore the door to the second floor, but she couldn't help a quick peek through the glass. The corridor was empty. Cyan was midway up the next flight of stairs but paused when she noted that the person above her had stopped. She waited for a door to open, but there was no sound. Instinct forced her to look up, even though she wouldn't be able to see who it was. What she did see was something dropping towards her.

Cyan pressed herself against the wall just as a book hit the spot where she had stood. It landed like a brick. The sound bounced off the walls and rattled through the metal banister. Cyan closed her eyes until it had died down. She opened her eyes slowly, bent slightly forward and looked down at the book. Her heart, which had gone into overdrive as the book fell, thumped again. The book was on its back with the cover open. It displayed a lot of pages. Cyan clutched the laptop and leant back hard against the wall. That book would have done some damage. Or worse.

Her knees wobbled and she sat down.

The door to the floor above opened and closed to the sound of receding footsteps. Cyan was surprised that no one stopped to find out if she was hurt. Maybe they were scared, or in shock. She shook as she got up slowly and picked up the book. It was as heavy as it looked.

When she walked into the small room Zoe glanced up in annoyance, but the look changed when she saw Cyan's face.

"What happened?"

"I-I found a book," Cyan said as she sat down.

She could tell that Zoe wasn't satisfied with her answer.

Zoe looked at the book, then at her laptop. "Item one," she said.

Dylan glanced at the book and then at Cyan as Zoe read the agenda. Cyan looked beyond the pedestal and through the window at the rain. Then she forced herself to focus on the meeting. Fortunately she didn't have to present a report and added fewer than a handful of comments.

More than once Cyan caught Dylan's eye after she had run her finger down the book's spine.

Zoe closed the 'any other business'.

"Why the book?" Dylan asked. He got up and stood beside Cyan and read the title. "And when did you take up oceanography?"

"I didn't," said Cyan with a nervous laugh. "Would you believe it just missed me?"

"Where?" asked Zoe.

"On the fire escape."

Zoe shook her head. "I have always argued that that fire escape should actually *be* a fire escape," she said.

"Sorry?" said Cyan.

"This happens too often," said Zoe. She turned to Dylan. "Weren't you nearly knocked flat by a book there?"

"Yeah." Dylan nodded. "Some nitwit PhD student nearly brained me with a text book. It was when I used the escape route to run from Dr Horsford."

"Dr Horsford?" asked Cyan.

"The Tea Man?" said Dylan.

"Oh him," said Cyan. "Once he starts talking he can keep you there all day."

"All night in this case – it was after five. I do wonder if that man has a home to go to." Dylan smiled. "Anyway. I heard the thunk. Saw the book. Looked up and didn't see anyone above me. I heard them run though."

"What, no apology?" said Cyan.

"Uh-uh. Not until the next day after I'd given the book back to the library. The poor love looked terrified. She couldn't have been more than four foot eleven. She had just stopped to look something up."

"On the side stairs?" said Cyan, eyebrows raised.

"Yeah, I know, daft place," said Dylan. "She explained that the book slipped from her hands. I was surprised that she could pick it up at all! She was mortified."

"See," said Zoe as she stood up. "No matter how many times that happens they insist on anytime access for staff and research students. Note it in the incident book, I'll make another report to Health and Safety."

Cyan followed her boss to the door.

"Hey! Don't forget the book," Dylan called after her.

Cyan took the heavy book from his hands. Back in the office she checked that it belonged to the library and then pushed it to the edge of her desk. She would take it back at lunch and maybe she would find out who borrowed it.

Cyan switched on her mobile phone to see that Cyrus had not replied to her message. Cyan smiled as she remembered an article she had read, which stated that mobile phones had taken over people's lives. She knew that this didn't apply to the professor. She had sat opposite him in meetings and watched as he picked up his phone and turned it off.

"If it's a dire emergency there's not much I can do here is there?" he had reasoned.

Cyan didn't share his opinion, but then she always had her phone on vibrate at work.

When Cyrus's reply came it was brief.

The government hasn't asked us to stay at home, so I don't think so.

We should really ask the other members, Cyan replied.

Half a minute later her phone vibrated.

Agreed, Cyrus replied.

Thanks.

A quarter of an hour later Cyrus's email arrived.

To all members of the Ealing Comedy Club

With Tropical Storm Alpha predicted to reach Corner Rise Islands shortly, would it be advisable to postpone tomorrow's event? We could watch and discuss Who Done It? *at a later date.*

Kind regards,

Cyrus Pepper

Chair, Ealing Comedy Club

Cyan replied that it should be postponed. Not long afterwards she was surprised at the number of members who were against the idea. She shook her head, people could be so stubborn. She would just have to watch the news and check online. Or she could send her apologies, or the Vice Chancellor could send a message closing the university or – Cyan's extension rang.

Without looking at the telephone she picked up the handset. "Hello. Crown Campus Registry."

"Good morning, Cyan, it's Fayval."

Cyan glanced at the time displayed on her computer. "And what a long one."

"You busy?"

"Not really," said Cyan.

"Can you spare a few minutes for tea?"

Less than five minutes later they were seated in the Hub cafe with two full, steaming mugs. Before Fayval could open her mouth Cyan told her about the book on the side stairs.

Fayval sighed. "I'm with Zoe on that one," she said. "Those stairs should become a fire escape only."

"Has this happened before?"

"Oh yes," said Fayval. "But you remember when a toilet roll was set alight before last summer's exams?"

"Oh yes."

Cyan remembered that well, the smell of smoke had told her it wasn't a drill. Nobody knew who did it, the culprit hid their face well from the security cameras, but there were rumours that it was to do with exam avoidance.

"Well," said Fayval. "I had a meeting that morning and you would not believe the panic when the alarm went off. There was a whiff of smoke and one man grabbed a large folder of papers and threw himself out of the door. Well, he lost his balance and had to grab the handrail, but not before he dropped that fat folder. There were several yells from below and someone said a few choice words."

"But that was an accident," said Cyan.

Fayval put her mug down. "Sorry?"

"What if this was deliberate?" she said.

"Of course not. How would anyone know where you'd be at that specific time?"

"True. But what if Katherine told her killer about me?" asked Cyan.

Fayval thought for a while. "I don't see why she would," she said. "No. Katherine was all about what was good for Katherine."

"I know, but—"

"No buts. Katherine barely did her job or spoke to anyone in your team. And Katherine failed to book the room right? So how could she tell anyone about it?"

Fayval was right of course. But something felt wrong.

"But Katherine must have known something," Cyan said.

"I agree with you on that. Did you read about her shoes?"

"And her bag."

"Bag?"

"She had a Terrance Warru bag."

Fayval nearly choked on her tea. "Wow!" she said. "That was some hush money. Then Katherine definitely thought she was in control. No wonder she turned her back on her killer."

"Really?"

"Oh yes. She was found on her front, near the window."

"Oh."

Cyan leant forward and looked into her mug. For a brief moment she could picture the victorious smirk on Katherine's face and the flick of her hair over her shoulder as she turned her back on the person who killed her. Cyan felt guilty and wished that she had better memories of Katherine. She had to change the subject.

"Sorry. You wanted to tell me something?"

"Yes I did," said Fayval. "It all started with Monisha."

"Who?"

"You know. Just joined SAS. Took over from Pauline, who retired? Monisha was a temp in Maths and Stats. She helped the students campaign for real tea mugs."

Cyan smiled to herself. That was genius and the slogan, 'Are you a mug?' She quickly pushed those thoughts away.

"So what did Monisha do?" she said and took a sip of tea.

"Monisha was on that tour for new members of staff and I had just finished giving a quick introduction to the museum when she nudged me and pointed."

Cyan put her mug down. "At what?"

"Someone with fantastic dress sense. I'm not sure whether she was student or staff."

Cyan picked up her mug. This was one of Fayval's slow reveals.

"What did this woman look like?" she asked.

"Completely out of place. She would have been better at some international fashion week. I mean, she really stood out."

Cyan had to stop Fayval or this would go on until lunchtime. "How," she said.

"She had shoulder-length black hair with reddish brown tips, needle-straight. And her eyes, they had to be colour contact lenses, they were amber."

"Really?"

"True," said Fayval. "I remember that because they matched her top. And her trousers, turquoise with, get this, snakeskin print on the outside and plain fabric on the inside leg."

Cyan could only think of one person who would dress like that. She wondered if Fayval had ever seen Orlanda.

"I'm not surprised you noticed her," said Cyan. "When was this?"

"This morning, during the tour."

"This morning?" said Cyan. "What happened next?"

"That Detective Brookes recognised this amber-eyed woman straight away," said Fayval. She took a sip of tea.

"She was there?"

"Didn't I say?"

Cyan shook her head.

"Sorry. Brookes was there with that detective man, you know him."

"Inspector Torrington?"

"That's him," said Fayval. "They caught me just before the tour started, and asked a few more questions. I'm surprised they haven't spoken to you yet."

"Maybe they were with Cyrus. That would explain why it took him so long to answer me this morning."

"Sorry?"

"What? Oh." Cyan hadn't realised that she had spoken out loud. "The Ealing Comedy Club," she said. "I tried to get him to cancel tomorrow's meet up."

"So he should," said Fayval. "Anyway, Brookes sees this woman and does a double take. Then she stepped back and pulled Torrington with her. Unfortunately they noticed me. They said goodbye and left, but before they did I'm sure Brookes was told to check up on this woman. Torrington didn't realise that I could see him through the glass."

"Wow. Did this student know she was watched?"

"I'm not sure. But she had vanished by the time the two detectives had left." Fayval looked at Cyan. "How do you know she's a student? She looked almost famous to me."

Cyan sighed. She wanted to protect Fayval, but she needed some advice, or at least someone to listen.

"It was the way she was dressed. I think she could be Orlanda."

"Who?"

"Katherine introduced me to her. I saw them arguing one lunchtime. And …" Cyan looked at Fayval. "Katherine tried not to say, but I just know that when Katherine left me alone in the registry she was going to see Orlanda."

"Well," said Fayval. "Katherine didn't see Orlanda, did she."

Cyan watched Fayval drain the last of her tea. "Why?"

"You've seen Katherine's friend more than I have," said Fayval. "Does she look like she could swing a full-sized flip chart easel to you?"

Cyan blinked at her friend. "No," she said slowly. "I doubt it."

Cyan swirled the dregs of tea in her mug. If Orlanda didn't murder Katherine and the book incident was an accident, then what now? Fayval must have read Cyan's mind.

"Like I said." Fayval put down her mug for emphasis. "Brookes and Torrington saw Orlanda. Maybe she'll lead them to who did kill Katherine. And," Fayval leant forward, "I bet that person killed Dayton as well."

Back in the registry Cyan logged in to her computer. Whoever waylaid Katherine had to be either a research student or a member of staff and there were a lot of those at the Crown Campus. Cyan stared at the screen. Brookes and Torrington had all the resources they needed to find this person, while she had none. Cyan looked sideways at the large book next to her. She would take it back to the library and that would be the end of it.

CHAPTER 20

The rain thumped against the windows like mud. Dylan got up and looked out. He stood for a bit and then turned towards Cyan.

"Bad day to go to the library," he said. "By the time you get there your umbrella will be a few bent wires and strips of cloth."

Cyan nodded slowly. "I might eat before I leave," she said. "Maybe the rain will have calmed down by then."

It hadn't. By the time Cyan left the Hub the rain fell even harder as if on a mission to destroy the campus. She ran most of the way to the Mann Building and after she gave the umbrella several shakes outside, she folded it and placed it in one of the reusable brolly bags by the entrance. Then she headed for the library.

Cyan always found the library's entry gates a challenge, the Perspex dividers that opened to allow entry made her think of large meat cleavers. She touched her card to the reader on top of one of the dividers and watched as the gates rose, then opened violently. Cyan rushed through and they closed silently behind her.

She walked past rows of tables towards the library's long counter. A young man looked up from his screen as Cyan approached, his hair was black at the sides and dyed red on the crown.

"Good afternoon," he said. "How can I help?"

"Good afternoon," said Cyan.

She put her bagged umbrella on the floor, pulled the book from her backpack and put it on the counter.

"There was an accident on the Hub's side staircase," Cyan said. "This book was dropped and I wondered who it belonged to."

The librarian looked as if he had plenty to say about the Hub's fire escape, but he stopped himself. Instead he pulled the book towards him and read the cover.

"*The Ocean is not Silent.* I remember this book for some reason."

He reached across to his computer and typed a few keys. He nodded.

"It has been reported missing. One of the natural science students lost it yesterday."

"Does it say who?" said Cyan.

The librarian swiftly checked Cyan's identity card, which had 'Staff' in large bold letters above her name.

"Sorry, you know I can't tell you that," he said. "But if you leave your name and contact information the student will probably get back to you. This book costs a fortune and I don't think they wanted to replace it."

Cyan nodded as she wrote down her name. She wondered how some of the investigators in her mother's beloved cosy mysteries would cope in this age of data protection. She was about to add her email address, but changed her mind and wrote down her telephone extension instead. Most students preferred to communicate by email, but it was worth a try, plus they could always find her email address if they wanted to.

Cyan returned the umbrella bag at the Mann Building's entrance before she splashed back to her office.

"Thank goodness," said Dylan as Cyan walked through the door. "I am famished."

Cyan glanced at her watch. "Sorry. I didn't realise I was late," she said.

"No panic." Dylan smiled. "Yet."

Dylan was out of the office before Cyan reached her desk. She had just sat down when her extension rang.

"Hi. Is that Cyan Butler?" a voice said before she could answer.

"Yes," Cyan said. "Registry Services."

"Good afternoon. I'm Nathan. Nathan Dale. The student who lost the book?"

Cyan sat upright. "Good afternoon, Nathan. Thanks for calling."

"Thanks for the book. Where did you find it?"

"It was on the main fire escape in the Portmore Building," Cyan said. She decided that the student didn't need any more details.

"How did it end up there? I left it in the King Canteen."

The student's voice had a pleasant smokey edge to it. An image of a tailored all-man band with seventies flared trousers popped into Cyan's head. She shook it away.

"Were you in the canteen with anyone?" she said. "That would explain it."

"No," said Nathan, "I was by myself. But there were some porters at a table nearby. I had hoped that one of them had picked it up."

"Why?"

"You know, to return it to the library, like you did."

"Yes of course," said Cyan. "But why the porters? Why not the canteen staff?"

"Oh I see," Nathan said. "I was halfway to the Mann Building when I realised I'd left it on the table. When I got back to the canteen both the book and the porters had gone. I did ask at the tea bar, but the canteen staff hadn't picked it up."

"Well I'm glad you got it back," she said.

"Me too. Thanks."

They said their goodbyes and the student hung up. Cyan looked beyond the desk next to her and through the window. Dylan, Fayval and Zoe had all told her that the book had been dropped by accident, even the library assistant looked like he had something to say about the side stairs. But something was wrong. Nathan was right, it was written in every staff and student handbook that a lost book was always returned to the library. If it didn't belong there, it would be redirected to lost property. So if a group of porters had picked up the book, how did it end up on the side stairs, where she was?

Cyan leant back in her chair. What if Trevor had been one of the porters in the King Canteen? Cyan dismissed that thought. Trevor had an alibi for the hours before Dayton's death and he could hardly have picked up that book and walked to the Hub in front of his colleagues. They would go past the Mann Building first and someone would have reminded him to take it to the library. Cyan sighed. She had to accept that Trevor never saw the book. Plus how would Trevor know where she was. Cyan's head began to hurt. Nathan had his book back, so that should have been the end of all her questions.

The rest of the afternoon passed slowly. Cyan sneaked a look at the news but just couldn't read any more about Katherine's death. She turned instead to the seasonal news about Christmas food and was soon lost in a roast turkey with roasted vegetables versus oven-baked chicken with rice and coleslaw debate. Cyan smiled. She planned to have seasoned lamb for Christmas dinner.

A message alert from Fayval appeared on her screen.

Are you free for a quick iced tea after work?

Cyan was nearly always free for an iced tea.

I am. I can let you know what happened when I took that book back to the library.

Oh? Okay then, the Spice Shack at five thirty? I might be a bit late, but I will be there.

See you then.

Cyan was glad to have something to look forward to. She went to the Spice Shack's web page and looked up their drinks menu. Five minutes later she still couldn't decide whether to go for Peach Melba or mango.

At the end of the work day Cyan reached under her desk for her umbrella.

"Oh for goodness' sake!"

"What?" said Dylan.

Cyan held up her umbrella, still inside the bag she picked up when she had walked into the Hub earlier that afternoon. She loosened the drawstring and pulled a wet mess out of the bag. A few drops of water fell on the carpet.

She held the umbrella away from her all the way to the ground floor and gave it a good shake as she left the Hub. She pulled its cover from her bag and fought to get the slippery umbrella inside while she stayed dry. A blur of bright colours stood out against the damp background. It pulled Cyan's eyes away from her private battle and to the main path on the way to the King Building. Cyan focused on a yellow and purple checked raincoat as it marched away from the Hub. The outfit was topped with brown hair that faded perfectly to orange ends. Cyan didn't see the student's face but knew it had to be Orlanda and wondered how the student made those colour combinations work.

Cyan rammed her umbrella into its cover, spun around and nearly collided with Daniella.

"Whoops. Sorry," Cyan said and managed a half smile.

Daniella was balanced on her toes, her whole body tense. She didn't reply.

"You okay?" asked Cyan.

"Well I was until you nearly ran me over. What's the rush?"

Cyan thought fast as Daniella lowered her heels. "I've got to go back to the office," she said. "And now I'll miss my bus."

"If you say so," said Daniella.

Cyan watched as Daniella slowly and dramatically loosened the rest of her pose. The professor shot Cyan a look of contempt before she left the Hub.

"I wish you well too," Cyan said. She stepped away from the entrance and took a few breaths. *So Brookes and Torrington have to make a few enquiries*, she thought. *Which doesn't mean that Orlanda has to be locked up.*

Cyan saw the door to the side staircase crack open and heard voices. She fled up the main stairs in the direction of her office. The last person she needed to see right now was Trevor.

She didn't go to her office. Instead she went to the second floor. She tried her staff card and the door bleeped open. Cyan stood at the end of a corridor lined with doors to meeting rooms of various sizes along both sides. The walls prevented shared discussions between rooms, but not enough to cover up loud noises, and Cyan knew from experience that flip chart easels did not fall in silence. She once had heard an easel hit the ground in another room and the sharp snap as it hit the floor had made her jump.

She stared through the glass doors into each room as she walked along the corridor. All the equipment was there. She came across one room with the blinds down. She paused briefly and then opened the door. She scanned the room quickly and found a flip chart easel propped up against the computer stand. Cyan closed the door behind her and moved on. She did wonder if she should wipe the door handle, but decided that the floor was now open and the police must have done all that they needed.

Cyan walked the whole floor in both directions and every room had an easel, pedestal, computer and drop-down screen. Cyan grunted, she had wasted her time. She went to the side staircase, but before she reached for her staff card she noticed a door to her right. She would have missed it, but it had a criss-cross of white police tape across it, with blue words that read 'Crime scene. Do not cross'. Cyan leant as close as she dared and peered through the door's small glass window. The room was small enough for her to see everything inside. She noted the computer stand, two desks but no flip chart easel.

"I bet that whole room smells like Katherine's desk."

Cyan turned away and swiped her card to leave the floor. The lock gave an alarmed bleep and stayed firmly shut. She tried again.

"That makes sense."

The police wouldn't have wanted members of staff walking around a crime scene. Cyan took one last look through the glass and headed back the way she came.

CHAPTER 21

Fayval wasn't at the bar when Cyan walked into the Sweet Orchid Spice Shack. She looked past the restaurant's open grill to see her at one of their favourite tables, deep in a book. Cyan ordered a lemon iced tea and went to join her friend. She was relieved to see that Fayval's glass was nearly full and the ice hadn't yet melted. Fayval hadn't been there long.

"Good evening," Cyan said.

Fayval looked up and smiled. "Hello, Cyan. How ya doing?"

"I," said Cyan, "am not doing well." She pulled of her raincoat and hung it over the back of her chair.

"Oh?"

"I nearly mowed Daniella down in the Hub entrance."

Fayval failed to stifle a giggle.

"And I foolishly went to see the room where Katherine's body was found."

Fayval snorted into her drink.

"But at least the student got his book back," said Cyan, and she told Fayval about her afternoon.

"Well," said Fayval. "I have a confession to make. I went up to that room too."

"Really?"

"How could I not? I'd been watching those SOCOs all day. The minute they walked out with their stuff I was up there. Oh don't look at me like that. I'm only human."

They both laughed in spite of the reason that drew them to the room.

"Thing is," said Cyan, "when I was outside that door I had that scary thought again."

"What thought?" said Fayval.

She lowered her voice. "What if Katherine did mention me to whoever killed Dayton."

Fayval rotated her almost empty glass between her palms. Cyan automatically took a sip of her tea.

"I don't think so," Fayval said. "Like I've said many times, Katherine was all about Katherine."

"But what if she did?" said Cyan. "If she is … was all about herself, she would try to save her own life. You know, 'Cyan knows I'm here.' Probably as some kind of security."

"Well that didn't work," said Fayval. "Look, if she was scared she wouldn't have been hit in the back of the head. The only time you turn your back on something that scares you is to run."

Cyan thought about it while Fayval drained her glass.

"But if she was hit in the back of the head, she must have been running."

"While looking out of the window?" said Fayval. "Her body was found lying away from the door. And she would have had to break the window to get out that way. No, Katherine thought she was in control."

Cyan looked at her friend. She wanted to believe Fayval, but she wasn't convinced. She was nearly brained by a book the day after Katherine was found dead. Maybe Katherine didn't plead for her life before she was killed, but Cyan could imagine the upward tilt of Katherine's chin as she reminded Orlanda that someone would miss her in the office.

"Cyan? Would you like another tea?" asked Fayval.

"Er. Sorry. Yes, please." Cyan would have liked something stronger.

"Same again? What was it?"

"What? Oh. Can I try the Peach Melba? Thanks."

Cyan watched Fayval walk through the restaurant, which had started to fill up since they arrived. She looked out of the window and in her mind saw the location and layout of the room sealed off with police tape. It was far enough from the rest of the rooms on the second floor to hide any sound and hidden enough for no one to notice as they walked past. If Katherine wanted to keep the meeting secret it was the perfect room to lead Orlanda to. But Cyan had to agree with Fayval, Orlanda couldn't have swung that easel.

Cyan sprang back to the present as Fayval put down the glasses.

"Katherine's pass didn't work on the side stairs."

"Hmm?" said Fayval.

"Katherine's pass. You had to let her in after she had that mini argument with Trevor."

"Actually," said Fayval, "where was Trevor?"

"I think the police have already found out," said Cyan. "He was probably next on their list after they spoke to you and me."

Fayval snorted. "I bet he told them that he was with the other porters or delivering post. Which of course would never give him enough time to swing an easel."

Cyan chuckled. "Sorry," she said. "That's not funny. So you think it would be Trevor?"

"Who else is tall, strong and argued with both Dayton and Katherine before they were murdered?"

Cyan nodded. "But there's no evidence."

"Is there any for this student Orlanda?"

"No."

They both took a sip of their drinks and Cyan wished that she had ordered the mango instead. Peach Melba iced tea was too sweet for her.

"So it sounds like both Orlanda and Trevor are off the hook," said Fayval.

Cyan nodded. As a technical college student, Orlanda's pass wouldn't open any door above the first floor of the Hub and Trevor would have been on the job.

Cyan sighed.

"Something else on your mind?" asked Fayval.

"A lot."

"Such as?"

"How could Dayton afford to live the way he did?"

"I read about the apartment and shoes," said Fayval. "Beats me."

"Last Sunday when I visited Mum she mentioned Pecunia."

"Pec who?" said Fayval.

"Pecunia."

Cyan reminded Fayval about the news reports on that gang and three of its members.

"So they're still on the island?"

"Probably. But it got me thinking about how Dayton could pay for all that stuff. I've been denying this for ages, but what if Dayton was mixed up with them?"

Fayval could only stare at Cyan.

"Think about it," said Cyan.

"Well," said Fayval, after a moment. "If that's the case then he is, was, the biggest hypocrite ever!"

Cyan thought about the way Dayton had made Cyrus feel like a failure. She had to agree with Fayval.

"All the time he used to say to people that they lacked focus," said Fayval. "Not focused enough, my backside!"

"Oh he was focused, alright," said Cyan. "He made sure that we all saw how successful he was."

"He wasn't successful," said Fayval. "He was just plain lucky. Until that ran out."

Cyan and Fayval sipped their tea.

"Normally I would have a lot to say now I know how much that King man lied," said Fayval. "But right now, I have had enough of him."

"I agree," said Cyan.

They spoke about Storm Alpha and the best food to cook in a hurry. Fayval turned up her nose at anything on toast, be it cheese or tinned sardines. After they had finished the second glass of tea Cyan got up to leave.

"Are you sure you won't buy something to take home?" asked Fayval, menu spread out in front of her.

"No. There's plenty of food in the fridge, plus cooking helps me relax."

Cyan didn't bother to reach for her book when she boarded the bus. She seated herself and looked at her own reflection in the window, as her brain tried to piece together what she believed she knew. The first thought was about Katherine. Had she really believed she had the upper hand when she left the registry? And what had Katherine said to end up dead herself? Then Cyan wondered about Dayton. After that conversation with Fayval, Cyan had no doubt that he had joined Pecunia, but no proof either. Orlanda was a puzzle, like

Fayval said, how would that well-dressed student have swung a large piece of office equipment, but she had to be involved somehow. Finally her mind went to Trevor. Last month he was a porter with a winning smile. But now? He still had an alibi for each death, but ... For the second time that day Cyan was stuck.

Cyan kept half an eye out for Gustavo when she entered her apartment block, but he was nowhere in sight. Loki was and ran meowing noisily to Cyan when she opened the door. She walked into her apartment and closed the door behind her.

"I have so much to talk to you about."

Cyan pulled a large bag of dried cat food from the cupboard and a clean food bowl from the drying rack. Loki continued to meow as she stretched herself up from the kitchen floor to the counter while Cyan dropped food into the bowl. Cyan watched Loki crunch on her dinner for a while and then left the kitchen and grabbed her laptop from a side table in the living room.

A moment later she sat back, her head buzzing. There were two members of Pecunia on Corner Rise at the time of the trial. Trevor joined the staff at Crown Campus about the time the gang members had vanished. Cyan was looking at the computer-generated E-FIT-V images of both Pecunia members – the only thing the second image had in common with Trevor was the skin tone. Cyan had just read an article written at the time the two men vanished. It stated that the police were looking for two men, but looking at the first image again, Cyan wasn't sure. She enlarged the first image and looked closely. She shrugged, she was getting off the point again. So neither looked like Trevor, but to Cyan it was too much of a coincidence that two people had died on campus since he started his job. Trevor was tall and would know where the security cameras were. He would also know that the fire door wasn't alarmed if opened from the inside. Cyan began to tremble. She got up and bolted the front door to her apartment. Trevor probably didn't know where she lived, but why take the chance?

Loki had already walked into the living room and jumped up into the armchair, then raised a paw and licked it. Cyan looked at the cat.

"Loki. What am I going to do?"

The cat cleaned behind her ears.

Cyan froze at the sound of her mobile phone. She shook herself back into movement and told herself to stop being silly before she answered it.

"Hello?" she said.

"Good evening, Cyan," said Vee.

Cyan gave a silent sigh of relief. "Good evening, Mum. How are you?"

"I'm good. How are you?"

Cyan decided not to tell Vee about the book incident.

"I'm good."

"You don't sound it," said Vee. "There have been two murders at that place now. Are you sure you still want to work there?"

"Of course. We went through this last night, plus I need to pay the rent."

"Well at least you won't be in tomorrow."

"Of course I will," said Cyan, "the campus will be open."

"What?"

Vee's tone made Cyan laugh.

"This is no joke," said Vee. "What with Alpha on the way. I had Mr Johns check on my shutters today. That's some real bad weather out there."

"Mum. The government hasn't ordered or asked us to stay at home and neither has the university."

"More fool them," Vee said with a sigh. "Give me a call after Alpha blows through. All that glass down there at the uni, without one shutter. You'll close your own shutters, won't you?"

"Of course," said Cyan, she hadn't thought of that. "And the Crown Campus has plenty of shutters."

Vee moved on to family news, and after she gave Cyan another order to call after the tropical storm had passed they said their goodbyes. Cyan walked to the living-room windows. She opened them and stood for a while in the cool evening breeze. She checked that Loki was stretched out on the armchair, and pulled the wooden shutters closed, bolting them from the inside.

Cyan's mobile phone whistled. She stood and stared at it.

"Oh for goodness' sake!" she snapped at herself. "Pull yourself together!"

She grabbed the mobile phone from her small bookshelf and unlocked the screen. There were several messages, the last one from Cyrus.

Good evening, ECC. Due to several concerns expressed about the coming weather, tomorrow's meet has been cancelled. I will be in touch with another date in a few weeks.

Cyan smiled. She hadn't listened to the news, but she could bet that the earlier bravery displayed by the other members of the ECC had been erased by endless reports about the tropical storm.

She reached for her TV remote control just as her stomach rumbled loud enough to make Loki look up. Cyan patted her tummy, stroked the cat and walked into the kitchen.

CHAPTER 22

Cyan slept badly that night. Every sound echoed around her head and filled her imagination with images of Dayton and Katherine. She was yanked awake by Loki's breakfast call and spent the morning with music from her mobile phone, drowning out her dreams perfectly. Cyan treble-checked that her shutters were down and her apartment door was locked behind her before she left for the bus stop. She dug her nose into a book and didn't notice that the bus was half empty until she got to the Crown Campus.

Cyan walked into the Gatehouse and showed her pass to security. "Not hiding from the storm?"

"Not this one," said Cyan. "Have many people been in?"

One of the security guards shrugged. "Slightly fewer than usual. I heard from one tutor that he set his class an online task for today."

"I doubt the campus will be open all day," said another. "Waste of time us being here. They should have closed it yesterday."

Cyan looked beyond the Gatehouse to the sky.

"The clouds look friendly enough," she said.

"Don't believe it," said the first security guard. "It won't be long before we get the order to clear the building."

They wished each other a good day and Cyan walked through the King Building and towards the Hub. She glanced up at the sky several more times. As she walked past the almost completed Student Centre she realised that she hadn't paid much attention to the radio.

Well, she thought, *the bus arrived and security are here, so there couldn't have been an order to stay at home.*

Cyan was relieved at the sight of an open Cinema Cafe and bought herself a large tea. In the registry the counter shutters were still down and she glanced quickly to the end of the counter where the post would usually be left. There wasn't a package in sight and she remembered that, like Fayval, Trevor had planned not to be in. If any other porters stayed away the post would be delayed.

Cyan raised the shutter, put her lunch in the fridge and sat down to log in for the day. The registry door opened.

"Good morning," said Zoe.

"Hello."

"I think this might be a short day."

"Oh?"

"Look at the sky."

"I have been," Cyan said. "It looks okay."

"Not any more."

Cyan looked out of the window, her friendly clouds had been chased out of the sky by clouds resembling clumps of iron wire that the sunlight struggled to penetrate. The first thing Cyan did when she logged on was to check the government's website. 'Persons are asked not to make any unnecessary journeys,' Cyan read.

"Still not a request to stay home," said Cyan to the empty office.

She began to envy Fayval, but there were only two student support administrators left so she couldn't have asked for the day off. Cyan scanned Katherine's desk. She shuddered, got up and went to open the registry door. Outside the corridor was empty.

Cyan found it hard to work, so instead she opened a private window on her browser and looked up everything on the Pecunia Gang, which included many versions of the E-FIT-V she had studied the night before. Once again she tried to find similarities between the images and Trevor's face, but the last time she had seen him was yesterday and she didn't have a photographic memory.

"Why the fixation on Trevor?" she asked the empty desk. "The police have checked him out already."

But Cyan knew why. He had lied about the reason for his argument with Dayton, he was tall enough to pull a statuette from any of the top shelves in the King Collection, he joined the university shortly after those two Pecunia Gang members went missing. It all fitted together so well in her mind that Cyan believed someone had lied for Trevor. That computer-generated image had to be him.

"And I bet that person was the other gang member."

Cyan rested her elbow on the table and her head in the palm of her hand. She turned idly towards the window. The sight made her sit up. The sky was almost filled with heavy grey clouds, and the sliver that was left had a pink tinge to it. Some of the lamps on the paths between the buildings had switched themselves on and the paths started to fill with people, some were students off towards the student accommodation above the campus, while others walked towards the King Building and away from the campus.

"It's come in quicker than anyone predicted," said Zoe.

Cyan looked up to see her line manager, cardigan in hand.

"You haven't seen the email?" said Zoe. "We've been told to leave."

Cyan switched her screen back to email and briefly read the message from HR.

Zoe pulled on her cardigan as Cyan shut down her desktop. Zoe lowered the shutters. The sound made Cyan wish that she hadn't drunk a large tea that morning.

"I need to pop to the ladies," she said.

"Okay, but hurry up," said Zoe. "I've called security to let them know we were leaving, so I'm sure they'll be around to check soon."

Cyan was back in record time. She pulled on her jacket, picked up her bags and grabbed her lunch from the fridge. Then she left the registry with Zoe.

They were startled when the door to the stairs opened.

"Hi," said one of the two security staff as they entered the first floor.

"Good morning," replied Zoe.

Cyan released her breath and smiled. "Hello," she said.

"I need to get out of here," whispered Zoe when the guards had walked past. "What with the storm and all, my nerves are shot."

Cyan nodded in agreement.

The two men moved fast. They reached the ground floor at the same time as Cyan and Zoe. Cyan noted that the canteen was already closed, and once the two registry staff had left the building the security staff locked the Hub's doors, waved Cyan and Zoe goodbye, and headed back to the Gatehouse.

"Get home safely and have a good weekend," said Zoe.

"Thanks. You too."

Zoe hurried towards the campus's other entrance, and Cyan sent up a private request for a bus.

The wind strengthened while Cyan made her way to the King Building. She looked up into the dark sky and then around her to see that all the lamps in the grounds were now on. Apart from the Estates vehicle on the main path the campus looked deserted. Cyan's mobile phone bleeped and she pulled it out of the bag. She had just unlocked the phone when she walked into someone.

"I'm—" Cyan said as she looked up.

It was Trevor.

"You've left it a bit late. Nearly everybody else has gone."

The Estates car passed and Trevor waved to the men inside.

"I-I thought you were at home," Cyan said. Her legs became as weak as wet cardboard.

"Whoa." Trevor caught her arm. "Let's get out of here."

He pulled her towards the King Building, but Cyan's brain locked in panic and she couldn't walk.

"Will you just move?" Trevor said. There was panic in his voice and his eyes swiftly scanned the campus.

"W-where are you taking me?"

"Away from here."

Cyan gulped. "You can't. I won't go!"

Trevor stopped abruptly and looked Cyan in the eye. "I want you off this campus!"

Cyan remained rooted.

"For goodness' sake!" said Trevor. "You're as stupid as that Katherine!"

"What?" said Cyan.

Trevor grabbed her arm and Cyan stumbled forward.

"Stupid woman," he muttered. "She tried to buy her off with a handbag and a pair of shoes. I told her to leave it."

"B-but Katherine didn't buy shoes for anyone."

"Not Katherine!" said Trevor. "I tried to stop that Dr King and was ignored. I saw the look in Katherine's eyes as she posed in those shoes and knew she would ignore me too. I wasn't about to take that risk again. The whole campus is full of greedy, craven people."

"I don't understand."

"You don't have to. Just walk. I've had enough corpses here already."

Cyan yelped as Trevor yanked her forward.

"Help!" Cyan shouted. "Please help me!"

"I'm trying to!" said Trevor.

Cyan's heels dragged along the path. She drew in a large breath to call again and stopped when she caught a whiff of mint. She heard a sound like a ripe melon dropped on hard ground, and Trevor's grip loosened. Cyan pulled her arm away quickly and watched as Trevor landed on his knees before he fell forward into the grass. A short piece of wood traced an arc through the air and landed next to him. Cyan spun around. Just behind her Orlanda stood dressed in grey trousers and a dark purple high-necked jacket, her hair hidden under an indigo and purple headscarf.

"Thank you." Cyan could have hugged the student. She watched as Orlanda knelt down beside Trevor and reached out a hand to his neck.

"Trevor's got a tough head," said Orlanda. "He's alive."

"We should call the police," Cyan said.

Cyan's and Orlanda's eyes met as the student stood up. Cyan's mind flicked back to Gustavo's comment – he had said something about the police looking for someone tall. Orlanda could get away with all those fancy clothes because she was so tall.

Cyan looked from Orlanda to Trevor and back. She was about to reach for her phone when Orlanda moved too fast to be seen. Before Cyan knew it Orlanda had grabbed her wrist with an unbreakable grip. Cyan shrieked. With one pull Cyan was dragged away from Trevor and the King Building.

"What," she said. "Where are we going?"

There was no reply.

Cyan glanced at Orlanda's profile. The student's jaw was clamped shut, her eyes focused on the Hub. Cyan's brain went from surprise to action and she tried to pull away.

"Stop that," said Orlanda.

"The Hub's been locked," said Cyan.

Orlanda stopped mid-stride. Cyan gave Orlanda a shove. The student wobbled, but stayed upright. Cyan just caught a glimpse of the student's hand before it struck. She didn't remember the blow. In her shock all she could do was watch her feet and wonder why they moved so fast. Cyan recovered at the sound of voices. She focused to see a few young people running up towards the student accommodation.

"Don't even think about it," said Orlanda.

Her voice sounded dangerous. Cyan's throat tightened up in response. Orlanda grunted and changed direction. She jerked Cyan towards the nearly completed Student Centre.

One of the concert blocks that held the temporary fence had been moved to create a gap. Cyan struggled as she was pulled towards it.

"Stop it," said Orlanda.

She spoke with a calm that alarmed Cyan.

Cyan pushed her heels against the ground.

"Do you want another slap?" The threat didn't make Cyan move so Orlanda shook Cyan into submission and then pulled her through the gap in the fence. She dragged her to the glass doors, which slid open to allow them into the Student Centre.

Orlanda swung Cyan onto the floor of the reception. Cyan landed hard and her mobile phone slid across the new cream stone tiles. She lay stunned for a few seconds. When Cyan regained movement she reached out and grabbed her mobile phone. In a move that would work in the best Ealing comedies, Cyan pushed herself up on her hands while her feet slipped on the stone floor. Cyan didn't look behind her when she managed to get to her feet. She didn't need to, she could hear Orlanda laughing at her. The sound made Cyan panic and she stumbled for the safety of the large, solid, circular reception desk straight in front of her. From behind the desk Cyan looked up at Orlanda, who was now bent double with laughter.

She's mad, Cyan thought. *I'm trapped with a—*

Cyan refused to finish the sentence, but her mind still made the link. Her knees weakened at the thought and she pulled out the office chair behind the desk. It was only when she sat down that she realised she still wore her backpack. She began to slide it from her shoulders.

"Slowly," said Orlanda.

Cyan froze. She wondered if Orlanda sounded like this before she killed Dayton. Then she focused on her backpack and took it off slowly as ordered.

"Slide it across the table."

Cyan did so. Orlanda grabbed it and dropped the pack onto the ground behind her.

"Now your phone," she ordered.

Cyan's grip tightened around her mobile phone. She felt as if it was the only thing that could save her. Orlanda stepped towards the desk, she seemed to fill the room. Cyan's hands shook as she put her mobile phone on the top of the desk. She jumped as Orlanda's hand whipped out and snatched it. Orlanda looked at the screen before she threw it on the ground behind her. Cyan winced at the crack when it hit the tiles. She fell back into the chair and pushed it as far away from the desk, and Orlanda, as she could. It wasn't far and she hit the wall behind her with one push. On Cyan's right was a single door with card access and to her left a turnstile. She wondered if her identity card would work on the locks. Then she looked up at Orlanda. The woman was built like an athlete and Cyan guessed that she wouldn't get to either exit before Orlanda caught her. Cyan then noticed the rubber mallet on the desk between them. Orlanda grabbed it and Cyan yelped.

"I'll just take this out of your reach," Orlanda said, pushing the mallet to the side of the large desk.

Cyan looked up into her kidnapper's face, then she looked at the glass doors behind her. Just beyond them a sheet of plywood, probably big enough to cover half of the reception desk, was tied to one of the bicycle racks in preparation for any strong winds.

Orlanda snapped her fingers. Cyan jumped and gave Orlanda her attention.

"Do you want to know what happened to Dayton?" Orlanda lifted her chin.

Cyan was about to answer when she thought she saw the plywood move. She looked closely. It shook slightly. She wondered if it had been fastened properly.

Cyan then looked above the door. She didn't see the slightly round tube along the top of the door, but knew that Corner Rise regulations stated that every large glass-fronted area should have shutters.

"We should close them," said Cyan.

No! shouted a voice in her head and Cyan wondered why she said that. But she still rose from her seat.

"Sit your backside down!" said Orlanda. "No one's gonna find us here. They've all gone home."

Behind Orlanda the plywood shook violently.

Orlanda moved closer to the reception desk and Cyan sat down hard.

"You haven't heard anything!"

Cyan swallowed and forced herself to look at Orlanda.

"I want you to know what happened."

Cyan looked into Orlanda's calm eyes. The sight frightened her even more. Cyan nodded.

"You've heard of the Pecunia, right?" said Orlanda.

She reached into her pocket and pulled out a packet of cigarettes. Cyan's eyes were fixed to the green wrapper. The student, now kidnapper, looked hungrily at the packet and slowly put them down on the desk. Menthol cigarettes. Cyan had been right to be afraid of that smell.

"I asked you a question."

"What?" said Cyan. "Yes. It's a gang—"

Orlanda thumped the desk and Cyan would have pushed the chair through the wall if she could.

"It's no gang! It's an organisation! It's no scam. There is big money. Like mega lottery jackpot big." Orlanda stood back from the desk. "Enough to pay loans. Buy houses," she said.

Cyan looked at the dark wood of the reception desk. "He *was* gambling," she said to herself.

Orlanda smiled. "You're impressed now, right?" she said.

Cyan thought about Dayton's apartment in Brixton, his shoes and his favourite phrase. He had been focused, but on the wrong thing.

"Didn't know 'bout your precious Mr King?" said Orlanda.

"Doctor," said Cyan automatically.

Cyan still believed that his title was real, unless he had paid someone else to write his thesis.

"Okay. *Dr* Dayton King. Doctor or not, he still owed us money."

Cyan could hear the satisfaction in the tall woman's voice. She raised her eyes from the table to Orlanda's face. The smile she saw was half pride and half contempt.

"How you think he got all that expensive stuff, eh?" said Orlanda. "He was good at numbers. He was good at gambling."

Orlanda paused dramatically. But Cyan didn't notice. Through the doors she saw the plywood rise at an angle, like a horse rearing on its hind legs. She realised that one of the ropes had come undone. Cyan got up from the chair.

"I really think—"

"You didn't hear me! I said sit your backside down!"

Orlanda moved slowly forward. Cyan sat. But her eyes stayed on the plywood.

"All those big college doctors and professors. All too scared of a little wind," said Orlanda.

The student spun quickly and looked out of the window. The plywood lay still against the bicycle racks. She snorted and fixed her eyes back on Cyan.

"*Doctor* Dayton King was good," said Orlanda. "He won a lot. And then he didn't. He borrowed money to make more money. But you can't owe money to Pecunia and not pay it back. They don't like that. They didn't like Dayton. So I had to get the money. Dr King had to pay his debts or else."

Cyan looked Orlanda in the eye. "Or else you'd kill him," she said.

"Do you think I planned this?" said Orlanda.

Cyan stared into Orlanda's expressionless face and it frightened her. "I-I don't know," she said.

"I didn't." Orlanda's voice rose. "This is Dayton's fault."

Orlanda's face became warped with anger. Cyan looked down at the desk.

"He wouldn't listen," said Orlanda. "Laughed in my face. *My* face! Do you know how hard I worked to get where I am?"

A sudden blast of wind made Cyan look up again, but it was all still outside. She looked at Orlanda, who was in her own world.

"You think it's easy to be a woman in an organisation run by men? They won't even give me a gun. *Me*. Do you know why I was sent to this rock?" Orlanda smiled wryly. "I was sent here because of that little fraud."

"Dancia?"

"Dinah Delany." Orlanda hurled the name out of her mouth. "Stupid woman. She thought she could rob the gang too. So I was sent to talk to her. And what did she do? She ran to the police and told them everything. Who we were. Why we were here."

Orlanda took a deep breath which she released as a snort.

"Dinah won't stay in prison for ever," she said. "Pecunia can wait."

Cyan studied Orlanda's face. The E-FIT-V pictures were not of two men. That morning Cyan had decided that one was Trevor. Now she knew that the other was Orlanda. Cyan's heart thumped so hard that she was certain Orlanda heard it. Cyan found another level of fear. She looked beyond Orlanda to the empty campus and prayed for help. Outside the plywood was still, but the ropes had slackened.

"Now that Dayton," said Orlanda. "He was way too proud to go to the police. I just had to speak to him. Get him to pay the money back."

"Then what?" said Cyan.

"Then I would be off this little piece of land. How do you live here? It's so small that they put a cinema in a college?"

Cyan stared up at Orlanda. "Corner Rise is my home!"

Orlanda raised an eyebrow and laughed. Her joyless eyes remained fixed on Cyan.

Outside all was quiet. Orlanda stepped forward.

"S-so. What happened?" said Cyan.

"Blame boastful Dayton. He comes to me and says, 'I can get in anywhere I want in this place.' Shows me the key to the museum. Then he arranges to meet me that Wednesday evening. I didn't realise the cinema would be shut."

"It closes most Wednesdays," said Cyan.

Orlanda shrugged. "Guess he didn't want to be seen. No cafe staff. No cinemagoers. No one. That suited me fine. So I went.

"He was such a fool. There I was, dressed in the darkest colours I owned. Because of all the cameras. All he said was 'Why so sombre?' I just meant to shake him up. But, when I told him to pay back the money he owed," Orlanda glowered at the reception desk, "he laughed. Then he pulled this little statue from the case. Ha! Him so short he had to stand on a seat to get it!" Orlanda pulled herself up to her full height.

Cyan gasped. Every time Cyan had seen Orlanda she had been dazzled by the clothes. Now that Orlanda was dressed plainly Cyan realised how tall the woman was.

"He smirked at me. He had that stupid statue in his hands. 'Silly little girl,' he says, 'what would happen if I went to the police?' Huh. He thought he could scare me. I watched him climb up onto the stool. He put the statue back and turned his back on me. I didn't need no stool to reach that statue. I picked it up and hit him hard."

Orlanda smiled.

"I wasn't such a little girl then."

"You killed him." Cyan winced as she realised she had spoken her

213

thought out loud.

"He tried to make a fool out of me. Expected me to cry and crawl away," said Orlanda. "Trevor was so angry. He had told me to leave after Dayton's death. There was no evidence, he said. I could be gone before the police had enough clues. He didn't care about Pecunia's business That's why he never tried to get Dayton to pay back the money. Instead he told me to be like him. Sit and wait until Pecunia called. But I want to be someone in the organisation."

The wind had quietened down. Maybe Alpha had passed and the builders would come back. Cyan needed more time.

"But what about Katherine?" Cyan said. "She was outside and—"

"That fool!" Orlanda's eyes flew open.

Cyan watched as her kidnapper took a few deep breaths.

"I thought she would be easy to use." Orlanda grunted. "I got to know her. Enough to find out that she liked to be around money. If only to brag about it."

Cyan nodded in spite of herself. Orlanda had got that right about Katherine.

"Yeah. You saw it too," said Orlanda. "So I gave her what she wanted. She said Daniella did it. I gave her the evidence."

"You told her that you were outside the Hub?"

Orlanda smiled. "I was by then."

"And then she went to the press."

"Huh. You should have seen her," Orlanda said. "She couldn't wait. And everyone knew about Daniella and Dayton. It was so easy."

"Really?" said Cyan.

She fixed her eyes on her captor and was pleased to see the smile slip from Orlanda's face.

"No. Daniella was cleared. Some student rubbish."

Cyan bit her tongue.

"Katherine said I made a fool of her. People at work had laughed at her. Huh!" said Orlanda. "She should have thought of that before."

She focused on Cyan.

"That crazy woman looked down at her shoes. Told me that another pair would be nice. 'Might stop a visit to the police.' She did what Dayton did. She turned her back on me. Like I was dismissed and should run along now. I wrapped my hands in my scarf, reached for that display thing and …" Orlanda shrugged, her face expressionless. "No loose ends. Right?" she said.

Cyan felt as if her blood had been pumped through ice.

"Is that why you dropped that book on me?" Cyan said.

"What else could I do," said Orlanda without a hint of regret in her voice. "Katherine just said your name one too many times. 'Cyan was in the Hub.' 'Cyan found the body.' 'Cyan asked some questions.' Regular little detective, aren't you?"

"If I was, I wouldn't be here," Cyan murmured.

Orlanda either didn't hear or chose to ignore her.

Cyan looked at the doors. "Trevor tried to save Katherine," she said.

"He tried. But she was scared of him. She thought he killed Dayton. I let her." Orlanda laughed. "The fool tried to save you too. I knew he was too soft."

Cyan looked out of the glass towards the Hub.

"But you didn't kill Trevor!" Cyan felt hope. He knew they were here.

"Trevor's a Pecunia member." Orlanda smiled. "He won't call the police for you."

Cyan's eyes grew large as Orlanda pulled on a pair of blue latex gloves. She picked up the mallet.

"Like I said. No loose ends." Orlanda looked down at Cyan.

The wind roared. Orlanda turned to the doors. Cyan jumped from her seat. She slid to the floor and crouched low under the desk.

Orlanda laughed. "That won't save you."

Whatever Orlanda said next was engulfed in an explosion of glass and wind that shook the whole Student Centre and made the reception desk vibrate. Cyan felt her inner ear tighten. She saw a shadow as the plywood flipped over the reception desk and hit the floor beside her. It formed a firm triangle with the wall.

Cyan stayed under the desk until her ears popped painfully. She heard the wind blow and the tinkle of glass, but no other sound. Cyan waited for a few seconds then she unfolded herself, crawled from under the desk, got slowly to her feet and looked straight into the dazed eyes of her kidnapper. Orlanda held her left arm across her chest and Cyan watched as the top of her left sleeve grew damp and sticky.

"Oh no, not now!" Cyan clutched at her stomach.

CHAPTER 23

Cyan staggered backwards from the desk and stopped when the backs of her knees hit the seat of the chair. She sat down hard. As the familiar embarrassing nausea started to take over Cyan fought to keep her eyes open. She stared at the table and listened. The air was still. The wind no longer whistled through the broken glass.

"I think Alpha's gone," Cyan said to herself.

She peeked up at her captor. Orlanda was as silent as the wind. She was still standing but her eyes were fixed wide open and she shook slightly. Cyan rose slowly. Orlanda's eyes flicked towards her, then they stared back at a point on the wall behind the desk. Behind Orlanda most of the doors had been reduced to glass gravel. A few hardy fingers of glass clung to the bottom of the frame, they were shattered but had not blown apart.

No 'little wind' did that, thought Cyan.

She kept both eyes on Orlanda then she glanced to her right. The desk curved to meet the wall and Cyan guessed that her staff card wouldn't open the door. To her left was a greater chance of escape. Cyan edged in that direction. She felt the narrow end of the plywood. Cyan gave it a push. It was wedged tight. She wondered if she could squeeze through the triangular hole the plywood had formed with the wall.

Cyan crouched down and examined the gap. She would never fit through that space. She braced herself and stood up. She needed a weapon.

Even though her arms trembled Cyan didn't feel afraid. She glanced across the desk's surface for something to use against her kidnapper. Then Cyan looked up into Orlanda's eyes. The student refocused on Cyan.

"You have caused me a lot of tro—"

"In here!"

The voice pulled Cyan's attention from Orlanda. Outside the broken building she saw two black uniforms. Police uniforms. What was left of the glass doors opened and in they rushed, followed by Brookes and Torrington.

The last of the glass doors fell to the ground behind the police with a tinkle. The glass in the reception area crunched underfoot by heavy, practical shoes. Orlanda glanced over her left shoulder and screamed. At first she sounded afraid. Then she sounded furious.

"Police! Stay where you are!"

"Desiree Orlanda Henry," said Torrington. "You are under arrest for the murders of Dr Dayton King and Ms Katherine Welman."

"Desiree?" said Cyan.

Then she caught Orlanda move in her peripheral vision. The tall woman had twisted back towards the desk, her right hand stretched out. She was reaching for the rubber mallet. Orlanda's gaze leapt from the mallet back to the police but Cyan moved fast. She grabbed the mallet and whammed it down on Orlanda's hand. Orlanda screamed and yanked her hand away. She held it against her chest while her left arm slid down to her side, unable to offer comfort. She snarled back at Cyan in anger.

The officers moved as one smooth machine. Orlanda was held and handcuffed before she could make another move. She squeaked once when her injured arm was touched, after that she was silent. Orlanda glared across the desk at Cyan before she was pulled away.

"Are you okay?" said DS Brookes.

Cyan wobbled and sat down as her adrenalin rush ended. She tried to smile at the officer, but her face would not cooperate, so she nodded in reply.

Behind Brookes Orlanda fought to free herself, her teeth bared. Cyan was amazed at the strength of her kidnapper. The two police officers struggled and, after he had made a quick call on his radio, Torrington added his size to the battle. Cyan breathed deeply. Orlanda had been wrong about the reception desk, it was a life saver.

After that it felt as if Cyan watched the world with the volume muted. She listened to words, but heard nothing. Orlanda continued to struggle as she was led out of the door. It was only when several more police cars arrived that Orlanda stopped. She kept her chin raised, even as she was folded into the back of the first police car.

Two new police officers entered the building and it took them a few minutes to remove the plywood. It had left a small hole in the wall.

Well that's a new paint job, thought Cyan.

"Cyan?"

Cyan turned at the sound of Brookes's voice.

"Can you stand up?"

"Yes," said Cyan.

Her legs trembled as she rose from the seat and she walked slowly to the second car. She looked out of the back-seat window to the Student Centre. After all those strong winds the glass walls were a mass of cracked spiderwebs. The doors were now just a pair of metal frames and the rope that had once held the plywood to the bicycle racks had long flown.

The rest of Corner Rise that she could see didn't look so bad, but then all the other buildings she saw had their shutters down.

By the time she got to the station she felt as shattered as the glass doors of the Student Centre. A police officer led her to a quiet room where she was given a cup of sweet tea.

"Sorry," said Cyan as the cup was placed in front of her. "I've lost my phone? It must be back at the uni."

The police office nodded. "I'll see what I can find out," she said before she left the room.

Cyan had finished her tea when the officer returned. She handed Cyan a plastic bag. Inside was her mobile phone in its pink and silver cover. She pulled it out of the bag, opened the cover and was relieved to see that the screen only had one crack. That would be easily repaired and the phone could still be used.

"Thank you," she said. "Can I make some calls?"

The officer nodded. Cyan quickly called Vee, who didn't believe her daughter could be all right and in a police station at the same time. Cyan was actually relieved when DS Brookes arrived to take her statement. She ended the call and took a deep breath after Vee had hung up. Brookes pulled out the chair next to Cyan and sat down.

After Cyan had recounted the events she looked up at Brookes. "H-how did you know I was in there?"

"The new Student Centre?"

Cyan nodded.

"We received two phone calls, one anonymous and one from Mrs Butler," said Brookes.

"Mum," said Cyan.

"The first call informed us that you were still at the Crown Campus and might be in danger. We were about to send a patrol car when Mrs Butler called. When she told us that you had gone to work and didn't return her call we became a lot more interested."

Cyan wanted to ask who the caller was, but bit her tongue.

"We were heading towards the Hub when the centre's glass door exploded, so we stopped to check it out. It was then that we saw Orlanda." Brookes shook her head. "She looked like a live version of the original CCTV footage from the evening Dr King was murdered."

"Would you believe that I wanted to close the shutters. The ones on the Student Centre?"

"I can," said Brookes. "We've all been taught the hurricane drill. But I can tell you now that they hadn't been fitted."

Cyan could only stare at the police officer. "I have to ask," she said.

"Yes?"

"Okay. You won't know who the other caller was. But was it a man or a woman?"

Brookes eyed Cyan before she replied. "Why?"

Cyan paused. If Trevor was part of Pecunia then he should be arrested. But if he saved her life? She took a deep breath.

"Trevor tried to get me off campus before Orlanda ... Orlanda hit him. He was still alive when she dragged me into the Student Centre. I forgot about him until you mentioned the anonymous phone call."

Brookes nodded slowly. Cyan could almost see the ideas as they formed behind the police officer's eyes.

"Excuse me for a moment."

Brookes swiftly left the room, closing the door behind her. Cyan felt a tiny ball of guilt form as she looked at the door. She shook herself. If she was right then Trevor could be dangerous, so why did she feel bad?

Cyan didn't have long with her thoughts. The door soon opened and Brookes walked back into the room.

"We've kept you long enough," said Brookes. "Do you have anyone you can stay with?"

"Yes. Oh wait. Loki."

"Who?"

"My cat," said Cyan.

She tried not to smile at the look on the police officer's face.

"I need to check she's okay," said Cyan. "But I'll call my mum when I get home. She'll come over for a bit."

Once again Cyan sat down in a police car, but this time she paid more attention to the island on the short journey home. She noticed that several businesses were either open or had their shutters partially raised. Cyan wondered if Vincent would open the Spice Shack that evening. She imagined the conversations in all the restaurants and bars and the tales of last-minute escapes before Alpha hit. Cyan was certain that at least one person would have been 'blown' through their door by the storm. She glanced at her watch, it was nearly twelve. Her stomach, reminded of the time, gave a tiny rumble.

Cyan didn't bother to check for any post when she reached her apartment, she doubted that any postal workers would have been allowed to brave the weather. Loki meowed loudly before Cyan put her key near the lock. She opened her front door and the cat rubbed herself against her legs. Cyan walked in, closed the door behind her and made a fuss of the cat. Then she raised all the shutters. Outside the sky was blue again and as hard as she looked, Cyan didn't see one broken branch. She made herself a cup of tea, pulled two biscuits from the tin and after a few minutes called Vee.

"Where are you?" asked Vee after they had exchanged greetings.

"At home. At last. Would you believe that Dr Dayton King was mixed up with that gambling gang."

"What, Peck?"

"Pecunia."

"You know. Hearing that doesn't make me feel good," said Vee. "I'm sending a taxi for you. You can stay here as long as you need to."

"Thanks, Mum. Give me a few moments to put food out for Loki and pack."

"Fifteen minutes. No more," warned Vee.

After they had hung up Cyan finished her tea and dug out two automatic cat feeders. Once Loki was dealt with she picked up her mobile phone. She looked at a number she usually just sent texts to. She sent one and a few minutes later her mobile phone rang.

"Good afternoon, Cyan. You survived Alpha then?" said Gustavo.

"Just about," said Cyan. "Call the police, they have the latest on Dayton's and Katherine's killer."

"What?"

"Call the police."

"Wait. What happened? Are you okay?"

"I'm okay now," Cyan said. "But you do need to call them."

Cyan wished Gustavo a good afternoon and smiled as she hung up.

That evening Cyan sat at Vee's dining table and inhaled the mouth-watering smells that floated from her mother's kitchen. Cyan had contributed a bottle of red wine to the meal, and it stood open and untouched in front of her.

Cyan looked at the sideboard, which held Vee's small collection of glasses. "No," she said softly to herself. "I'll have a glass if Mum does."

Instead she pushed the book she had tried to read aside and opened her laptop. Cyan went straight to *The Corner Rise Tribune* and read Gustavo's scoop on an abduction and an arrest. It was too early to name names, but he had done wonders with the police statement.

After dinner Cyan gave Vee a summarised version of the events of the day. Vee sat opened-mouthed throughout. Afterwards she got up and gave Cyan a big, tight hug.

"Wow," she said after she had released her daughter. "My daughter was saved by plywood. So that Orlanda planned the murder."

"I don't think so," said Cyan. "Dayton stole the key to the Collection and didn't want to be seen. Someone would have reported it, or walked in, or mentioned it in gossip. No. Dayton made Orlanda so angry and she lashed out."

Vee shook her head slowly, then rose to clear the table.

Cyan spent the next day with Vee. They watched as everything to do with the case, from the way Dayton made his money to Orlanda's membership of Pecunia, the illegal gambling organisation, was reported, reviewed and discussed. Vee put down two mugs of tea on two large coasters that protected the Queen Anne style oval coffee table, and seated herself in the living room's one armchair.

"Thanks," said Cyan as she uncurled her legs beneath her and reached for her tea. "Funny how Dayton never mentioned the money he owed," she said.

"Not really," said Vee. "Once that Dr King started to lie like that, he had to keep it up. What would people say if he gave up that place in Mimosa Drive?"

"You make it sound like he was trapped."

"That's because he was," said Vee.

They sipped their tea and continued to watch the midday news. Cyan shuddered at the sight of Orlanda and felt a pang of sadness when she saw Trevor's face appear on-screen. She knew that there would be a lot of talk on campus next week, especially among the portering staff.

"Enough news," said Vee. "I've got some silver that needs polishing."

Cyan smiled. "And some weeding."

"Of course!"

The next morning Cyan thanked her mum for a large breakfast, assured her that she would be okay in her own apartment, and left just as a taxi filled with Vee's church friends arrived. Cyan waved to the people in the taxi and they waved back. She wondered how so many large hats could fit into one route taxi. Cyan rearranged her light backpack and felt the tub of marinaded chicken move. In spite of breakfast she felt her mouth water. Nobody cooked chicken like her mum.

The sun wasn't at its hottest and Cyan looked forward to a pleasant walk to Three Trees. Her mobile phone rang.

"Good morning," she said.

"Good morning. DS Phyllida Brookes here."

"Oh hello." Cyan stopped walking and stepped to the side of the pavement.

"I thought I should tell you that we arrested Trevor Furley last night. He was brought into East Point Hospital after collapsing."

"Is he okay?" Cyan said.

"He was a bit dazed, but that's all."

Brookes didn't say much after that and Cyan thanked her for the message. She looked at her phone for a few seconds. She had hoped Trevor would get away, but she didn't need to ask Brookes what Trevor was charged with. He had protected a murderer.

Cyan put her phone away and joined the main road just as a bus to Light House arrived. Cyan shrugged to herself and stepped onto the bus. She had just sat down when her mobile phone rang again. This time when she looked at the screen it was Fayval.

"Good morning."

"Good morning," said Fayval. "Did you watch the news this weekend?"

"All day yesterday."

Cyan listened to Fayval's excited voice. "Sounds like the Student Centre is all broken glass."

Cyan felt her stomach clench. She had managed her emotions well when she told Vee about the Student Centre, but now the thought of all that had happened was beginning to sink in. Cyan wondered if she would ever be able to walk into that building again.

Fayval was still talking as Cyan approached her stop. "Sorry, Fayval, I'm on the bus and it's my stop. I-I had dinner at Mum's last night."

"Not a problem," said Fayval.

Cyan made a mental note to tell Fayval everything once she could.

The End

ABOUT THE AUTHOR

A K Summer lives in London with her husband and a fussy senior cat. She got the idea for Murder on Corner Rise after many years of working in various universities. The location came while sailing from the Caribbean to the Azores when she saw a map of Corner Seamount on the charts.

Printed in Great Britain
by Amazon